ROSEMARY'S BABY

'It is a terrifying book: offhand, I can think of no other in which fear of an unknown evil strikes with greater chill.' Violet Grant, *Daily Telegraph*

'The pay-off is so fiendish, it made me sweat. Diabolically good.' Peter Phillips, *The Sun*

'. . . a terrifying, wholly devilish book. Gripping, starkly spine-chilling.' Maurice Prior, *Spectator*

'This horror story will grip you and chill you.' Peter Grosvenor, *Daily Express*

'Brilliant.' Maurice Richardson, *Observer*

'. . . if you read this book in the dead of night, do not be surprised if you feel the urge to keep glancing behind you.' Campbell Black, *Queen*

'a darkly brilliant tale of modern deviltry that, like James' *Turn of the Screw*, induces the reader to believe the unbelievable. I believed it and was altogether enthralled.' Truman Capote

Rosemary's Baby

IRA LEVIN

UNABRIDGED

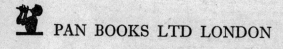 PAN BOOKS LTD LONDON

First published in UK 1967 by Michael Joseph Ltd.
This edition published 1968 by
PAN BOOKS LTD.
33 Tothill Street, London, SW1

Printed in Great Britain by
Richard Clay (The Chaucer Press), Ltd.,
Bungay, Suffolk

Completed in August, 1966,
in Wilton, Connecticut,
and dedicated to Gabrielle

Part One

CHAPTER ONE

ROSEMARY AND Guy Woodhouse had signed a lease on a five-room apartment in a geometric white house on First Avenue when they received word, from a woman named Mrs Cortez, that a four-room apartment in the Bramford had become available. The Bramford, old, black, and elephantine, is a warren of high-ceilinged apartments prized for their fireplaces and Victorian detail. Rosemary and Guy had been on its waiting list since their marriage but had finally given up.

Guy relayed the news to Rosemary, stopping the phone against his chest. Rosemary groaned 'Oh *no*!' and looked as if she would weep.

'It's too late,' Guy said to the phone. 'We signed a lease yesterday.' Rosemary caught his arm. 'Couldn't we get out of it?' she asked him. 'Tell them something?'

'Hold on a minute, will you, Mrs Cortez?' Guy stopped the phone again. 'Tell them what?' he asked.

Rosemary floundered and raised her hands helplessly. 'I don't know, the truth. That we have a chance to get into the Bramford.'

'Honey,' Guy said, 'they're not going to care about that.'

'You'll think of *something*, Guy. Let's just look, all right? Tell her we'll look. Please. Before she hangs up.'

'We signed a *lease*, Ro; we're stuck.'

'Please! She'll hang up!' Whimpering with mock anguish, Rosemary pried the phone from Guy's chest and tried to push it up to his mouth.

Guy laughed and let the phone be pushed. 'Mrs Cortez? It turns out there's a chance we'll be able to get out of it, because we haven't signed the actual lease yet. They were out of the forms so we only signed a letter of agreement. Can we take a look at the apartment?'

Mrs Cortez gave instructions: they were to go to the

Bramford between eleven and eleven-thirty, find Mr Micklas or Jerome, and tell whichever they found that they were the party she had sent to look at 7E. Then they were to call her. She gave Guy her number.

'You see how you can think of things?' Rosemary said, putting Peds and yellow shoes on her feet. 'You're a *marvellous* liar.'

Guy, at the mirror, said, 'Christ, a pimple.'

'Don't squeeze it.'

'It's only four rooms, you know. No nursery.'

'I'd rather have four rooms in the Bramford,' Rosemary said, 'than a whole floor in that – that white cellblock.'

'Yesterday you loved it.'

'I liked it. I never loved it. I'll bet not even the architect loves it. We'll make a dining area in the living-room and have a beautiful nursery, when and if.'

'Soon,' Guy said. He ran an electric razor back and forth across his upper lip, looking into his eyes, which were brown and large. Rosemary stepped into a yellow dress and squirmed the zipper up the back of it.

They were in one room, that had been Guy's bachelor apartment. It had posters of Paris and Verona, a large day bed and a pullman kitchen.

It was Tuesday, the third of August.

Mr Micklas was small and dapper but had fingers missing from both hands, which made shaking hands an embarrassment, though not apparently for him. 'Oh, an actor,' he said, ringing for the elevator with a middle finger. 'We're very popular with actors.' He named four who were living at the Bramford, all of them well known. 'Have I seen you in anything?'

'Let's see,' Guy said. 'I did *Hamlet* a while back, didn't I, Liz? And then we made *The Sandpiper* ...'

'He's joking,' Rosemary said. 'He was in *Luther* and *Nobody Loves An Albatross* and a lot of television plays and television commercials.'

'That's where the money is, isn't it?' Mr Micklas said; 'the commercials.'

'Yes,' Rosemary said, and Guy said, 'And the artistic thrill, too.'

Rosemary gave him a pleading look; he gave back one of stunned innocence and then made a leering vampire face at the top of Mr Micklas's head.

The elevator – oak-panelled, with a shining brass hand-rail all around – was run by a uniformed Negro boy with a locked-in-place smile. 'Seven,' Mr Micklas told him; to Rosemary and Guy he said, 'This apartment has four rooms, two baths, and five closets. Originally the house consisted of very large apartments – the smallest was a nine – but now they've almost all been broken up into fours, fives, and sixes. Seven E is a four that was originally the back part of a ten. It has the original kitchen and master bath, which are enormous, as you'll soon see. It has the original master bedroom for its living-room, another bedroom for its bedroom, and two servant's rooms thrown together for its dining-room or second bedroom. Do you have children?'

'We plan to,' Rosemary said.

'It's an ideal child's room, with a full bathroom and a large closet. The whole set-up is made to order for a young couple like yourselves.'

The elevator stopped and the Negro boy, smiling, chivied it down, up, and down again for a closer alignment with the floor rail outside; and still smiling, pulled in the brass inner gate and the outer rolling door. Mr Micklas stood aside and Rosemary and Guy stepped out – into a dimly lighted hallway walled and carpeted in dark green. A workman at a sculptured green door marked 7B looked at them and turned back to fitting a peepscope into its cut-out hole.

Mr Micklas led the way to the right and then to the left, through short branches of dark green hallway. Rosemary and Guy, following, saw rubbed-away places in the wall-paper and a seam where it had lifted and was curling inward; saw a dead light bulb in a cut-glass sconce and a patched place of light green tape on the dark green carpet. Guy looked at Rosemary: *Patched carpet?* She looked away and smiled brightly: *I love it; everything's lovely!*

'The previous tenant, Mrs Gardenia,' Mr Micklas said,

not looking back at them, 'passed away only a few days ago and nothing has been moved out of the apartment yet. Her son asked me to tell whoever looks at it that the rugs, the air conditioners, and some of the furniture can be had practically for the asking.' He turned into another branch of hallway papered in newer-looking green and gold stripes.

'Did she die in the apartment?' Rosemary asked. 'Not that it —'

'Oh, no, in a hospital,' Mr Micklas said. 'She'd been in a coma for weeks. She was very old and passed away without ever waking. I'll be grateful to go that way myself when the time comes. She was chipper right to the end; cooked her own meals, shopped the department stores . . . She was one of the first women lawyers in New York State.'

They came now to a stairwell that ended the hallway. Adjacent to it, on the left, was the door of apartment 7E, a door without sculptured garlands, narrower than the doors they had passed. Mr Micklas pressed the pearl bell button – *L. Gardenia* was mounted above it in white letters on black plastic – and turned a key in the lock. Despite lost fingers he worked the knob and threw the door smartly. 'After you, please,' he said, leaning forward on his toes and holding the door open with the length of an outstretched arm.

The apartment's four rooms were divided two and two on either side of a narrow central hallway that extended in a straight line from the front door. The first room on the right was the kitchen, and at the sight of it Rosemary couldn't keep from giggling, for it was as large if not larger than the whole apartment in which they were then living. It had a six-burner gas stove with two ovens, a mammoth refrigerator, a monumental sink; it had dozens of cabinets, a window on Seventh Avenue, a high *high* ceiling, and it even had – imagining away Mrs Gardenia's chrome table and chairs and roped bales of *Fortune* and *Musical America* – the perfect place for something like the blue-and-ivory breakfast nook she had clipped from last month's *House Beautiful*.

Opposite the kitchen was the dining-room or second bedroom, which Mrs Gardenia had apparently used as a combination study and greenhouse. Hundreds of small plants, dying and dead, stood on jerry-built shelves under spirals of unlighted fluorescent tubing; in their midst a roll-top desk spilled over with books and papers. A handsome desk it was, broad and gleaming with age. Rosemary left Guy and Mr Micklas talking by the door and went to it, stepping over a shelf of withered brown fronds. Desks like this were displayed in antique-store windows; Rosemary wondered, touching it, if it was one of the things that could be had practically for the asking. Graceful blue penmanship on mauve paper said *than merely the intriguing pastime I believed it to be. I can no longer associate myself*—and she caught herself snooping and looked up at Mr Micklas turning from Guy. 'Is this desk one of the things Mrs Gardenia's son wants to sell?' she asked.

'I don't know,' Mr Micklas said. 'I could find out for you, though.'

'It's a beauty,' Guy said.

Rosemary said 'Isn't it?' and smiling, looked about at walls and windows. The room would accommodate almost perfectly the nursery she had imagined. It was a bit dark – the windows faced on a narrow courtyard – but the white-and-yellow wallpaper would brighten it tremendously. The bathroom was small but a bonus, and the closet, filled with potted seedlings that seemed to be doing quite well, was a good one.

They turned to the door, and Guy asked, 'What are all these?'

'Herbs, mostly,' Rosemary said. 'There's mint and basil ... I don't know what these are.'

Farther along the hallway there was a guest closet on the left, and then, on the right, a wide archway opening on to the living-room. Large bay windows stood opposite, two of them, with diamond panes and three-sided window seats. There was a small fireplace in the right-hand wall, with a scrolled white marble mantel, and there were high oak bookshelves on the left.

'Oh, Guy,' Rosemary said, finding his hand and squeezing

it. Guy said 'Mm' non-committally but squeezed back; Mr Micklas was beside him.

'The fireplace works, of course,' Mr Micklas said.

The bedroom, behind them, was adequate – about twelve by eighteen, with its windows facing on the same narrow courtyard as those of the dining-room–second-bedroom–nursery. The bathroom, beyond the living-room, was big, and full of bulbous white brass-knobbed fixtures.

'It's a marvellous apartment!' Rosemary said, back in the living-room. She spun about with opened arms, as if to take and embrace it. 'I love it!'

'What she's trying to do,' Guy said, 'is get you to lower the rent.'

Mr Micklas smiled. 'We would raise it if we were allowed,' he said. 'Beyond the fifteen-per-cent increase, I mean. Apartments with this kind of charm and individuality are as rare as hen's teeth today. The new —' He stopped short, looking at a mahogany secretary at the head of the central hallway. 'That's odd,' he said. 'There's a closet behind that secretary. I'm sure there is. There are five: two in the bedroom, one in the second bedroom, and two in the hallway, there and there.' He went closer to the secretary.

Guy stood high on tiptoes and said, 'You're right. I can see the corners of the door.'

'She moved it,' Rosemary said. 'The secretary; it used to be there.' She pointed to a peaked silhouette left ghostlike on the wall near the bedroom door, and the deep prints of four ball feet in the burgundy carpet. Faint scuff-trails curved and crossed from the four prints to the secretary's feet where they stood now against the narrow adjacent wall.

'Give me a hand, will you?' Mr Micklas said to Guy.

Between them they worked the secretary bit by bit back towards its original place. 'I see why she went into a coma,' Guy said, pushing.

'She couldn't have moved this by herself,' Mr Micklas said; 'she was eighty-nine.'

Rosemary looked doubtfully at the closet door they had uncovered. 'Should we open it?' she asked. 'Maybe her son should.'

14

The secretary lodged neatly in its four footprints. Mr Micklas massaged his fingers-missing hands. 'I'm authorized to show the apartment,' he said, and went to the door and opened it. The closet was nearly empty; a vacuum cleaner stood at one side of it and three or four wood boards at the other. The overhead shelf was stacked with blue and green bath towels.

'Whoever she locked in got out,' Guy said.

Mr Micklas said, 'She probably didn't need five closets.'

'But why would she cover up her vacuum cleaner and her towels?' Rosemary asked.

Mr Micklas shrugged. 'I don't suppose we'll ever know. She may have been getting senile after all.' He smiled. 'Is there anything else I can show you or tell you?'

'Yes,' Rosemary said. 'What about the laundry facilities? Are there washing machines downstairs?'

They thanked Mr Micklas, who saw them out on to the sidewalk, and then they walked slowly uptown along Seventh Avenue.

'It's cheaper than the other,' Rosemary said, trying to sound as if practical considerations stood foremost in her mind.

'It's one room less, honey,' Guy said.

Rosemary walked in silence for a moment, and then said, 'It's better located.'

'God, yes,' Guy said. 'I could walk to all the theatres.'

Heartened, Rosemary leaped from practicality. 'Oh, Guy, let's take it! Please! Please! It's *such* a wonderful apartment! She didn't do *anything* with it, old Mrs Gardenia! That living-room could be – it could be *beautiful*, and *warm*, and – oh, please, Guy, let's take it, all right?'

'Well sure,' Guy said, smiling. 'If we can get out of the other thing.'

Rosemary grabbed his elbow happily. 'We will!' she said. 'You'll think of something, I know you will!'

Guy telephoned Mrs Cortez from a glass-walled booth while Rosemary, outside, tried to lip-read. Mrs Cortez said she would give them until three o'clock; if she hadn't heard from them by then she would call the next party on the waiting list.

They went to the Russian Tea Room and ordered Bloody Marys and chicken salad sandwiches on black bread.

'You could tell them I'm sick and have to go into the hospital,' Rosemary said.

But that was neither convincing nor compelling. Instead Guy spun a story about a call to join a company of *Come Blow Your Horn* leaving for a four-month USO tour of Vietnam and the Far East. The actor playing Alan had broken his hip and unless he, Guy, who knew the part from stock, stepped in and replaced him, the tour would have to be postponed for at least two weeks. Which would be a damn shame, the way those kids over there were slugging away against the Commies. His wife would have to stay with her folks in Omaha...

He ran it twice and went to find the phone.

Rosemary sipped her drink, keeping her left hand all-fingers-crossed under the table. She thought about the First Avenue apartment she didn't want and made a conscientious mental list of its good points; the shiny new kitchen, the dishwasher, the view of the East River, the central air conditioning...

The waitress brought the sandwiches.

A pregnant woman went by in a navy blue dress. Rosemary watched her. She must have been in her sixth or seventh month, talking back happily over her shoulder to an older woman with packages, probably her mother.

Someone waved from the opposite wall – the red-haired girl who had come into CBS a few weeks before Rosemary left. Rosemary waved back. The girl mouthed something and, when Rosemary didn't understand, mouthed it again. A man facing the girl turned to look at Rosemary, a starved-looking waxen-faced man.

And there came Guy, tall and handsome, biting back his grin, with *yes* glowing all over him.

'Yes?' Rosemary asked as he took his seat opposite her.

'Yes,' he said. 'The lease is void; the deposit will be returned; I'm to keep an eye open for Lieutenant Hartman of the Signal Corps. Mrs Cortez awaits us at two.'

'You called her?'

'I called her.'

The red-haired girl was suddenly with them, flushed and bright-eyed. 'I said "Marriage certainly agrees with you, you look marvellous,"' she said.

Rosemary, ransacking for the girl's name, laughed and said, 'Thank you! We're celebrating. We just got an apartment in the Bramford!'

'The Bram?' the girl said. 'I'm *mad* about it! If you ever want to sub-let, I'm first, and don't you forget it! All those weird gargoyles and creatures climbing up and down between the windows!'

CHAPTER TWO

HUTCH, SURPRISINGLY, tried to talk them out of it, on the grounds that the Bramford was a 'danger zone'.

When Rosemary had first come to New York in June of 1962 she had joined another Omaha girl and two girls from Atlanta in an apartment on lower Lexington Avenue. Hutch lived next door, and though he declined to be the full-time father-substitute the girls would have made of him – he had raised two daughters of his own and that was quite enough, thank you – he was none the less on hand in emergencies, such as The Night Someone Was on The Fire Escape and The Time Jeanne Almost Choked to Death. His name was Edward Hutchins, he was English, he was fifty-four. Under three different pen-names he wrote three different series of boys' adventure books.

To Rosemary he gave another sort of emergency assistance. She was the youngest of six children, the other five of whom had married early and made homes close to their parents; behind her in Omaha she had left an angry, suspicious father, a silent mother, and four resenting brothers and sisters. (Only the next-to-the-oldest, Brian, who had a drink problem, had said, 'Go on, Rosie, do what you want to do,' and had slipped her a plastic handbag with eighty-five dollars in it.) In New York Rosemary felt guilty and selfish, and Hutch bucked her up with strong tea and talks about parents and children and one's duty to oneself. She asked him questions that had been unspeakable in Catholic High; he sent her to a night course in philosophy at NYU. 'I'll make a duchess out of this cockney flower girl yet,' he said, and Rosemary had had wit enough to say 'Garn!'

Now, every month or so, Rosemary and Guy had dinner with Hutch, either in their apartment or, when it was his turn, in a restaurant. Guy found Hutch a bit boring but always treated him cordially; his wife had been a cousin of

Terence Rattigan, the playwright, and Rattigan and Hutch corresponded. Connections often proved crucial in the theatre, Guy knew, even connections at second-hand.

On the Thursday after they saw the apartment, Rosemary and Guy had dinner with Hutch at Klube's, a small German restaurant on Twenty-third Street. They had given his name to Mrs Cortez on Tuesday afternoon as one of three references she had asked for, and he had already received and answered her letter of inquiry.

'I was tempted to say that you were drug addicts or litter-bugs,' he said, 'or something equally repellent to managers of apartment houses.'

They asked why.

'I don't know whether or not you know it,' he said, buttering a roll, 'but the Bramford had rather an unpleasant reputation early in the century.' He looked up, saw that they didn't know, and went on. (He had a broad shiny face, blue eyes that darted enthusiastically, and a few strands of wetted-down black hair combed crossways over his scalp.) 'Along with the Isadora Duncans and Theodore Dreisers,' he said, 'the Bramford has housed a considerable number of less attractive personages. It's where the Trench sisters performed their little dietary experiments, and where Keith Kennedy held his parties. Adrian Marcato lived there too; and so did Pearl Ames.'

'Who were the Trench sisters?' Guy asked, and Rosemary asked, 'Who was Adrian Marcato?'

'The Trench sisters,' Hutch said, 'were two proper Victorian ladies who were occasional cannibals. They cooked and ate several young children, including a niece.'

'Lovely,' Guy said.

Hutch turned to Rosemary. 'Adrian Marcato practised witchcraft,' he said. 'He made quite a splash in the eighteen-nineties by announcing that he had succeeded in conjuring up the living Satan. He showed off a handful of hair and some claw-parings, and apparently people believed him; enough of them, at least, to form a mob that attacked and nearly killed him in the Bramford lobby.'

'You're joking,' Rosemary said.

'I'm quite serious. A few years later the Keith Kennedy business began, and by the twenties the house was half empty.'

Guy said, 'I knew about Keith Kennedy and about Pearl Ames, but I didn't know Adrian Marcato lived there.'

'And those sisters,' Rosemary said with a shudder.

'It was only World War Two and the housing shortage,' Hutch said, 'that filled the place up again, and now it's acquired a bit of Grand-Old-Apartment-House prestige; but in the twenties it was called Black Bramford and sensible people stayed away. The melon is for the lady, isn't it, Rosemary?'

The waiter placed their appetizers. Rosemary looked questioningly at Guy; he pursed his brow and gave a quick headshake: *It's nothing, don't let him scare you.*

The waiter left. 'Over the years,' Hutch said, 'the Bramford has had far more than its share of ugly and unsavoury happenings. Nor have all of them been in the distant past. In 1959 a dead infant was found wrapped in newspaper in the basement.'

Rosemary said, 'But – awful things probably happen in *every* apartment house now and then.'

'Now and then,' Hutch said. 'The point is, though, that at the Bramford awful things happen a good deal more frequently than "now and then". There are less spectacular irregularities too. There've been more suicides there, for instance, than in houses of comparable size and age.'

'What's the answer, Hutch?' Guy said, playing serious-and-concerned. 'There must be some kind of explanation.'

Hutch looked at him for a moment. 'I don't know,' he said. 'Perhaps it's simply that the notoriety of a pair of Trench sisters attracts an Adrian Marcato, and his notoriety attracts a Keith Kennedy, and eventually a house becomes a – a kind of rallying place for people who are more prone than others to certain types of behaviour. Or perhaps there are things we don't know yet – about magnetic fields or electrons or whatever – ways in which a place can quite literally be malign. I do know this, though: the Bramford is by no means unique. There was a house in

London, on Praed Street, in which five separate brutal murders took place within sixty years. None of the five was in any way connected with any of the others; the murderers weren't related nor were the victims, nor were all the murders committed for the same moonstone or Maltese falcon. Yet five separate brutal murders took place within sixty years. In a small house with a shop on the street and an apartment overhead. It was demolished in 1954 – for no especially pressing purpose, since as far as I know the plot was left empty.'

Rosemary worked her spoon in melon. 'Maybe there are good houses too,' she said; 'houses where people keep falling in love and getting married and having babies.'

'And becoming stars,' Guy said.

'Probably there are,' Hutch said. 'Only one never hears of them. It's the stinkers that get the publicity.' He smiled at Rosemary and Guy. 'I wish you two would look for a good house instead of the Bramford,' he said.

Rosemary's spoon of melon stopped halfway to her mouth. 'Are you honestly trying to talk us out of it?' she asked.

'My dear girl,' Hutch said, 'I had a perfectly good date with a charming woman this evening and broke it solely to see you and say my say. I am honestly trying to talk you out of it.'

'Well, Jesus, Hutch —' Guy began.

'I am not saying,' Hutch said, 'that you will walk into the Bramford and be hit on the head with a piano or eaten by spinsters or turned to stone. I am simply saying that the record is there and ought to be considered along with the reasonable rent and the working fireplace: the house has a high incidence of unpleasant happenings. Why deliberately enter a danger zone? Go to the Dakota or the Osborne if you're dead set on nineteenth-century splendour.'

'The Dakota is co-op,' Rosemary said, 'and the Osborne's going to be torn down.'

'Aren't you exaggerating a little bit, Hutch?' Guy said. 'Have there been any other "unpleasant happenings" in the past few years? Besides that baby in the basement?'

'An elevator man was killed last winter,' Hutch said. 'In a not-at-the-dinner-table kind of accident. I was at the library this afternoon with the *Times Index* and three hours of microfilm; would you care to hear more?'

Rosemary looked at Guy. He put down his fork and wiped his mouth. 'It's silly,' he said. 'All right, a lot of unpleasant things have happened there. That doesn't mean that more of them are going to happen. I don't see why the Bramford is any more of a "danger zone" than any other house in the city. You can flip a coin and get five heads in a row; that doesn't mean that the next five flips are going to be heads too, and it doesn't mean that the coin is any different from any other coin. It's coincidence, that's all.'

'If there were *really* something wrong,' Rosemary said, 'wouldn't it have been demolished? Like the house in London?'

'The house in London,' Hutch said, 'was owned by the family of the last chap murdered there. The Bramford is owned by the church next door.'

'There you are,' Guy said, lighting a cigarette; 'we've got divine protection.'

'It hasn't been working,' Hutch said.

The waiter lifted away their plates.

Rosemary said, 'I didn't know it was owned by a church,' and Guy said, 'The whole city is, honey.'

'Have you tried the Wyoming?' Hutch asked. 'It's in the same block, I think.'

'Hutch,' Rosemary said, 'we've tried everywhere. There's nothing, absolutely nothing, except the *new* houses, with neat square rooms that are all exactly alike and television cameras in the elevators.'

'Is that so terrible?' Hutch asked, smiling.

'Yes,' Rosemary said, and Guy said, 'We were set to go into one, but we backed out to take this.'

Hutch looked at them for a moment, then sat back and struck the table with wide-apart palms. 'Enough,' he said. 'I shall mind my own business, as I ought to have done from the outset. Make fires in your working fireplace! I'll give you a bolt for the door and keep my mouth shut from this day forward. I'm an idiot; forgive me.'

Rosemary smiled. 'The door already has a bolt,' she said. 'And one of those chain things and a peephole.'

'Well, mind you use all three,' Hutch said. 'And don't go wandering through the halls introducing yourself to all and sundry. You're not in Iowa.'

'Omaha.'

The waiter brought their main courses.

On the following Monday afternoon Rosemary and Guy signed a two-year lease on apartment 7E at the Bramford. They gave Mrs Cortez a check for five hundred and eighty-three dollars – a month's rent in advance and a month's rent as security – and were told that if they wished they could take occupancy of the apartment earlier than September first, as it would be cleared by the end of the week and the painters could come in on Wednesday the eighteenth.

Later on Monday they received a telephone call from Martin Gardenia, the son of the apartment's previous tenant. They agreed to meet him at the apartment on Tuesday evening at eight, and, doing so, found him to be a tall man past sixty with a cheerful open manner. He pointed out the things he wanted to sell and named his prices, all of which were attractively low. Rosemary and Guy conferred and examined, and bought two air conditioners, a rosewood vanity with a petit-point bench, the living-room's Persian rug, and the andirons, firescreen, and tools. Mrs Gardenia's rolltop desk, disappointingly, was not for sale. While Guy wrote a cheque and helped tag the items to be left behind, Rosemary measured the living-room and the bedroom with a six-foot folding rule she had bought that morning.

The previous March Guy had played a role on *Another World*, a daytime television series. The character was back now for three days, so for the rest of the week Guy was busy. Rosemary winnowed a folder of decorating schemes she had collected since high school, found two that seemed appropriate to the apartment, and with those to guide her

23

went looking at furnishings with Joan Jellico, one of the girls from Atlanta she had roomed with on coming to New York. Joan had the card of a decorator, which gave them entrance to wholesale houses and showrooms of every sort. Rosemary looked and made shorthand notes and drew sketches to bring to Guy, and hurried home spilling over with fabric and wallpaper samples in time to catch him on *Another World* and then run out again and shop for dinner. She skipped her sculpture class and cancelled, happily, a dental appointment.

On the Friday evening the apartment was theirs; an emptiness of high ceilings and unfamiliar dark into which they came with a lamp and a shopping bag, striking echoes from the farthest rooms. They turned on their air conditioners and admired their rug and their fireplace and Rosemary's vanity; admired too their bathtub, doorknobs, hinges, moulding, floors, stove, refrigerator, bay windows, and view. They picnicked on the rug, on tuna sandwiches and beer, and made floor plans of all four rooms, Guy measuring and Rosemary drawing. On the rug again, they unplugged the lamp and stripped and made love in the nightglow of shadeless windows. 'Shh!' Guy hissed afterwards, wide-eyed with fear. 'I hear – the Trench sisters chewing!' Rosemary hit him on the head, hard.

They bought a sofa and a king-size bed, a table for the kitchen, and two bentwood chairs. They called Con Ed and the phone company and stores and workmen and the Padded Wagon.

The painters came on Wednesday the eighteenth; patched, spackled, primed, painted, and were gone on Friday the twentieth, leaving colours very much like Rosemary's samples. A solitary paperhanger came in and grumbled and papered the bedroom.

They called stores and workmen and Guy's mother in Montreal. They bought an armoire and a dining table and hi-fi components and new dishes and silverware. They were flush. In 1964 Guy had done a series of Anacin commercials that, shown time and time again, had earned him eighteen thousand dollars and was still producing a sizable income.

They hung window shades and papered shelves, watched carpet go down in the bedroom and white vinyl in the hallway. They got a plug-in-phone with three jacks; paid bills and left a forwarding notice at the post office.

On Friday, August 27th, they moved. Joan and Dick Jellico sent a large potted plant and Guy's agent a small one. Hutch sent a telegram: *The Bramford will change from a bad house to a good house when one of its doors is marked R. and G. Woodhouse.*

CHAPTER THREE

AND THEN Rosemary was busy and happy. She bought
and hung curtains, found a Victorian glass lamp for the
living-room, hung pots and pans on the kitchen wall. One
day she realized that the four boards in the hall closet were
shelves, fitting across to sit on wood cleats on the side walls.
She covered them with gingham contact paper and, when
Guy came home, showed him a neatly filled linen closet.
She found a supermarket on Sixth Avenue and a Chinese
laundry on Fifty-fifth Street for the sheets and Guy's shirts.

Guy was busy too, away every day like other women's
husbands. With Labour Day past, his vocal coach was back
in town; Guy worked with him each morning and audi-
tioned for plays and commercials most afternoons. At
breakfast he was touchy reading the theatrical page –
everyone else was out of town with *Skyscraper* or *Drat! The
Cat!* or *The Impossible Years* or *Hot September*; only he
was in New York with residuals-from-Anacin – but Rosemary knew that very soon he'd get something good, and
quietly she set his coffee before him and quietly took for
herself the newspaper's other section.

The nursery was, for the time being, a den, with off-white
walls and the furniture from the old apartment. The white-
and-yellow wallpaper would come later, clean and fresh.
Rosemary had a sample of it lying ready in *Picasso's
Picassos*, along with a Saks ad showing the crib and
bureau.

She wrote to her brother Brian to share her happiness.
No one else in the family would have welcomed it; they
were all hostile now – parents, brothers, sisters – not for-
giving her for (a) marrying a Protestant, (b) marrying in
only a civil ceremony, and (c) having a mother-in-law who
had had two divorces and was married now to a Jew up in
Canada.

She made Guy chicken Marengo and *vitello tonnato*, baked a mocha layer cake and a jarful of butter cookies.

They heard Minnie Castevet before they met her; heard her through their bedroom wall, shouting in a hoarse midwestern bray. 'Roman, come to bed! It's twenty past eleven!' And five minutes later: 'Roman? Bring me in some root beer when you come!'

'I didn't know they were still making Ma and Pa Kettle movies,' Guy said, and Rosemary laughed uncertainly. She was nine years younger than Guy, and some of his references lacked clear meaning for her.

They met the Goulds in 7F, a pleasant elderly couple, and the German-accented Bruhns and their son Walter in 7C. They smiled and nodded in the hall to the Kelloggs, 7G, Mr Stein, 7H, and the Messrs Dubin and DeVore, 7B. (Rosemary learned everyone's name immediately, from doorbells and from face-up mail on doormats, which she had no qualms about reading.) The Kapps in 7D, unseen and with no mail, were apparently still away for the summer; and the Castevets in 7A, heard ('Roman! Where's Terry?') but unseen, were either recluses or comers-and-goers-at-odd-hours. Their door was opposite the elevator, their doormat supremely readable. They got air mail letters from a surprising variety of places: Hawick, Scotland; Langeac, France; Vitória, Brazil; Cessnock, Australia. They subscribed to both *Life* and *Look*.

No sign at all did Rosemary and Guy see of the Trench sisters, Adrian Marcato, Keith Kennedy, Pearl Ames, or their latter-day equivalents. Dublin and DeVore were homosexuals; everyone else seemed entirely commonplace.

Almost every night the midwestern bray could be heard, from the apartment which, Rosemary and Guy came to realize, had originally been the bigger front part of their own. 'But it's *impossible* to be a hundred per cent sure!' the woman argued, and, 'If you want *my* opinion, we shouldn't tell her at *all*; that's *my* opinion!'

One Saturday night the Castevets had a party, with a dozen or so people talking and singing. Guy fell asleep easily but Rosemary lay awake until after two, hearing flat unmusical singing and a flute or clarinet that piped along beside it.

The only time Rosemary remembered Hutch's misgivings and was made uneasy by them was when she went down to the basement every fourth day or so to do the laundry. The service elevator was in itself unsettling – small, unmanned, and given to sudden creaks and tremors – and the basement was an eerie place of once-whitewashed brick passageways where footfalls whispered distantly and unseen doors thudded closed, where cast-off refrigerators faced the wall under glary bulbs in wire cages.

It was here, Rosemary would remember, that a dead baby wrapped in newspaper had not so long ago been found. Whose baby had it been, and how had it died? Who had found it? Had the person who left it been caught and punished? She thought of going to the library and reading the story in old newspapers as Hutch had done; but that would have made it more real, more dreadful than it already was. To know the spot where the baby had lain, to have perhaps to walk past it on the way to the laundry room and again on the way back to the elevator, would have been unbearable. Partial ignorance, she decided, was partial bliss. *Damn Hutch and his good intentions!*

The laundry room would have done nicely in a prison: steamy brick walls, more bulbs in cages, and scores of deep double sinks in iron-mesh cubicles. There were coin-operated washers and dryers and, in most of the padlocked cubicles, privately owned machines. Rosemary came down on weekends or after five; earlier on weekdays a bevy of Negro laundresses ironed and gossiped and had abruptly fallen silent at her one unknowing intrusion. She had smiled all around and tried to be invisible, but they hadn't spoken another word and she had felt self-conscious, clumsy, and Negro-oppressing.

One afternoon, when she and Guy had been in the Bramford a little over two weeks, Rosemary was sitting in the laundry room at 5.15 reading *The New Yorker* and waiting to add softener to the rinse water when a girl her own age came in – a dark-haired cameo-faced girl who, Rosemary realized with a start, was Anna Maria Alberghetti. She was wearing white sandals, black shorts, and an apricot silk blouse, and was carrying a yellow plastic laundry basket. Nodding at Rosemary and then not looking at her, she went to one of the washers, opened it, and began feeding dirty clothes into it.

Anna Maria Alberghetti, as far as Rosemary knew, did not live at the Bramford, but she could well have been visiting someone and helping out with the chores. A closer look, though, told Rosemary that she was mistaken; this girl's nose was too long and sharp and there were other less definable differences of expression and carriage. The resemblance, however, was a remarkable one – and suddenly Rosemary found the girl looking at her with an embarrassed questioning smile, the washer beside her closed and filling.

'I'm sorry,' Rosemary said. 'I thought you were Anna Maria Alberghetti, so I've been staring at you. I'm sorry.'

The girl blushed and smiled and looked at the floor a few feet to her side. 'That happens a lot,' she said. 'You don't have to apologize. People have been thinking I'm Anna Maria since I was, oh, just a kid, when she first started out in *Here Comes The Groom*.' She looked at Rosemary, still blushing but no longer smiling. 'I don't see a resemblance at all,' she said. 'I'm of Italian parentage like she is, but no *physical* resemblance.'

'There's a very strong one,' Rosemary said.

'I guess there is,' the girl said; 'everyone's always telling me. I don't see it though. I wish I did, believe me.'

'Do you know her?' Rosemary asked.

'No.'

'The way you said "Anna Maria" I thought —'

'Oh no, I just call her that. I guess from talking about her so much with everyone.' She wiped her hand on her shorts and stepped forward, holding it out and smiling. 'I'm Terry Gionoffrio,' she said, 'and *I* can't spell it so don't *you* try.'

Rosemary smiled and shook hands. 'I'm Rosemary

Woodhouse,' she said. 'We're new tenants here. Have you been here long?'

'I'm not a tenant at all,' the girl said. 'I'm just staying with Mr and Mrs Castevet, up on the seventh floor. I'm their guest, sort of, since June. Oh, you know them?'

'No,' Rosemary said, smiling, 'but our apartment is right behind theirs and used to be the back part of it.'

'Oh for goodness' sake,' the girl said, 'you're the party that took the old lady's apartment! Mrs – the old lady who died!'

'Gardenia.'

'That's right. She was a good *friend* of the Castevets. She used to grow herbs and things and bring them in for Mrs Castevet to cook with.'

Rosemary nodded. 'When we first looked at the apartment,' she said, 'one room was full of plants.'

'And now that she's dead,' Terry said, 'Mrs Castevet's got a miniature greenhouse in the kitchen and grows things herself.'

'Excuse me, I have to put softener in,' Rosemary said. She got up and got the bottle from the laundry bag on the washer.

'Do you know who *you* look like?' Terry asked her; and Rosemary, unscrewing the cap, said, 'No, who?'

'Piper Laurie.'

Rosemary laughed. 'Oh, no,' she said. 'It's funny your saying that, because my husband used to date Piper Laurie before she got married.'

'No kidding? In Hollywood?'

'No, here.' Rosemary poured a capful of the softener. Terry opened the washer door and Rosemary thanked her and tossed the softener in.

'Is he an actor, your husband?' Terry asked.

Rosemary nodded complacently, capping the bottle.

'No kidding! What's his name?'

'Guy Woodhouse,' Rosemary said. 'He was in *Luther* and *Nobody Loves An Albatross*, and he does a lot of work in television.'

'Gee, I watch TV all day long,' Terry said. 'I'll bet I've

seen him!' Glass crashed somewhere in the basement; a bottle smashing or a windowpane. 'Yow,' Terry said.

Rosemary hunched her shoulders and looked uneasily towards the laundry room's doorway. 'I hate this basement,' she said.

'Me too,' Terry said. 'I'm glad you're here. If I was alone now I'd be scared stiff.'

'A delivery boy probably dropped a bottle,' Rosemary said.

Terry said, 'Listen, we could come down together regular. Your door is by the service elevator, isn't it? I could ring your bell and we could come down together. We could call each other first on the house phone.'

'That would be great,' Rosemary said. 'I hate coming down here alone.'

Terry laughed happily, seemed to seek words, and then, still laughing, said, 'I've got a good luck charm that'll maybe do for both of us!' She pulled away the collar of her blouse, drew out a silver neckchain, and showed Rosemary on the end of it a silver filigree ball a little less than an inch in diameter.

'Oh, that's *beautiful*,' Rosemary said.

'Isn't it?' Terry said. 'Mrs Castevet gave it to me the day before yesterday. It's three hundred years old. She grew the stuff inside it in that little greenhouse. It's good luck, or anyway it's supposed to be.'

Rosemary looked more closely at the charm Terry held out between thumb and fingertip. It was filled with a greenish-brown spongy substance that pressed out against the silver openwork. A bitter smell made Rosemary draw back.

Terry laughed again. 'I'm not mad about the smell either,' she said. 'I hope it works!'

'It's a beautiful charm,' Rosemary said. 'I've never seen anything like it.'

'It's European,' Terry said. She leaned a hip against a washer and admired the ball, turning it one way and another. 'The Castevets are the most wonderful people in the world, bar none,' she said. 'They picked me up off the sidewalk – and I mean that literally; I conked out on Eighth Avenue – and they brought me here and adopted me like a mother and father. Or like a grandmother and grandfather, I guess.'

'You were sick?' Rosemary asked.

'That's putting it mildly,' Terry said. 'I was starving and on dope and doing a lot of other things that I'm so ashamed of I could throw up just thinking about them. And Mr and Mrs Castevet completely rehabilitated me. They got me off the H, the dope, and got food into me and clean clothes on me, and now nothing is too good for me as far as they're concerned. They give me all kinds of health food and vitamins, they even have a doctor come give me regular checkups! It's because they're childless. I'm like the daughter they never had, you know?'

Rosemary nodded.

'I thought at first that maybe they had some kind of ulterior motive,' Terry said. 'Maybe some kind of sex thing they would want me to do, or he would want, or she. But they've really been like real grandparents. Nothing like that. They're going to put me through secretarial school in a little while and later on I'm going to pay them back. I only had three years of high school but there's a way of making it up.' She dropped the filigree ball back into her blouse.

Rosemary said, 'It's nice to know there are people like that, when you hear so much about apathy and people who are afraid of getting involved.'

'There aren't many like Mr and Mrs Castevet,' Terry said. 'I would be dead now if it wasn't for them. That's an absolute fact. Dead or in jail.'

'You don't have any family that could have helped you?'

'A brother in the Navy. The less said about *him* the better.'

Rosemary transferred her finished wash to a dryer and waited with Terry for hers to be done. They spoke of Guy's occasional role on *Another World* ('Sure I remember! You're married to *him*?'), the Bramford's past (of which Terry knew nothing), and the coming visit to New York of

32

Pope Paul. Terry was, like Rosemary, Catholic but no longer observing; she was anxious, though, to get a ticket to the papal mass to be celebrated at Yankee Stadium. When her wash was done and drying the two girls walked together to the service elevator and rode to the seventh floor. Rosemary invited Terry in to see the apartment, but Terry asked if she could take a rain check; the Castevets ate at six and she didn't like to be late. She said she would call Rosemary on the house phone later in the evening so they could go down together to pick up their dry laundry.

Guy was home, eating a bag of Fritos and watching a Grace Kelly movie. 'Them sure must be clean clothes,' he said.

Rosemary told him about Terry and the Castevets, and that Terry had remembered him from *Another World*. He made light of it, but it pleased him. He was depressed by the likelihood that an actor named Donald Baumgart was going to beat him out for a part in a new comedy for which both had read a second time that afternoon. 'Jesus Christ,' he said, 'what kind of a name is *Donald Baumgart?*' His own name, before he changed it, had been Sherman Peden.

Rosemary and Terry picked up their laundry at eight o'clock, and Terry came in with Rosemary to meet Guy and see the apartment. She blushed and was flustered by Guy, which spurred him to flowery compliments and the bringing of ashtrays and the striking of matches. Terry had never seen the apartment before; Mrs Gardenia and the Castevets had had a falling-out shortly after her arrival, and soon afterwards Mrs Gardenia had gone into the coma from which she had never emerged. 'It's a lovely apartment,' Terry said.

'It will be,' Rosemary said. 'We're not even halfway furnished yet.'

'I've *got* it!' Guy cried with a handclap. He pointed triumphantly at Terry. 'Anna Maria Alberghetti!'

CHAPTER FOUR

A PACKAGE CAME from Bonniers, from Hutch; a tall
teakwood ice bucket with a bright orange lining. Rosemary
called him at once and thanked him. He had seen the
apartment after the painters left but not since she and Guy
had moved in; she explained about the chairs that were a
week late and the sofa that wasn't due for another month.
'For God's sake don't even think yet about entertaining,'
Hutch said. 'Tell me how everything is.'

Rosemary told him, in happy detail. 'And the neighbours
certainly don't *seem* abnormal,' she said. 'Except normal
abnormal like homosexuals; there are two of them, and
across the hall from us there's a nice old couple named
Gould with a place in Pennsylvania where they breed Persian cats. We can have one any time we want.'

'They shed,' Hutch said.

'And there's another couple that we haven't actually met
yet who took in this girl who was hooked on drugs, whom
we *have* met, and they completely cured her and are putting her through secretarial school.'

'It sounds as if you've moved into Sunnybrook Farm,'
Hutch said; 'I'm delighted.'

'The basement is kind of creepy,' Rosemary said. 'I curse
you every time I go down there.'

'Why on earth me?'

'Your *stories*.'

'If you mean the ones I write, I curse me too; if you mean
the ones I told you, you might with equal justification curse
the fire alarm for the fire and the weather bureau for the
typhoon.'

Rosemary, cowed, said, 'It won't be so bad from now on.
That girl I mentioned is going down there with me.'

Hutch said, 'It's obvious you've exerted the healthy influence I predicted and the house is no longer a chamber of

horrors. Have fun with the ice bucket and say hello to Guy.'

The Kapps in apartment 7D appeared; a stout couple in their middle thirties with an inquisitive two-year-old daughter named Lisa. 'What's your name?' Lisa asked, sitting in her stroller. 'Did you eat your egg? Did you eat your Captain Crunch?'

'My name is Rosemary,' Rosemary said. 'I ate my egg but I've never even *heard* of Captain Crunch. Who is he?'

On Friday night, September 17th, Rosemary and Guy went with two other couples to a preview of a play called *Mrs Dally* and then to a party given by a photographer, Dee Bertillon, in his studio on West Forty-eighth Street. An argument developed between Guy and Bertillon over Actors Equity's policy of blocking the employment of foreign actors – Guy thought it was right, Bertillon thought it was wrong – and though the others present buried the disagreement under a quick tide of jokes and gossip, Guy took Rosemary away soon after, at a few minutes past twelve-thirty.

The night was mild and balmy and they walked; and as they approached the Bramford's blackened mass they saw on the sidewalk before it a group of twenty or so people gathered in a semicircle at the side of a parked car. Two police cars waited double-parked, their roof lights spinning red.

Rosemary and Guy walked faster, hand in hand, their senses sharpening. Cars on the avenue slowed questioningly; windows scraped open in the Bramford and heads looked out beside gargoyles' heads. The night doorman Toby came from the house with a tan blanket that a policeman turned to take from him.

The roof of the car, a Volkswagen, was crumpled to the side; the windshield was crazed with a million fractures. 'Dead,' someone said, and someone else said, 'I look up and I think it's some kind of a big bird zooming down, like an eagle or something.'

Rosemary and Guy stood on tiptoes, craned over people's shoulders. 'Get back now, will you?' a policeman at the centre said. The shoulders separated, a sport-shirted back moved away. On the sidewalk Terry lay, watching the sky with one eye, half of her face gone to red pulp. Tan blanket flipped over her. Settling, it reddened in one place and then another.

Rosemary wheeled, eyes shut, right hand making an automatic cross. She kept her mouth tightly closed, afraid she might vomit.

Guy winced and drew air in under his teeth. 'Oh, Jesus,' he said, and groaned. 'Oh my God.'

A policeman said, 'Get back, will you?'

'We know her,' Guy said.

Another policeman turned and said, 'What's her name?'

'Terry.'

'Terry what?' He was forty or so and sweating. His eyes were blue and beautiful, with thick black lashes.

Guy said, 'Ro? What was her name? Terry what?'

Rosemary opened her eyes and swallowed. 'I don't remember,' she said. 'Italian, with a G. A long name. She made a joke about spelling it. Not being able to.'

Guy said to the blue-eyed policeman. 'She was staying with people named Castevet, in apartment seven A.'

'We've got that already,' the policeman said.

Another policeman came up, holding a sheet of pale yellow notepaper. Mr Micklas was behind him, tight-mouthed, in a raincoat over striped pyjamas. 'Short and sweet,' the policeman said to the blue-eyed one, and handed him the yellow paper. 'She stuck it to the window sill with a band-aid so it wouldn't blow away.'

'Anybody there?'

The other shook his head.

The blue-eyed policeman read what was written on the sheet of paper, sucking thoughtfully at his front teeth. 'Theresa Gionoffrio,' he said. He pronounced it as an Italian would. Rosemary nodded.

Guy said, 'Wednesday night you wouldn't have guessed she had a sad thought in her mind.'

'Nothing but sad thoughts,' the policeman said, opening his pad holder. He laid the paper inside it and closed the holder with a width of yellow sticking out.

'Did you know her?' Mr Micklas asked Rosemary.

'Only slightly,' she said.

'Oh, of course,' Mr Micklas said; 'you're on seven too.'

Guy said to Rosemary, 'Come on, honey, let's go upstairs.'

The policeman said, 'Do you have any idea where we can find these people Castevet?'

'No, none at all,' Guy said. 'We've never even met them.'

'They're usually at home now,' Rosemary said. 'We hear them through the wall. Our bedroom is next to theirs.'

Guy put his hand on Rosemary's back. 'Come on, hon,' he said. They nodded to the policeman and Mr Micklas, and started towards the house.

'Here they come now,' Mr Micklas said. Rosemary and Guy stopped and turned. Coming from downtown, as they themselves had come, were a tall, broad, white-haired woman and a tall, thin, shuffling man. 'The Castevets?' Rosemary asked. Mr Micklas nodded.

Mrs Castevet was wrapped in light blue, with snow-white dabs of gloves, purse, shoes, and hat. Nurse-like she supported her husband's forearm. He was dazzling, in an every-colour seersucker jacket, red slacks, a pink bow tie, and a grey fedora with a pink band. He was seventy-five or older; she was sixty-eight or nine. They came closer with expressions of young alertness, with friendly quizzical smiles. The policeman stepped forward to meet them and their smiles faltered and fell away. Mrs Castevet said something worryingly; Mr Castevet frowned and shook his head. His wide, thin-lipped mouth was rosy-pink, as if lipsticked; his cheeks were chalky, his eyes small and bright in deep sockets. She was big-nosed, with a sullen fleshy underlip. She wore pink-rimmed eyeglasses on a neckchain that dipped down from behind plain pearl earrings.

The policeman said, 'Are you folks the Castevets on the seventh floor?'

'We are,' Mr Castevet said in a dry voice that had to be listened for.

'You have a young woman named Theresa Gionoffrio living with you?'

'We do,' Mr Castevet said. 'What's wrong? Has there been an accident?'

'You'd better brace yourselves for some bad news,' the policeman said. He waited, looking at each of them in turn and then he said, 'She's dead. She killed herself.' He raised a hand, the thumb pointing back over his shoulder. 'She jumped out of the window.'

They looked at him with no change of expression at all, as if he hadn't spoken yet; then Mrs Castevet leaned sideways, glanced beyond him at the red-stained blanket, and stood straight again and looked him in the eyes. 'That's not possible,' she said in her loud midwestern Roman-bring-me-some-root-beer voice. 'It's a mistake. Somebody else is under there.'

The policeman, not turning from her, said, 'Artie, would you let these people take a look, please?'

Mrs Castevet marched past him, her jaw set.

Mr Castevet stayed where he was. 'I knew this would happen,' he said. 'She got deeply depressed every three weeks or so. I noticed it and told my wife, but she pooh-poohed me. She's an optimist who refuses to admit that everything doesn't always turn out the way she wants it to.'

Mrs Castevet came back. 'That doesn't mean that she killed herself,' she said. 'She was a very happy girl with no *reason* for self-destruction. It must have been an accident. She must have been cleaning the windows and lost her hold. She was always surprising us by cleaning things and doing things for us.'

'She wasn't cleaning windows at midnight,' Mr Castevet said.

'Why not?' Mrs Castevet said angrily. 'Maybe she was!'

The policeman held out the pale yellow paper, having taken it from his pad holder.

Mrs Castevet hesitated, then took it and turned it around and read it. Mr Castevet tipped his head in over her arm and read it too, his thin vivid lips moving.

38

'Is that her handwriting?' the policeman asked.

Mrs Castevet nodded. Mr Castevet said, 'Definitely. Absolutely.'

The policeman held out his hand and Mrs Castevet gave him the paper. He said, 'Thank you. I'll see you get it back when we're done with it.'

She took off her glasses, dropped them on their neckchain, and covered both her eyes with white-gloved fingertips. 'I don't believe it,' she said. 'I just don't believe it. She was so happy. All her troubles were in the past.' Mr Castevet put his hand on her shoulder and looked at the ground and shook his head.

'Do you know the name of her next-of-kin?' the policeman asked.

'She didn't have any,' Mrs Castevet said. 'She was all alone. She didn't have anyone, only us.'

'Didn't she have a brother?' Rosemary asked.

Mrs Castevet put on her glasses and looked at her. Mr Castevet looked up from the ground, his deep-socketed eyes glinting under his hat brim.

'Did she?' the policeman asked.

'She said she did,' Rosemary said. 'In the Navy.'

The policeman looked to the Castevets.

'It's news to me,' Mrs Castevet said, and Mr Castevet said, 'To both of us.'

The policeman asked Rosemary, 'Do you know his rank or where he's stationed?'

'No, I don't,' she said, and to the Castevets: 'She mentioned him to me the other day, in the laundry room. I'm Rosemary Woodhouse.'

Guy said, 'We're in seven E.'

'I feel just the way you do, Mrs Castevet,' Rosemary said. 'She seemed so happy and full of – of good feelings about the future. She said *wonderful* things about you and your husband; how grateful she was to both of you for all the help you were giving her.'

'Thank you,' Mrs Castevet said, and Mr Castevet said 'It's nice of you to tell us that. It makes it a little easier.'

The policeman said, 'You don't know anything else about

this brother except that he's in the Navy?'

'That's all,' Rosemary said. 'I don't think she liked him very much.'

'It should be easy to find him,' Mr Castevet said, 'with an uncommon name like Gionoffrio.'

Guy put his hand on Rosemary's back again and they withdrew towards the house. 'I'm so stunned and so sorry,' Rosemary said to the Castevets; and Guy said, 'It's such a pity. It's —'

Mrs Castevet said, 'Thank you,' and Mr Castevet said something long and sibilant of which only the phrase 'her last days' was understandable.

They rode upstairs ('Oh, my!' the night elevator man Diego said; 'Oh, my! Oh, my!'), looked ruefully at the now-haunted door of 7A, and walked through the branching hallway to their own apartment. Mr Kellogg in 7G peered out from behind his chained door and asked what was going on downstairs. They told him.

They sat on the edge of their bed for a few minutes, speculating about Terry's reason for killing herself. Only if the Castevets told them some day what was in the note, they agreed, would they ever learn for certain what had driven her to the violent death they had nearly witnessed. And even knowing what was in the note, Guy pointed out, they might still not know the full answer, for part of it had probably been beyond Terry's own understanding. Something had led her to drugs and something had led her to death; what that something was, it was too late now for anyone to know.

'Remember what Hutch said?' Rosemary asked. 'About there being more suicides here than in other buildings?'

'Ah, Ro,' Guy said, 'that's crap, honey, that "danger zone" business.'

'Hutch believes it.'

'Well, it's *still* crap.'

'I can imagine what he's going to say when he hears about this.'

'Don't tell him,' Guy said. 'He sure as hell won't read

40

about it in the papers.' A strike against the New York newspapers had begun that morning, and there were rumours that it might continue a month or longer.

They undressed, showered, resumed a stopped game of Scrabble, stopped it, made love, and found milk and a dish of cold spaghetti in the refrigerator. Just before they put the lights out at two-thirty, Guy remembered to check the answering service and found that he had got a part in a radio commercial for Cresta Blanca wines.

Soon he was asleep, but Rosemary lay awake beside him, seeing Terry's pulped face and her one eye watching the sky. After a while, though, she was at Our Lady. Sister Agnes was shaking her fist at her, ousting her from leadership of the second-floor monitors. 'Sometimes I wonder how come you're the leader of *anything*!' she said. A bump on the other side of the wall woke Rosemary, and Mrs Castevet said, 'And please don't tell me what Laura-Louise said because I'm not interested!' Rosemary turned over and burrowed into her pillow.

Sister Agnes was furious. Her piggy-eyes were squeezed to slits and her nostrils were bubbling the way they always did at such moments. Thanks to Rosemary it had been necessary to brick up all the windows, and now Our Lady had been taken out of the beautiful-school competition being run by the *World-Herald*. 'If you'd listened to *me*, we wouldn't have *had* to do it!' Sister Agnes cried in a hoarse midwestern bray. 'We'd have been all set to go now instead of starting all over from scratch!' Uncle Mike tried to hush her. He was the principal of Our Lady, which was connected by passageways to his body shop in South Omaha. 'I *told* you not to tell her anything in advance,' Sister Agnes continued lower, piggy-eyes glinting hatefully at Rosemary. 'I *told* you she wouldn't be open-minded. Time enough *later* to let her in on it.' (Rosemary had told Sister Veronica about the windows being bricked up and Sister Veronica had withdrawn the school from the competition; otherwise no one would have noticed and they would have won. It had been right to tell, though, Sister Agnes notwithstanding. A Catholic school shouldn't win by trickery.) 'Anybody! Anybody!' Sister Agnes said. 'All she has to be is young, healthy, and not a virgin. She doesn't have to be a no-good drug-addict whore out of the gutter. Didn't I say that in the beginning? Anybody. As long as she's young and healthy and not a virgin.' Which didn't make sense at all, not even to Uncle Mike; so Rosemary turned over and it was Saturday afternoon, and she and Brian and Eddie and Jean were at the candy counter in the Orpheum, going in to see Gary Cooper and Patricia Neal in *The Fountainhead*, only it was live, not a movie.

CHAPTER FIVE

ON THE FOLLOWING Monday morning Rosemary was putting away the last of a double armload of groceries when the doorbell rang; and the peephole showed Mrs Castevet, white hair in curlers under a blue-and-white kerchief, looking solemnly straight ahead as if waiting for the click of a passport photographer's camera.

Rosemary opened the door and said, 'Hello. How are you?'

Mrs Castevet smiled bleakly. 'Fine,' she said. 'May I come in for a minute?'

'Yes, of course; please do.' Rosemary stood back against the wall and held the door wide open. A faint bitter smell brushed across her as Mrs Castevet came in, the smell of Terry's silver good luck charm filled with spongy greenish-brown. Mrs Castevet was wearing toreador pants and shouldn't have been; her hips and thighs were massive, slabbed with wide bands of fat. The pants were lime green under a blue blouse; the blade of a screwdriver poked from her hip pocket. Stopping between the doorways of the den and kitchen, she turned and put on her neckchained glasses and smiled at Rosemary. A dream Rosemary had had a night or two earlier sparked in her mind – something about Sister Agnes bawling her out for bricking up windows – and she shook it away and smiled attentively, ready to hear what Mrs Castevet was about to say.

'I just came over to thank you,' Mrs Castevet said, 'for saying those nice things to us the other night, poor Terry telling you she was grateful to us for what we done. You'll never know how comforting it was to hear something like that in such a shock moment, because in both of our minds was the thought that maybe we had failed her in some way and *drove* her to it, although her note made it crystal clear, of course, that she did it of her own free will; but anyway it was a blessing to hear the words spoken out loud like that by somebody Terry had confided in just before the end.'

'Please, there's no reason to thank me,' Rosemary said. 'All I did was tell you what she said to me.'

'A lot of people wouldn't have bothered,' Mrs Castevet said. 'They'd have just walked away without wanting to spend the air and the little bit of muscle power. When you're older you'll come to realize that acts of kindness are few and far between in this world of ours. So I *do* thank you, and Roman does too. Roman is my hubby.'

Rosemary ducked her head in concession, smiled, and said, 'You're welcome. I'm glad that I helped.'

'She was cremated yesterday morning with no ceremony,' Mrs Castevet said. 'That's the way she wanted it. Now we have to forget and go on. It certainly won't be easy; we took a lot of pleasure in having her around, not having children of our own. Do you have any?'

'No, we don't,' Rosemary said.

Mrs Castevet looked into the kitchen. 'Oh, that's nice,' she said, 'the pan's hanging on the wall that way. And look how you put the table, isn't that interesting.'

'It was in a magazine,' Rosemary said.

'You certainly got a nice paint job,' Mrs Castevet said, fingering the door jamb appraisingly. 'Did the house do it? You must have been mighty openhanded with the painters; they didn't do this kind of work for *us*.'

'All we gave them was five dollars each,' Rosemary said.

'Oh, is that all?' Mrs Castevet turned around and looked into the den. 'Oh, that's nice,' she said, 'a TV room.'

'It's only temporary,' Rosemary said. 'At least I hope it is. It's going to be a nursery.'

'Are you pregnant?' Mrs Castevet asked, looking at her.

'Not yet,' Rosemary said, 'but I hope to be, as soon as we're settled.'

'That's wonderful,' Mrs Castevet said. 'You're young and healthy; you ought to have lots of children.'

'We plan to have three,' Rosemary said. 'Would you like to see the rest of the apartment?'

'I'd love to,' Mrs Castevet said. 'I'm dying to see what

you've done to it. I used to be in here almost every day. The woman who had it before you was a dear friend of mine.'

'I know,' Rosemary said, easing past Mrs Castevet to lead the way; 'Terry told me.'

'Oh, did she,' Mrs Castevet said, following along. 'It sounds like you two had some long talks together down there in the laundry room.'

'Only one,' Rosemary said.

The living-room startled Mrs Castevet. 'My goodness!' she said. 'I can't get over the change! It looks so much *brighter*! Oh and look at that chair. Isn't that handsome?'

'It just came Friday,' Rosemary said.

'What did you pay for a chair like that?'

Rosemary, disconcerted, said, 'I'm not sure. I think it was about two hundred dollars.'

'You don't mind my asking, do you?' Mrs Castevet said, and tapped her nose. 'That's how I got a big nose, by being nosy.'

Rosemary laughed and said, 'No, no, it's all right. I don't mind.'

Mrs Castevet inspected the living-room, the bedroom, and the bathroom, asking how much Mrs Gardenia's son had charged them for the rug and the vanity, where they had got the night-table lamps, exactly how old Rosemary was, and if an electric toothbrush was really any better than the old kind. Rosemary found herself enjoying this open forthright old woman with her loud voice and her blunt questions. She offered coffee and cake to her.

'What does your hubby do?' Mrs Castevet asked, sitting at the kitchen table idly checking prices on cans of soup and oysters. Rosemary, folding a Chemex paper, told her. 'I knew it!' Mrs Castevet said. 'I said to Roman yesterday, "He's so good-looking I'll bet he's a movie actor!" There's three-four of them in the building, you know. What movies was he in?'

'No movies,' Rosemary said. 'He was in two plays called *Luther* and *Nobody Loves An Albatross* and he does a lot of work in television and radio.'

They had the coffee and cake in the kitchen, Mrs Castevet refusing to let Rosemary disturb the living-room on her account. 'Listen, Rosemary,' she said, swallowing cake and coffee at once, 'I've got a two-inch-thick sirloin steak sitting defrosting right this minute, and half of it's going to go to waste with just Roman and me there to eat it. Why don't you and Guy come over and have supper with us tonight, what do you say?'

'Oh, no, we couldn't,' Rosemary said.

'Sure you could; why not?'

'No, really, I'm sure you don't want to —'

'It would be a big help to us if you would,' Mrs Castevet said. She looked into her lap, then looked up at Rosemary with a hard-to-carry smile. 'We had friends with us last night and Saturday,' she said, 'but this'll be the first night we'll be alone since – the other night.'

Rosemary leaned forward feelingly. 'If you're *sure* it won't be trouble for you,' she said.

'Honey, if it was trouble I wouldn't ask you,' Mrs Castevet said. 'Believe me, I'm as selfish as the day is long.'

Rosemary smiled. 'That isn't what Terry told me,' she said.

'Well,' Mrs Castevet said with a pleased smile, 'Terry didn't know what she was talking about.'

'I'll have to check with Guy,' Rosemary said, 'but you go ahead and count on us.'

Mrs Castevet said happily, 'Listen! You tell him I won't take no for an answer! I want to be able to tell folks I knew him when!'

They ate their cake and coffee, talking of the excitements and hazards of an acting career, the new season's television shows and how bad they were, and the continuing newspaper strike.

'Will six-thirty be too early for you?' Mrs Castevet asked at the door.

'It'll be perfect,' Rosemary said.

'Roman don't like to eat any later than that,' Mrs Castevet said. 'He has stomach trouble and if he eats too late he can't get to sleep. You know where we are, don't you?

Seven A, at six-thirty. We'll be looking forward. Oh, here's your mail, dear; I'll get it. Ads. Well, it's better than getting nothing, isn't it?'

Guy came home at two-thirty in a bad mood; he had learned from his agent that, as he had feared, the grotesquely named Donald Baumgart had won the part he had come within a hair of getting. Rosemary kissed him and installed him in his new easy chair with a melted cheese sandwich and a glass of beer. She had read the script of the play and not liked it; it would probably close out of town, she told Guy, and Donald Baumgart would never be heard of again.

'Even if it folds,' Guy said, 'it's the kind of part that gets noticed. You'll see; he'll get something else right after.' He opened the corner of his sandwich, looked in bitterly, closed it, and started eating.

'Mrs Castevet was here this morning,' Rosemary said. 'To thank me for telling them that Terry was grateful to them. I think she really just wanted to see the apartment. She's absolutely the nosiest person I've ever seen. She actually asked the prices of things.'

'No kidding,' Guy said.

'She comes right out and *admits* she's nosy, though, so it's kind of funny and forgivable instead of annoying. She even looked into the medicine chest.'

'Just like that?'

'Just like that. And guess what she was wearing.'

'A Pillsbury sack with three X's on it.'

'No, toreador pants.'

'*Toreador* pants?'

'Lime-green ones.'

'Ye gods.'

Kneeling on the floor between the bay windows, Rosemary drew a line on brown paper with crayon and a yardstick and then measured the depth of the window seats. 'She invited us to have dinner with them this evening,' she said, and looked at Guy. 'I told her I'd have to check with you, but that it would probably be okay.'

'Ah, Jesus, Ro,' Guy said, 'we don't want to do that, do we?'

'I think they're lonely,' Rosemary said. 'Because of Terry.'

'Honey,' Guy said, 'if we get friendly with an old couple like that we're *never* going to get them off our necks. They're right here on the same floor with us, they'll be looking in six times a day. Especially if she's nosy to begin with.'

'I told her she could count on us,' Rosemary said.

'I thought you told her you had to check first.'

'I did, but I told her she could count on us too.' Rosemary looked helplessly at Guy. 'She was so anxious for us to come.'

'Well, it's not my night for being kind to Ma and Pa Kettle,' Guy said. 'I'm sorry, honey, call her up and tell her we can't make it.'

'All right, I will,' Rosemary said, and drew another line with the crayon and the yardstick.

Guy finished his sandwich. 'You don't have to sulk about it,' he said.

'I'm not sulking,' Rosemary said. 'I see exactly what you mean about them being on the same floor. It's a valid point and you're absolutely right. I'm not sulking at all.'

'Oh hell,' Guy said, 'we'll go.'

'No, no, what for? We don't have to. I shopped for dinner before she came, so *that's* no problem.'

'We'll go,' Guy said.

'We don't have to if you don't want to. That sounds so phony but I really mean it, really I do.'

'We'll go. It'll be my good deed for the day.'

'All right, but only if you want to. And we'll make it very clear to them that it's only this one time and not the beginning of anything. Right?'

'Right.'

CHAPTER SIX

AT A FEW minutes past six-thirty Rosemary and Guy left their apartment and walked through the branches of dark green hallway to the Castevets' door. As Guy rang the doorbell the elevator behind them clanged open and Mr Dubin or Mr DeVore (they didn't know which was which) came out carrying a suit swathed in cleaner's plastic. He smiled and, unlocking the door of 7B next to them, said, 'You're in the wrong place, aren't you?' Rosemary and Guy made friendly laughs and he let himself in, calling 'Me!' and allowing them a glimpse of a black sideboard and red-and-gold wallpaper.

The Castevets' door opened and Mrs Castevet was there, powdered and rouged and smiling broadly in light green silk and a frilled pink apron. 'Perfect timing!' she said. 'Come on in! Roman's making Vodka Blushes in the blender. My, I'm glad you could come, Guy! I'm fixing to tell people I knew you when! "Had dinner right off that plate, he did – Guy Woodhouse in person!" I'm not going to wash it when you're done; I'm going to leave it just as is!'

Guy and Rosemary laughed and exchanged glances; *Your friend,* his said, and hers said, *What can I do?*

There was a large foyer in which a rectangular table was set for four, with an embroidered white cloth, plates that didn't all match, and bright ranks of ornate silver. To the left the foyer opened on a living-room easily twice the size of Rosemary and Guy's but otherwise much like it. It had one large bay window instead of two smaller ones, and a huge pink marble mantel sculptured with lavish scrollwork. The room was oddly furnished; at the fireplace end there were a settee and a lamp table and a few chairs, and at the opposite end an officelike clutter of file cabinets, bridge tables piled with newspapers, overfilled bookshelves, and a typewriter on a metal stand. Between the two ends of the

49

room was a twenty-foot field of brown wall-to-wall carpet, deep and new-looking, marked with the trail of a vacuum cleaner. In the centre of it, entirely alone, a small round table stood holding *Life* and *Look* and *Scientific American*.

Mrs Castevet showed them across the brown carpet and seated them on the settee; and as they sat Mr Castevet came in, holding in both hands a small tray on which four cocktail glasses ran over with clear pink liquid. Staring at the rims of the glasses he shuffled forward across the carpet, looking as if with every step he would trip and fall disastrously. 'I seem to have overfilled the glasses,' he said. 'No, no, don't get up. Please. Generally I pour these out as precisely as a bartender, don't I, Minnie?'

Mrs Castevet said, 'Just watch the carpet.'

'But this evening,' Mr Castevet continued, coming closer, 'I made a little too much, and rather than leave the surplus in the blender, I'm afraid I thought I . . . There we are. Please, sit down. Mrs Woodhouse?'

Rosemary took a glass, thanked him, and sat. Mrs Castevet quickly put a paper cocktail napkin in her lap.

'Mr Woodhouse? A Vodka Blush. Have you ever tasted one?'

'No,' Guy said, taking one and sitting.

'Minnie,' Mr Castevet said.

'It looks delicious,' Rosemary said, smiling vividly as she wiped the base of her glass.

'They're very popular in Australia,' Mr Castevet said. He took the final glass and raised it to Rosemary and Guy. 'To our guests,' he said. 'Welcome to our home.' He drank and cocked his head critically, one eye partway closed, the tray at his side dripping on the carpet.

Mrs Castevet coughed in mid-swallow. 'The carpet!' she choked, pointing.

Mr Castevet looked down. 'Oh dear,' he said, and held the tray up uncertainly.

Mrs Castevet thrust aside her drink, hurried to her knees, and laid a paper napkin carefully over the wetness. 'Brand-new carpet,' she said. 'Brand-new carpet. This man is so clumsy!'

The Vodka Blushes were tart and quite good.

'Do you come from Australia?' Rosemary asked, when the carpet had been blotted, the tray safely kitchened, and the Castevets seated in straight-backed chairs.

'Oh no,' Mr Castevet said, 'I'm from right here in New York City. I've been there though. I've been everywhere. Literally.' He sipped Vodka Blush, sitting with his legs crossed and a hand on his knee. He was wearing black loafers with tassels, grey slacks, a white blouse, and a blue-and-gold striped ascot. 'Every continent, every country,' he said. 'Every major city. You name a place and I've been there. Go ahead. Name a place.'

Guy said, 'Fairbanks, Alaska.'

'I've been there,' Mr Castevet said. 'I've been all over Alaska; Fairbanks, Juneau, Anchorage, Nome, Seward; I spent four months there in 1938 and I've made a lot of one-day stop-overs in Fairbanks and Anchorage on my way to places in the Far East. I've been in small towns in Alaska too; Dillingham and Akulurak.'

'Where are *you* folks from?' Mrs Castevet asked, fixing the folds at the bosom of her dress.

'I'm from Omaha,' Rosemary said, 'and Guy is from Baltimore.'

'Omaha is a good city,' Mr Castevet said. 'Baltimore is too.'

'Did you travel for business reasons?' Rosemary asked him.

'Business and pleasure both,' he said. 'I'm seventy-nine years old and I've been going one place or another since I was ten. You name it, I've been there.'

'What business were you in?' Guy asked.

'Just about every business,' Mr Castevet said. 'Wool, sugar, toys, machine parts, marine insurance, oil . . .'

A bell pinged in the kitchen. 'Steak's ready,' Mrs Castevet said, standing up with her glass in her hand. 'Don't rush your drinks now; take them along to the table. Roman, take your pill.'

'It will end on October third,' Mr Castevet said; 'the day

before the Pope gets here. No Pope ever visits a city where the newspapers are on strike.'

'I heard on TV that he's going to postpone and wait till it's over,' Mrs Castevet said.

Guy smiled. 'Well,' he said, 'that's show biz.'

Mr and Mrs Castevet laughed, and Guy along with them. Rosemary smiled and cut her steak. It was overdone and juiceless, flanked by peas and mashed potatoes under flour-laden gravy.

Still laughing, Mr Castevet said, 'It *is*, you know! That's *just* what it is; show biz!'

'You can say *that* again,' Guy said.

'The costumes, the rituals,' Mr Castevet said; 'every re-ligion, not only Catholicism. Pageants for the ignorant.'

Mrs Castevet said, 'I think we're offending Rosemary.'

'No, no, not at all,' Rosemary said.

'You aren't religious, my dear, are you?' Mr Castevet asked.

'I was brought up to be,' Rosemary said, 'but now I'm an agnostic. I wasn't offended. Really I wasn't.'

'And you, Guy?' Mr Castevet asked. 'Are you an agnostic too?'

'I guess so,' Guy said. 'I don't see how anyone can be anything else. I mean, there's no absolute proof one way or the other, is there?'

'No, there isn't,' Mr Castevet said.

Mrs Castevet, studying Rosemary, said, 'You looked un-comfortable before, when we were laughing at Guy's little joke about the Pope.'

'Well he *is* the Pope,' Rosemary said. 'I guess I've been conditioned to have respect for him and I still do, even if I don't think he's holy any more.'

'If you don't think he's holy,' Mr Castevet said, 'you should have no respect for him at *all*, because he's going around deceiving people and pretending he *is* holy.'

'Good point,' Guy said.

'When I *think* what they spend on robes and jewels,' Mrs Castevet said.

'A good picture of the hypocrisy behind organized religion,' Mr Castevet said, 'was given, in *Luther*. Did you ever get to play the leading part, Guy?'

'Me? No,' Guy said.

'Weren't you Albert Finney's understudy?' Mr Castevet asked.

'No,' Guy said, 'the fellow who played Weinand was. I just covered two of the smaller parts.'

'That's strange,' Mr Castevet said; 'I was quite certain that *you* were his understudy. I remember being struck by a gesture you made and checking in the programme to see who you were; and I could swear you were listed as Finney's understudy.'

'What gesture do you mean?' Guy asked.

'I'm not sure now; a movement of your —'

'I used to do a thing with my arms when Luther had the fit, a sort of involuntary reaching —'

'Exactly,' Mr Castevet said. 'That's just what I meant. It had a wonderful authenticity to it. In contrast, may I say, to everything Mr Finney was doing.'

'Oh, come on now,' Guy said.

'I thought his performance was considerably overrated,' Mr Castevet said. 'I'd be most curious to see what *you* would have done with the part.'

Laughing, Guy said, 'That makes two of us,' and cast a bright-eyed glance at Rosemary. She smiled back, pleased that Guy was pleased; there would be no reproofs from him now for an evening wasted talking with Ma and Pa Settle. No, Kettle.

'My father was a theatrical producer,' Mr Castevet said, 'and my early years were spent in the company of such people as Mrs Fiske and Forbes-Robertson, Otis Skinner and Modjeska. I tend, therefore, to look for something more than mere competence in actors. You have a most interesting inner quality, Guy. It appears in your television work, too, and it should carry you very far indeed; provided, of course, that you get those initial "breaks" upon which even the greatest actors are to some degree dependent. Are you preparing for a show now?'

'I'm up for a couple of parts,' Guy said.

'I can't believe that you won't get them,' Mr Castevet said.

'*I* can,' Guy said.

Mr Castevet stared at him. 'Are you serious?' he asked.

Dessert was a homemade Boston cream pie that, though better than the steak and vegetables, had for Rosemary a peculiar and unpleasant sweetness. Guy, however, praised it heartily and ate a second helping. Perhaps he was only acting, Rosemary thought; repaying compliments with compliments.

After dinner Rosemary offered to help with the cleaning up. Mrs Castevet accepted the offer instantly and the two women cleared the table while Guy and Mr Castevet went into the living-room.

The kitchen, opening off the foyer, was small, and made smaller still by the miniature greenhouse Terry had mentioned. Some three feet long, it stood on a large white table near the room's one window. Goosenecked lamps leaned close around it, their bright bulbs reflecting in the glass and making it blinding white rather than transparent. In the remaining space the sink, stove, and refrigerator stood close together with cabinets jutting out above them on all sides. Rosemary wiped dishes at Mrs Castevet's elbow, working diligently and conscientiously in the pleasing knowledge that her own kitchen was larger and more graciously equipped. 'Terry told me about that greenhouse,' she said.

'Oh yes,' Mrs Castevet said. 'It's a nice hobby. You ought to do it too.'

'I'd like to have a spice garden some day,' Rosemary said. 'Out of the city, of course. If Guy ever gets a movie offer we're going to grab it and go live in Los Angeles. I'm a country girl at heart.'

'Do you come from a big family?' Mrs Castevet asked.

'Yes,' Rosemary said. 'I have three brothers and two sisters. I'm the baby.'

'Are your sisters married?'

'Yes, they are.'

Mrs Castevet pushed a soapy sponge up and down inside

a glass. 'Do they have children?' she asked.

'One has two and the other has four,' Rosemary said. 'At least that was the count the last I heard. It could be three and five by now.'

'Well, that's a good sign for *you*,' Mrs Castevet said, still soaping the glass. She was a slow and thorough washer. 'If your sisters have lots of children, chances are you will too. Things like that go in families.'

'Oh, we're fertile, all right,' Rosemary said, waiting towel in hand for the glass. 'My brother Eddie has *eight* already and he's only twenty-six.'

'My goodness!' Mrs Castevet said. She rinsed the glass and gave it to Rosemary.

'All told I've got twenty nieces and nephews,' Rosemary said. 'I haven't even *seen* half of them.'

'Don't you go home every once in a while?' Mrs Castevet asked.

'No, I don't,' Rosemary said. 'I'm not on the best of terms with my family, except one brother. They feel I'm the black sheep.'

'Oh? How is that?'

'Because Guy isn't Catholic, and we didn't have a church wedding.'

'Tsk,' Mrs Castevet said. 'Isn't it something the way people fuss about religion? Well, it's *their* loss, not yours; don't you let it bother you any.'

'That's more easily said than done,' Rosemary said, putting the glass on a shelf. 'Would you like me to wash and you wipe for a while?'

'No, this is fine, dear,' Mrs Castevet said.

Rosemary looked outside the door. She could see only the end of the living-room that was bridge tables and file cabinets; Guy and Mr Castevet were at the other end. A plane of blue cigarette smoke lay motionless in the air.

'Rosemary?'

She turned. Mrs Castevet, smiling, held out a wet plate in a green rubber-gloved hand.

It took almost an hour to do the dishes and pans and silver, although Rosemary felt she could have done them alone in less than half that time. When she and Mrs Castevet came out of the kitchen and into the living-room, Guy and Mr Castevet were sitting facing each other on the settee, Mr Castevet driving home point after point with repeated strikings of his forefinger against his palm.

'Now Roman, you stop bending Guy's ear with your Modjeska stories,' Mrs Castevet said. 'He's only listening 'cause he's polite.'

'No, it's interesting, Mrs Castevet,' Guy said.

'You see?' Mr Castevet said.

'*Minnie*,' Mrs Castevet told Guy. 'I'm Minnie and he's Roman; okay?' She looked mock-defiantly at Rosemary. 'Okay?'

Guy laughed. 'Okay, Minnie,' he said.

They talked about the Goulds and the Bruhns and Dubin-and-DeVore; about Terry's sailor brother who had turned out to be in a civilian hospital in Saigon; and, because Mr Castevet was reading a book critical of the Warren Report, about the Kennedy assassination. Rosemary, in one of the straight-backed chairs, felt oddly out of things, as if the Castevets were old friends of Guy's to whom she had just been introduced. 'Do *you* think it could have been a plot of some kind?' Mr Castevet asked her, and she answered awkwardly, aware that a considerate host was drawing a left-out guest into conversation. She excused herself and followed Mrs Castevet's directions to the bathroom, where there were flowered paper towels inscribed *For Our Guest* and a book called *Jokes for The John* that wasn't especially funny.

They left at ten-thirty, saying 'Goodbye, Roman' and 'Thank you, Minnie' and shaking hands with an enthusiasm and an implied promise of more such evenings together that, on Rosemary's part, was completely false. Rounding the first bend in the hallway and hearing the door close behind them, she blew out a relieved sigh and grinned happily at Guy when she saw him doing exactly the same.

'Naow Roman,' he said, working his eyebrows comically,

'yew stop bendin' Guy's ee-yurs with them thar Mojesky sto-rees!'

Laughing, Rosemary cringed and hushed him, and they ran hand in hand on ultra-quiet tiptoes to their own door, which they unlocked, opened, slammed, locked, bolted, chained; and Guy nailed it over with imaginary beams, pushed up three imaginery boulders, hoisted an imaginary drawbridge, and mopped his brow and panted while Rosemary bent over double and laughed into both hands.

'About that steak,' Guy said.

'Oh my God!' Rosemary said. 'The pie! How did you eat two pieces of it? It was *weird*!'

'Dear girl,' Guy said, 'that was an act of superhuman courage and self-sacrifice. I said to myself, "Ye gods, I'll bet nobody's ever asked this old bat for seconds on *anything* in her entire life!" So I did it.' He waved a hand grandly. 'Now and again I get these noble urges.'

They went into the bedroom. 'She raises herbs and spices,' Rosemary said, 'and when they're full-grown she throws them out the window.'

'Shh, the walls have ears,' Guy said. 'Hey, how about that silverware?'

'Isn't that funny?' Rosemary said, working her feet against the floor to unshoe them; 'only three dinner plates that match, and they've got that beautiful, beautiful silver.'

'Let's be nice; maybe they'll will it to us.'

'Let's be nasty and buy our own. Did you go to the bathroom?'

'There? No.'

'Guess what they've got in it.'

'A bidet.'

'No, *Jokes for The John*.'

'No.'

Rosemary shucked off her dress. 'A book on a hook,' she said. 'Right next to the toilet.'

Guy smiled and shook his head. He began taking out his cufflinks, standing beside the armoire. 'Those stories of Roman's, though,' he said, 'were pretty damn interesting, actually. I'd never even heard of Forbes-Robertson before, but he was a very big star in his day.' He worked at the second link, having trouble with it. 'I'm going to go over there again tomorrow night and hear some more,' he said.

Rosemary looked at him, disconcerted. 'You are?' she asked.

'Yes,' he said, 'he asked me.' He held out his hand to her. 'Can you get this off for me?'

She went to him and worked at the link, feeling suddenly lost and uncertain. 'I thought we were going to do something with Jimmy and Tiger,' she said.

'Was that definite?' he asked. His eyes looked into hers. 'I thought we were just going to call and see.'

'It wasn't *definite*,' she said.

He shrugged. 'We'll see them Wednesday or Thursday.'

She got the link out and held it on her palm. He took it. 'Thanks,' he said. 'You don't have to come along if you don't want to; you can stay here.'

'I think I will,' she said. 'Stay here.' She went to the bed and sat down.

'He knew Henry Irving too,' Guy said. 'It's really terrifically interesting.'

Rosemary unhooked her stockings. 'Why did they take down the pictures,' she said.

'What do you mean?'

'Their pictures; they took them down. In the living-room and in the hallway leading back to the bathroom. There are hooks in the wall and clean places. And the one picture that *is* there, over the mantel, doesn't fit. There are two inches of clean at both sides of it.'

Guy looked at her. 'I didn't notice,' he said.

'And why do they have all those files and things in the living-room?' she asked.

'*That* he told me,' Guy said, taking off his shirt. 'He puts out a newsletter for stamp collectors. All over the world. That's why they get so much foreign mail.'

'Yes, but why in the living-room?' Rosemary said. 'They have three or four other rooms, all with the doors closed. Why doesn't he use one of those?'

Guy went to her, shirt in hand, and pressed her nose with

a firm fingertip. 'You're getting nosier than Minnie,' he said, kissed air at her, and went out to the bathroom.

Ten or fifteen minutes later, while in the kitchen putting on water for coffee, Rosemary got the sharp pain in her middle that was the night-before signal of her period. She relaxed with one hand against the corner of the stove, letting the pain have its brief way, and then she got out a Chemex paper and the can of coffee, feeling disappointed and forlorn.

She was twenty-four and they wanted three children two years apart; but Guy 'wasn't ready yet' – nor would he ever be ready, she feared, until he was as big as Marlon Brando and Richard Burton put together. Didn't he know how handsome and talented he was, how sure to succeed? So her plan was to get pregnant by 'accident'; the pills gave her headaches, she said, and rubber gadgets were repulsive. Guy said that subconsciously she was still a good Catholic, and she protested enough to support the explanation. Indulgently he studied the calendar and avoided the 'dangerous days', and she said, 'No, it's safe today, darling; I'm sure it is.'

And again this month he had won and she had lost, in this undignified contest in which he didn't even know they were engaged. 'Damn!' she said, and banged the coffee can down on the stove. Guy, in the den, called, 'What happened?'

'I bumped my elbow!' she called back.

At least she knew now why she had become depressed during the evening.

Double damn! If they were living together and not married she would have been pregnant fifty times by now!

CHAPTER SEVEN

THE FOLLOWING evening after dinner Guy went over to the Castevets'. Rosemary straightened up the kitchen and was debating whether to work on the window-seat cushions or get into bed with *Manchild in The Promised Land* when the doorbell rang. It was Mrs Castevet, and with her another woman, short, plump, and smiling, with a Buckley-for-Mayor button on the shoulder of a green dress.

'Hi, dear, we're not bothering you, are we?' Mrs Castevet said when Rosemary had opened the door. 'This is my dear friend Laura-Louise McBurney, who lives up on twelve. Laura-Louise, this is Guy's wife Rosemary.'

'Hello, Rosemary. Welcome to the Bram!'

'Laura-Louise just met Guy over at our place and she wanted to meet you too, so we came on over. Guy said you were staying in not doing anything. Can we come in?'

With resigned good grace Rosemary showed them into the living-room.

'Oh, you've got new chairs,' Mrs Castevet said. 'Aren't they beautiful!'

'They came this morning,' Rosemary said.

'Are you all right, dear? You look worn.'

'I'm fine,' Rosemary said and smiled. 'It's the first day of my period.'

'And you're up and around?' Laura-Louise asked, sitting. 'On *my* first days I experienced such pain that I couldn't move or eat or *anything*. Dan had to give me gin through a straw to kill the pain and we were one-hundred-per-cent Temperance at the time, with that one exception.'

'Girls today take things more in their stride than we did,' Mrs Castevet said, sitting too. 'They're healthier than we were, thanks to vitamins and better medical care.'

Both women had brought identical green sewing bags and, to Rosemary's surprise, were opening them now and taking out crocheting (Laura-Louise) and darning (Mrs

Castevet); settling down for a long evening of needlework and conversation. 'What's that over there?' Mrs Castevet asked. 'Seat covers?'

'Cushions for the window seats,' Rosemary said, and thinking *Oh all right, I will*, went over and got the work and brought it back and joined them.

Laura-Louise said, 'You've certainly made a tremendous change in the apartment, Rosemary.'

'Oh, before I forget,' Mrs Castevet said, 'this is for you. From Roman and me.' She put a small packet of pink tissue paper into Rosemary's hand, with a hardness inside it.

'For me?' Rosemary asked. 'I don't understand.'

'It's just a little present is all,' Mrs Castevet said, dismissing Rosemary's puzzlement with quick hand-waves. 'For moving in.'

'But there's no reason for you to . . .' Rosemary unfolded the leaves of used-before tissue paper. Within the pink was Terry's silver filigree ball-charm and its clustered-together neck-chain. The smell of the ball's filling made Rosemary pull her head away.

'It's real old,' Mrs Castevet said. 'Over three hundred years.'

'It's lovely,' Rosemary said, examining the ball and wondering whether she should tell that Terry had shown it to her. The moment for doing so slipped by.

'The green inside is called tannis root,' Mrs Castevet said. 'It's good luck.'

Not for Terry, Rosemary thought, and said, 'It's lovely, but I can't accept such a —'

'You already have,' Mrs Castevet said, darning a brown sock and not looking at Rosemary. 'Put it on.'

Laura-Louise said, 'You'll get used to the smell before you know it.'

'Go on,' Mrs Castevet said.

'Well, thank you,' Rosemary said; and uncertainly she put the chain over her head and tucked the ball into the collar of her dress. It dropped down between her breasts, cold for a moment and obtrusive. *I'll take it off when they go*, she thought.

Laura-Louise said, 'A friend of ours made the chain entirely by hand. He's a retired dentist and his hobby is making jewellery out of silver and gold. You'll meet him at Minnie and Roman's on – on some night soon, I'm sure, because they entertain so much. You'll probably meet all their friends, all *our* friends.'

Rosemary looked up from her work and saw Laura-Louise pink with embarrassment that had hurried and confused her last words. Minnie was busy darning, unaware. Laura-Louise smiled and Rosemary smiled back.

'Do you make your own clothes?' Laura-Louise asked.

'No, I don't,' Rosemary said, letting the subject be changed. 'I try to every once in a while but nothing ever hangs right.'

It turned out to be a fairly pleasant evening. Minnie told some amusing stories about her girlhood in Oklahoma, and Laura-Louise showed Rosemary two useful sewing tricks and explained feelingly how Buckley, the Conservative mayoral candidate, could win the coming election despite the high odds against him.

Guy came back at eleven, quiet and oddly self-contained. He said hello to the women and, by Rosemary's chair, bent and kissed her cheek. Minnie said. '*Eleven*? My land! Come on, Laura-Louise.' Laura-Louise said, 'Come and visit me any time you want, Rosemary; I'm in twelve F.' The two women closed their sewing bags and went quickly away.

'Were his stories as interesting as last night?' Rosemary asked.

'Yes,' Guy said. 'Did you have a nice time?'

'All right. I got some work done.'

'So I see.'

'I got a present too.'

She showed him the charm. 'It was Terry's,' she said. 'They gave it to her; she showed it to me. The police must have – given it back.'

'She probably wasn't even wearing it,' Guy said.

'I'll bet she was. She was as proud of it as – as if it was the first gift anyone had ever given her.' Rosemary lifted the chain off over her head and held the chain and the charm on her palm, jiggling them and looking at them.

'Aren't you going to wear it?' Guy asked.

'It smells,' she said. 'There's stuff in it called tannis root.' She held out her hand. 'From the famous greenhouse.'

Guy smelled and shrugged. 'It's not bad,' he said.

Rosemary went into the bedroom and opened a drawer in the vanity where she had a tin Louis Sherry box full of odds and ends. 'Tannis, anybody?' she asked herself in the mirror, and put the charm in the box, closed it, and closed the drawer.

Guy, in the doorway, said, 'If you took it, you ought to wear it.'

That night Rosemary awoke and found Guy sitting beside her smoking in the dark. She asked him what was the matter. 'Nothing,' he said. 'A little insomnia, that's all.'

Roman's stories of old-time stars, Rosemary thought, might have depressed him by reminding him that his own career was lagging behind Henry Irving's and Forbes-Whos-it's. His going back for more of the stories might have been a form of masochism.

She touched his arm and told him not to worry.

'About what?'

'About anything.'

'All right,' he said, 'I won't.'

'You're the greatest,' she said. 'You know? You are. And it's all going to come out right. You're going to have to learn karate to get rid of the photographers.'

He smiled in the glow of his cigarette.

'Any day now,' she said. 'Something big. Something worthy of you.'

'I know,' he said. 'Go to sleep, honey.'

'Okay. Watch the cigarette.'

'I will.'

'Wake me if you can't sleep.'

'Sure.'

'I love you.'

'I love *you*, Ro.'

A day or two later Guy brought home a pair of tickets for the Saturday night performance of *The Fantasticks*, given to him, he explained, by Dominick, his vocal coach. Guy had seen the show years before when it first opened; Rosemary had always been meaning to see it. 'Go with Hutch,' Guy said; 'it'll give me a chance to work on the *Wait Until Dark* scene.'

Hutch had seen it too, though, so Rosemary went with Joan Jellico, who confided during dinner at the Bijou that she and Dick were separating, no longer having anything in common except their address. The news upset Rosemary. For days Guy had been distant and preoccupied, wrapped in something he would neither put aside nor share. Had Joan and Dick's estrangement begun in the same way? She grew angry at Joan, who was wearing too much make-up and applauding too loudly in the small theatre. No wonder she and Dick could find nothing in common; she was loud and vulgar, he was reserved, sensitive; they should never have married in the first place.

When Rosemary came home Guy was coming out of the shower, more vivacious and *there* than he had been all week. Rosemary's spirits leaped. The show had been even better than she expected, she told him, and bad news, Joan and Dick were separating. They really were birds of completely different feathers though, weren't they? How had the *Wait Until Dark* scene gone? Great. He had it down cold.

'Damn that tannis root,' Rosemary said. The whole bedroom smelled of it. The bitter prickly odour had even found its way into the bathroom. She got a piece of aluminium foil from the kitchen and wound the charm in a tight triple wrapping, twisting the ends to seal them.

'It'll probably lose its strength in a few days,' Guy said.

'It better,' Rosemary said, spraying the air with a deodorant bomb. 'If it doesn't, I'm going to throw it away and tell Minnie I lost it.'

They made love – Guy was wild and driving – and later, through the wall, Rosemary heard a party in progress at Minnie and Roman's; the same flat unmusical singing she

64

had heard the last time, almost like religious chanting, and the same flute or clarinet weaving in and around and underneath it.

Guy kept his keyed-up vivacity all through Sunday, building shelves and shoe racks in the bedroom closets and inviting a bunch of *Luther* people over for Moo Goo Gai Woodhouse; and on Monday he painted the shelves and shoe racks and stained a bench Rosemary had found in a thrift shop, cancelling his session with Dominick and keeping his ear stretched for the phone, which he caught every time before the first ring was finished. At three in the afternoon it rang again, and Rosemary, trying out a different arrangement of the living-room chairs, heard him say, 'Oh God, no. Oh, the poor guy.'

She went to the bedroom door.

'Oh God,' Guy said.

He was sitting on the bed, the phone in one hand and a can of Red Devil paint remover in the other. He didn't look at her. 'And they don't have any idea what's causing it?' he said. 'My God, that's awful, just awful.' He listened, and straightened as he sat. 'Yes, I am,' he said. And then, 'Yes, I would. I'd hate to get it this way, but I —' He listened again. 'Well, you'd have to speak to Allan about that end of it,' he said,—Allan Stone, his agent—'but I'm sure there won't be any problem, Mr Weiss, not as far as we're concerned.'

He had it. The Something Big. Rosemary held her breath, waiting.

'Thank *you*, Mr Weiss,' Guy said. 'And will you let me know if there's any news? Thanks.'

He hung up and shut his eyes. He sat motionless, his hand staying on the phone. He was pale and dummylike, a Pop Art wax statue with real clothes and props, real phone, real can of paint remover.

'Guy?' Rosemary said.

He opened his eyes and looked at her.

'What is it?' she asked.

He blinked and came alive. 'Donald Baumgart,' he said.

- 65

'He's gone blind. He woke up yesterday and – he can't see.'

'Oh no,' Rosemary said.

'He tried to hang himself this morning. He's in Bellevue now, under sedation.'

They looked painfully at each other.

'I've got the part,' Guy said. 'It's a hell of a way to get it.' He looked at the paint remover in his hand and put it on the night table. 'Listen,' he said, 'I've got to get out and walk around.' He stood up. 'I'm sorry. I've got to get outside and absorb this.'

'I understand, go ahead,' Rosemary said, standing back from the doorway.

He went as he was, down the hall and out the door, letting it swing closed after him with its own soft slam.

She went into the living-room, thinking of poor Donald Baumgart and lucky Guy; lucky she-and-Guy, with the good part that would get attention even if the show folded, would lead to other parts, to movies maybe, to a house in Los Angeles, a spice garden, three children two years apart. Poor Donald Baumgart with his clumsy name that he didn't change. He must have been good, to have won out over Guy, and there he was in Bellevue, blind and wanting to kill himself, under sedation.

Kneeling on a window seat, Rosemary looked out the side of its bay and watched the house's entrance far below, waiting to see Guy come out. When would rehearsals begin? she wondered. She would go out of town with him, of course; what fun it would be! Boston? Philadelphia? Washington would be exciting. She had never been there. While Guy was rehearsing afternoons, she could sightsee; and evenings, after the performance, everyone would meet in a restaurant or club to gossip and exchange rumours . . .

She waited and watched but he didn't come out. He must have used the Fifty-fifth Street door.

Now, when he should have been happy, he was dour and troubled, sitting with nothing moving except his cigarette hand and his eyes. His eyes followed her around the apartment; tensely, as if she were dangerous. 'What's *wrong*?' she asked a dozen times.

'Nothing,' he said. 'Don't you have your sculpture class today?'

'I haven't gone in two months.'

'Why don't you go?'

She went; tore away old plasticine, reset the armature, and began anew, doing a new model among new students. 'Where've you been?' the instructor asked. He had eyeglasses and an Adam's apple and made miniatures of her torso without watching his hands.

'In Zanzibar,' she said.

'Zanzibar is no more,' he said, smiling nervously. 'It's Tanzania.'

One afternoon she went down to Macy's and Gimbels, and when she came home there were roses in the kitchen, roses in the living-room, and Guy coming out of the bedroom with one rose and a forgive-me smile, like a reading he had once done for her of Chance Wayne in *Sweet Bird*.

'I've been a living turd,' he said. 'It's from sitting around hoping that Baumgart won't regain his sight, which is what I've been doing, rat that I am.'

'That's natural,' she said. 'You're bound to feel two ways about —'

'Listen,' he said, pushing the rose to her nose, 'even if this thing falls through, even if I'm Charley Cresta Blanca for the rest of my days, I'm going to stop giving you the short end of the stick.'

'You haven't —'

'Yes I have. I've been so busy tearing my hair out over *my* career that I haven't given Thought One to yours. Let's have a baby, okay? Let's have three, one at a time.'

She looked at him.

'A baby,' he said. 'You know. Goo, goo? Diapers? Waa, waa?'

'Do you mean it?' she asked.

'Sure I mean it,' he said. 'I even figured out the right time to start. Next Monday and Tuesday. Red circles on the calendar, please.'

67

'You *really* mean it, Guy?' she asked, tears in her eyes.

'No, I'm kidding,' he said. '*Sure* I mean it. Look, Rosemary, for God's sake don't cry, all right? Please. It's going to upset me very much if you cry, so stop right now, all right?'

'All right,' she said. 'I won't cry.'

'I really went rose-nutty, didn't I?' he said, looking around brightly. 'There's a bunch in the bedroom too.'

CHAPTER EIGHT

S H E   W E N T   T O upper Broadway for swordfish steaks and
across town to Lexington Avenue for cheeses; not because
she couldn't get swordfish steaks and cheeses right there in
the neighbourhood but simply because on that snappy
bright-blue morning she wanted to be all over the city,
walking briskly with her coat flying, drawing second
glances for her prettiness, impressing tough clerks with the
precision and know-how of her orders. It was Monday,
October fourth, the day of Pope Paul's visit to the city, and
the sharing of the event made people more open and com-
municative than they ordinarily were; *How nice it is*, Rosemary thought, *that the whole city is happy on a day when
I'm so happy*.

She followed the Pope's rounds on television during the
afternoon, moving the set out from the wall of the den
(soon nursery) and turning it so she could watch from the
kitchen while readying the fish and vegetables and salad
greens. His speech at the UN moved her, and she was sure
it would help ease the Vietnam situation. 'War never again,'
he said; wouldn't his words give pause to even the most
hardheaded statesman?

At four-thirty, while she was setting the table before the
fireplace, the telephone rang.

'Rosemary? How are you?'

'Fine,' she said. 'How are you?' It was Margaret, the older
of her two sisters.

'Fine,' Margaret said.

'Where are you?'

'In Omaha.'

They had never got on well. Margaret had been a sullen,
resentful girl, too often used by their mother as the care-
taker of the younger children. To be called by her like this
was strange; strange and frightening.

'Is everyone all right?' Rosemary asked. *Someone's dead,* she thought. *Who? Ma? Pa? Brian?*

'Yes, everyone's fine.'

'They are?'

'Yes. Are you?'

'Yes; I said I was.'

'I've had the funniest feeling all day long, Rosemary. That something happened to you. Like an accident or something. That you were hurt. Maybe in the hospital.'

'Well, I'm not,' Rosemary said, and laughed. 'I'm fine. Really I am.'

'It was such a strong feeling,' Margaret said. 'I was *sure* something had happened. Finally Gene said why don't I call you and find out.'

'How is he?'

'Fine.'

'And the children?'

'Oh, the usual scrapes and scratches, but they're fine too. I've got another one on the way, you know.'

'No, I didn't know. That's wonderful. When is it due?' *We'll have one on the way soon too.*

'The end of March. How's your husband, Rosemary?'

'He's fine. He's got an important part in a new play that's going into rehearsal soon.'

'Say, did you get a good look at the Pope?' Margaret asked. 'There must be terrific excitement there.'

'There is,' Rosemary said. 'I've been watching it on television. It's in Omaha too, isn't it?'

'Not live? You didn't go out and see him live?'

'No, I didn't.'

'Really?'

'Really.'

'Honest to goodness, Rosemary,' Margaret said. 'Do you know Ma and Pa were going to *fly there* to see him but they couldn't because there's going to be a strike vote and Pa's seconding the motion? Lots of people did fly, though: the Donovans, and Dot and Sandy Wallingford; and you're right there, *living* there, and didn't go out and see him?'

'Religion doesn't mean as much to me now as it did back home,' Rosemary said.

'Well,' Margaret said, 'I guess that's inevitable,' and Rosemary heard, unspoken, *when you're married to a Protestant*. She said, 'It was nice of you to call, Margaret. There's nothing for you to worry about. I've never been healthier or happier.'

'It was such a strong feeling,' Margaret said. 'From the minute I woke up. I'm so used to taking care of you little brats . . .'

'Give my love to everyone, will you? And tell Brian to answer my letter.'

'I will. Rosemary —?'

'Yes?'

'I still have the feeling. Stay home tonight, will you?'

'That's just what we're planning to do,' Rosemary said, looking over at the partially set table.

'Good,' Margaret said. 'Take care of yourself.'

'I will,' Rosemary said. 'You too, Margaret.'

'I will. Goodbye.'

'Goodbye.'

She went back to setting the table, feeling pleasantly sad and nostalgic for Margaret and Brian and the other kids, for Omaha and the irretrievable past.

With the table set, she bathed; then powdered and perfumed herself, did her eyes and lips and hair, and put on a pair of burgundy silk lounging pyjamas that Guy had given her the previous Christmas.

He came home late, after six. 'Mmmm,' he said, kissing her. 'you look good enough to eat. Shall we? Damn!'

'What?'

'I forgot the pie.'

He had told her not to make a dessert; he would bring home his absolute all-time favourite, a Horn and Hardart pumpkin pie.

'I could *kick* myself,' he said. 'I passed *two* of those damn retail stores; not one but two.'

'It's all right,' Rosemary said. 'We **can** have fruit and

71

cheese. That's the best dessert anyway, really.'

'It is not; Horn and Hardart pumpkin pie is.'

He went in to wash up and she put a tray of stuffed mushrooms into the oven and mixed the salad dressing.

In a few minutes Guy came to the kitchen door, buttoning the collar of a blue velour shirt. He was bright-eyed and a bit on edge, the way he had been the first time they slept together, when he knew it was going to happen. It pleased Rosemary to see him that way.

'Your pal the Pope really loused up traffic today,' he said.

'Did you see any of the television?' she asked. 'They've had fantastic coverage.'

'I got a glimpse up at Allan's,' he said. 'Glasses in the Leezer?'

'Yes. He made a wonderful speech at the UN. "War never again," he told them.'

'Rotsa ruck. Hey, *those* look good.'

They had Gibsons and the stuffed mushrooms in the living-room. Guy put crumpled newspaper and sticks of kindling on the fireplace grate, and two big chunks of cannel coal. 'Here goes nothing,' he said, and struck a match and lit the paper. It flamed high and caught the kindling. Dark smoke began spilling out over the front of the mantel and up towards the ceiling. 'Good grief,' Guy said, and groped inside the fireplace. 'The paint, the paint!' Rosemary cried.

He got the flue opened; and the air conditioner, set at exhaust, drew out the smoke.

'Nobody, but nobody, has a fire tonight,' Guy said.

Rosemary, kneeling with her drink and staring into the spitting flame-wrapped coals, said, 'Isn't it gorgeous? I hope we have the coldest winter in eighty years.'

Guy put on Ella Fitzgerald singing Cole Porter.

They were halfway through the swordfish when the doorbell rang. 'Shit,' Guy said. He got up, tossed down his napkin, and went to answer it. Rosemary cocked her head and listened.

The door opened and Minnie said, 'Hi, Guy!' and more that was unintelligible. *Oh, no*, Rosemary thought. *Don't*

72

let her in, Guy. Not now, not tonight.

Guy spoke, and then Minnie again: '... extra. We don't need them.' Guy again and Minnie again. Rosemary eased out held-in breath; it didn't sound as if she was coming in, thank God.

The door closed and was chained (*Good!*) and bolted (*Good!*). Rosemary watched and waited, and Guy sidled into the archway, smiling smugly, with both hands behind his back. '*Who* says there's nothing to ESP?' he said, and coming towards the table brought forth his hands with two white custard cups sitting one on each palm. 'Madame and Monsieur shall have ze dessairt after all,' he said, setting one cup by Rosemary's wineglass and the other by his own. '*Mousse au chocolat*,' he said, 'or "chocolate mouse", as Minnie calls it. Of course with her it could *be* chocolate mouse, so eat with care.'

Rosemary laughed happily. 'That's wonderful,' she said. 'It's what *I* was going to make.'

'See?' Guy said, sitting. 'ESP.' He replaced his napkin and poured more wine.

'I was afraid she was going to come charging in and stay all evening,' Rosemary said, forking up carrots.

'No,' Guy said, 'she just wanted us to try her chocolate mouse, seein' as how it's one of her speci-*al*-ities.'

'It *looks* good.'

'It does, doesn't it.'

The cups were filled with peaked swirls of chocolate. Guy's was topped with a sprinkling of chopped nuts, and Rosemary's with a half walnut.

'It's sweet of her, really,' Rosemary said. 'We shouldn't make fun of her.'

'You're right,' Guy said, 'you're right.'

The mousse was excellent, but it had a chalky undertaste that reminded Rosemary of blackboards and grade school. Guy tried but could find no 'undertaste' at all, chalky or otherwise. Rosemary put her spoon down after two swallows. Guy said, 'Aren't you going to finish it? That's silly, honey; there's no "undertaste".'

Rosemary said there was.

'Come on,' Guy said, 'the old bat slaved all day over a hot stove; eat it.'

'But I don't like it,' Rosemary said.

'It's delicious.'

'You can have mine.'

Guy scowled. 'All right, don't eat it,' he said; 'you don't wear the charm she gave you, you might as well not eat her dessert too.'

Confused, Rosemary said, 'What does one thing have to do with the other?'

'They're both examples of – well, unkindness, that's all,' Guy said. 'Two minutes ago you said we should stop making fun of her. That's a form of making fun too, accepting something and then not using it.'

'Oh —' Rosemary picked up her spoon. 'If it's going to turn into a big scene —' She took a full spoonful of the mousse and thrust it into her mouth.

'It isn't going to turn into a big scene,' Guy said. 'Look, if you really can't stand it, don't eat it.'

'Delicious,' Rosemary said, full-mouthed and taking another spoonful, 'no undertaste at all. Turn the records over.'

Guy got up and went to the record player. Rosemary doubled her napkin in her lap and plopped two spoonfuls of the mousse into it, and another half-spoonful for good measure. She folded the napkin closed and then showily scraped clean the inside of the cup and swallowed down the scrapings as Guy came back to the table. 'There, Daddy,' she said, tilting the cup towards him. 'Do I get a gold star on my chart?'

'Two of them,' he said. 'I'm sorry if I was stuffy.'

'You were.'

'I'm sorry.' He smiled.

Rosemary melted. 'You're forgiven,' she said. 'It's nice that you're considerate of old ladies. It means you'll be considerate of me when I'm one.'

They had coffee and crème de menthe.

'Margaret called this afternoon,' Rosemary said.

'Margaret?'

'My sister.'

'Oh. Everything okay?'

'Yes. She was afraid something had happened to me. She had a feeling.'

'Oh?'

'We're to stay home tonight.'

'Drat. And I made a reservation at Nedick's. In the Orange Room.'

'You'll have to cancel it.'

'How come you turned out sane when the rest of your family is nutty?'

The first wave of dizziness caught Rosemary at the kitchen sink as she scraped the uneaten mousse from her napkin into the drain. She swayed for a moment, then blinked and frowned. Guy, in the den, said, 'He isn't there yet. Christ, what a mob.' The Pope at Yankee Stadium.

'I'll be in in a minute,' Rosemary said.

Shaking her head to clear it, she rolled the napkins up inside the tablecloth and put the bundle aside for the hamper. She put the stopper in the drain, turned on the hot water, squeezed in some Joy, and began loading in the dishes and pans. She would do them in the morning, let them soak overnight.

The second wave came as she was hanging up the dish towel. It lasted longer, and this time the room turned slowly around and her legs almost slued out from under her. She hung on to the edge of the sink.

When it was over she said 'Oh boy,' and added up two Gibsons, two glasses of wine (or had it been three?), and one crème de menthe. No wonder.

She made it to the doorway of the den and kept her footing through the next wave by holding on to the knob with one hand and the jamb with the other.

'What is it?' Guy asked, standing up anxiously.

'Dizzy,' she said, and smiled.

He snapped off the TV and came to her, took her arm and held her surely around the waist. 'No wonder,' he said.

75

'All that booze. You probably had an empty stomach, too.'

He helped her towards the bedroom and, when her legs buckled, caught her up and carried her. He put her down on the bed and sat beside her, taking her hand and stroking her forehead sympathetically. She closed her eyes. The bed was a raft that floated on gentle ripples, tilting and swaying pleasantly. 'Nice,' she said.

'Sleep is what you need,' Guy said, stroking her forehead. 'A good night's sleep.'

'We have to make a baby.'

'We will. Tomorrow. There's plenty of time.'

'Missing the mass.'

'Sleep. Get a good night's sleep. Go on . . .'

'Just a nap,' she said, and was sitting with a drink in her hand on President Kennedy's yacht. It was sunny and breezy, a perfect day for a cruise. The President, studying a large map, gave terse and knowing instructions to a Negro mate.

Guy had taken off the top of her pyjamas. 'Why are you taking them off?' she asked.

'To make you more comfortable,' he said.

'I'm comfortable.'

'Sleep, Ro.'

He undid the snaps at her side and slowly drew off the bottoms. Thought she was asleep and didn't know. Now she had nothing on at all except a red bikini, but the other women on the yacht – Jackie Kennedy, Pat Lawford, and Sarah Churchill – were wearing bikinis too, so it was all right, thank goodness. The President was in his Navy uniform. He had completely recovered from the assassination and looked better than ever. Hutch was standing on the dock with armloads of weather-forecasting equipment. 'Isn't Hutch coming with us?' Rosemary asked the President.

'Catholics only,' he said, smiling. 'I wish we weren't bound by these prejudices, but unfortunately we are.'

'But what about Sarah Churchill?' Rosemary asked. She turned to point, but Sarah Churchill was gone and the family was there in her place: Ma, Pa, and everybody, with the husbands, wives, and children. Margaret was pregnant, and so were Jean and Dodie and Ernestine.

Guy was taking off her wedding ring. She wondered why, but was too tired to ask. 'Sleep,' she said, and slept.

It was the first time the Sistine Chapel had been opened to the public and she was inspecting the ceiling on a new elevator that carried the visitor through the chapel horizontally, making it possible to see the frescoes exactly as Michelangelo, painting them, had seen them. How glorious they were! She saw God extending his finger to Adam, giving him the divine spark of life; and the underside of a shelf partly covered with gingham contact paper as she was carried backward through the linen closet. 'Easy,' Guy said, and another man said, 'You've got her too high.'

'Typhoon!' Hutch shouted from the dock amid all his weather-forecasting equipment. 'Typhoon! It killed fifty-five people in London and it's heading this way!' And Rosemary knew he was right. She must warn the President. The ship was heading for disaster.

But the President was gone. Everyone was gone. The deck was infinite and bare, except for, far away, the Negro mate holding the wheel unremittingly on its course.

Rosemary went to him and saw at once that he hated all white people, hated her. 'You'd better go down below, Miss,' he said, courteous but hating her, not even waiting to hear the warning she had brought.

Below was a huge ballroom where on one side a church burned fiercely and on the other a black-bearded man stood glaring at her. In the centre was a bed. She went to it and lay down, and was suddenly surrounded by naked men and women, ten or a dozen, with Guy among them. They were elderly, the women grotesque and slack-breasted. Minnie and her friend Laura-Louise were there, and Roman in a black mitre and a black silk robe. With a thin black wand he was drawing designs on her body, dipping the wand's point in a cup of red held for him by a sun-browned man with a white moustache. The point moved back and forth across her stomach and down ticklingly to the insides of her thighs. The naked people were chanting – flat, unmusical,

77

foreign-tongued syllables – and a flute or clarinet accompanied them. 'She's awake, she sees!' Guy whispered to Minnie. He was large-eyed, tense. 'She *don't* see,' Minnie said. 'As long as she ate the mouse she can't see nor hear. She's like dead. Now sing.'

Jackie Kennedy came into the ballroom in an exquisite gown of ivory satin embroidered with pearls. 'I'm so sorry to hear you aren't feeling well,' she said, hurrying to Rosemary's side.

Rosemary explained about the mouse-bite, minimizing it so Jackie wouldn't worry.

'You'd better have your legs tied down,' Jackie said, 'in case of convulsions.'

'Yes, I suppose so,' Rosemary said. 'There's always a chance it was rabid.' She watched with interest as white-smocked interns tied her legs, and her arms too, to the four bedposts.

'If the music bothers you,' Jackie said, 'let me know and I'll have it stopped.'

'Oh, no,' Rosemary said. 'Please don't change the programme on my account. It doesn't bother me at all, really it doesn't.'

Jackie smiled warmly at her. 'Try to sleep,' she said. 'We'll be waiting up on deck.' She withdrew, her satin gown whispering.

Rosemary slept a while, and then Guy came in and began making love to her. He stroked her with both hands – a long, relishing stroke that began at her bound wrists, slid down over her arms, breasts, and loins, and became a voluptuous tickling between her legs. He repeated the exciting stroke again and again, his hands hot and sharp-nailed, and then, when she was ready-ready-more-than-ready, he slipped a hand in under her buttocks, raised them, lodged his hardness against her, and pushed it powerfully in. Bigger he was than always; painfully, wonderfully big. He lay forward upon her, his other arm sliding under her back to hold her, his broad chest crushing her breasts. (He was wearing, because it was to be a costume party, a suit of coarse leathery armour.) Brutally, rhythmically, he drove

78

his new hugeness. She opened her eyes and looked into yellow furnace-eyes, smelled sulphur and tannis root, felt wet breath on her mouth, heard lust-grunts and the breathing of onlookers.

This is no dream, she thought. *This is real, this is happening.* Protest woke in her eyes and throat, but something covered her face, smothering her in a sweet stench.

The hugeness kept driving in her, the leathery body banging itself against her again and again and again.

The Pope came in with a suitcase in his hand and a coat over his arm. 'Jackie tells me you've been bitten by a mouse,' he said.

'Yes,' Rosemary said. 'That's why I didn't come to see you.' She spoke sadly, so he wouldn't suspect she had just had an orgasm.

'That's all right,' he said. 'We wouldn't want you to jeopardize your health.'

'Am I forgiven, Father?' she asked.

'Absolutely,' he said. He held out his hand for her to kiss the ring. Its stone was a silver filigree ball less than an inch in diameter; inside it, very tiny, Anna Maria Alberghetti sat waiting.

Rosemary kissed it and the Pope hurried out to catch his plane.

CHAPTER NINE

'HEY, IT'S AFTER nine,' Guy said, shaking her shoulder.

She pushed his hand away and turned over on to her stomach. 'Five minutes,' she said, deep in the pillow.

'*No*,' he said, and yanked her hair. 'I've got to be at Dominick's at ten.'

'Eat out.'

'The hell I will.' He slapped her behind through the blanket.

Everything came back: the dreams, the drinks, Minnie's chocolate mousse, the Pope, that awful moment of not-dreaming. She turned back over and raised herself on her arms, looking at Guy. He was lighting a cigarette, sleep-rumpled, needing a shave. He had pyjamas on. She was nude.

'What time is it?' she asked.

'Ten after nine.'

'What time did I go to sleep?' She sat up.

'About eight-thirty,' he said. 'And you didn't go to sleep, honey; you passed out. From now on you get cocktails *or* wine, not cocktails *and* wine.'

'The dreams I had,' she said, rubbing her forehead and closing her eyes. 'President Kennedy, the Pope, Minnie and Roman . . .' She opened her eyes and saw scratches on her left breast; two parallel hairlines of red running down into the nipple. Her thighs stung; she pushed the blanket from them and saw more scratches, seven or eight going this way and that.

'Don't yell,' Guy said. 'I already filed them down.' He showed short smooth fingernails.

Rosemary looked at him uncomprehendingly.

'I didn't want to miss Baby Night,' he said.

'You mean you —'

'And a couple of my nails were ragged.'

'While I was – out?'

He nodded and grinned. 'It was kind of fun,' he said, 'in a necrophile sort of way.'

She looked away, her hands pulling the blanket back over her thighs. 'I dreamed someone was – raping me,' she said. 'I don't know who. Someone – unhuman.'

'Thanks a lot,' Guy said.

'You were there, and Minnie and Roman, other people . . . It was some kind of ceremony.'

'I tried to wake you,' he said, 'but you were out like a light.'

She turned further away and swung her legs out on the other side of the bed.

'What's the matter?' Guy asked.

'Nothing,' she said, sitting there, not looking around at him. 'I guess I feel funny about your doing it that way, with me unconscious.'

'I didn't want to miss the night,' he said.

'We could have done it this morning or tonight. Last night wasn't the only split second in the whole month. And even if it *had* been . . .'

'I thought you would have wanted me to,' he said, and ran a finger up her back.

She squirmed away from it. 'It's supposed to be shared, not one awake and one asleep,' she said. Then: 'Oh, I guess I'm being silly.' She got up and went to the closet for her housecoat.

'I'm sorry I scratched you,' Guy said. 'I was a wee bit loaded myself.'

She made breakfast and, when Guy had gone, did the sinkful of dishes and put the kitchen to rights. She opened windows in the living-room and bedroom – the smell of last night's fire still lingered in the apartment – made the bed, and took a shower; a long one, first hot and then cold. She stood capless and immobile under the downpour, waiting for her head to clear and her thoughts to find an order and conclusion.

Had last night really been, as Guy had put it, Baby Night? Was she now, at this moment, actually pregnant?

Oddly enough, she didn't care. She was unhappy – whether or not it was silly to be so. Guy had taken her without her knowledge, had made love to her as a mindless body ('kind of fun in a necrophile sort of way') rather than as the complete mind-and-body person she was; and had done so, moreover, with a savage gusto that had produced scratches, aching soreness, and a nightmare so real and intense that she could almost see on her stomach the designs Roman had drawn with his red-dipped wand. She scrubbed soap on herself vigorously, resentfully. True, he had done it for the best motive in the world, to make a baby, and true too he had drunk as much as she had; but she wished that no motive and no number of drinks could have enabled him to take her that way, taking only her body without her soul or self or she-ness – whatever it was he presumably loved. Now, looking back over the past weeks and months, she felt a disturbing presence of overlooked signals just beyond memory, signals of a shortcoming in his love for her, of a disparity between what he said and what he felt. He was an actor; could anyone know when an actor was true and not acting?

It would take more than a shower to wash away these thoughts. She turned the water off and, between both hands, pressed out her streaming hair.

On the way out to shop she rang the Castevets' doorbell and returned the cups from the mousse. 'Did you like it, dear?' Minnie asked. 'I think I put a little too much cream de cocoa in it.'

'It was delicious,' Rosemary said. 'You'll have to give me the recipe.'

'I'd love to. You going marketing? Would you do me a teeny favour? Six eggs and a small Instant Sanka; I'll pay you later. I hate going out for just one or two things, don't you?'

There was distance now between her and Guy, but he seemed not to be aware of it. His play was going into rehearsal November first – *Don't I Know You From Somewhere?* was the name of it – and he spent a great deal of time studying his part, practising the use of the crutches and leg-braces it called for, and visiting the Highbridge section of the Bronx, the play's locale. They had dinner with friends more evenings than not; when they didn't, they made natural-sounding conversation about furniture and the ending-any-day-now newspaper strike and the World Series. They went to a preview of a new musical and a screening of a new movie, to parties and the opening of a friend's exhibit of metal constructions. Guy seemed never to be looking at her, always at a script or TV or at someone else. He was in bed and asleep before she was. One evening he went to the Castevets' to hear more of Roman's theatre stories, and she stayed in the apartment and watched *Funny Face* on TV.

'Don't you think we ought to talk about it?' she said the next morning at breakfast.

'About what?'

She looked at him; he seemed genuinely unknowing. 'The conversations we've been making,' she said.

'What do you mean?'

'The way you haven't been looking at me.'

'What are you *talking* about? I've been looking at you.'

'No you haven't.'

'I have *so*. Honey, what is it? What's the matter?'

'Nothing. Never mind.'

'No, don't say that. What is it? What's bothering you?'

'Nothing.'

'Ah look, honey, I know I've been kind of preoccupied, with the part and the crutches and all; is that it? Well gee whiz, Ro, it's *important*, you know? But it doesn't mean I don't love you, just because I'm not riveting you with a passionate *gaze* all the time. I've got to think about *practical* matters too.' It was awkward and charming and sincere, like his playing of the cowboy in *Bus Stop*.

'All right,' Rosemary said. 'I'm sorry I'm being pesty.'

'You? You couldn't be pesty if you tried.'

He leaned across the table and kissed her.

Hutch had a cabin near Brewster where he spent occasional

weekends. Rosemary called him and asked if she might use it for three or four days, possibly a week. 'Guy's getting into his new part,' she explained, 'and I really think it'll be easier for him with me out of the way.'

'It's yours,' Hutch said, and Rosemary went down to his apartment on Lexington Avenue and Twenty-fourth Street to pick up the key.

She looked in first at a delicatessen where the clerks were friends from her own days in the neighbourhood, and then she went up to Hutch's apartment, which was small and dark and neat as a pin, with an inscribed photo of Winston Churchill and a sofa that had belonged to Madame Pompadour. Hutch was sitting barefoot between two bridge tables, each with its typewriter and piles of paper. His practice was to write two books at once, turning to the second when he struck a snag on the first, and back to the first when he struck a snag on the second.

'I'm really looking forward to it,' Rosemary said, sitting on Madame Pompadour's sofa. 'I suddenly realized the other day that I've never been alone in my whole life – not for more than a few hours, that is. The idea of three or four days is heaven.'

'A chance to sit quietly and find out who you are; where you've been and where you're going.'

'Exactly.'

'All right, you can stop forcing that smile,' Hutch said. 'Did he hit you with a lamp?'

'He didn't hit me with anything,' Rosemary said. 'It's a very difficult part, a crippled boy who *pretends* that he's adjusted to his crippled-ness. He's got to work with crutches and leg-braces, and naturally he's preoccupied and – and, well, preoccupied.'

'I see,' Hutch said. 'We'll change the subject. The *News* had a lovely rundown the other day of all the gore we missed during the strike. Why didn't you tell me you'd had another suicide up there at Happy House?'

'Oh, didn't I tell you?' Rosemary asked.

'No, you didn't,' Hutch said.

'It was someone we knew. The girl I told you about; the

84

one who'd been a drug addict and was rehabilitated by the Castevets, these people who live on our floor. I'm *sure* I told you *that*.'

'The girl who was going to the basement with you.'

'That's right.'

'They didn't rehabilitate her very successfully, it would seem. Was she living with them?'

'Yes,' Rosemary said. 'We've gotten to know them fairly well since it happened. Guy goes over there once in a while to hear stories about the theatre. Mr Castevet's father was a producer around the turn of the century.'

'I shouldn't have thought Guy would be interested,' Hutch said. 'An elderly couple, I take it?'

'He's seventy-nine; she's seventy or so.'

'It's an odd name,' Hutch said. 'How is it spelled?'

Rosemary spelled it for him.

'I've never heard it before,' he said. 'French, I suppose.'

'The name may be but they aren't,' Rosemary said. 'He's from right here and she's from a place called – believe it or not – Bushyhead, Oklahoma.'

'My God,' Hutch said. 'I'm going to use that in a book. That one. I know just where to put it. Tell me, how are you planning to get to the cabin? You'll need a car, you know.'

'I'm going to rent one.'

'Take mine.'

'Oh no, Hutch, I couldn't.'

'Do, please,' Hutch said. 'All I do is move it from one side of the street to the other. Please. You'll save me a great deal of bother.'

Rosemary smiled. 'All right,' she said. 'I'll do you a favour and take your car.'

Hutch gave her the keys to the car and the cabin, a sketch-map of the route, and a typed list of instructions concerning the pump, the refrigerator, and a variety of possible emergencies. Then he put on shoes and a coat and walked her down to where the car, an old light-blue Oldsmobile, was parked. 'The registration papers are in the glove compartment,' he said. 'Please feel free to stay as long as you like. I have no immediate plans for either the car or the cabin.'

'I'm sure I won't stay more than a week,' Rosemary said. 'Guy might not even want me to stay that long.'

When she was settled in the car, Hutch leaned in at the window and said, 'I have all kinds of good advice to give you but I'm going to mind my own business if it kills me.'

Rosemary kissed him. 'Thank you,' she said. 'For that and for this and for everything.'

She left on the morning of Saturday, October 16th, and stayed five days at the cabin. The first two days she never once thought about Guy – a fitting revenge for the cheerfulness with which he had agreed to her going. Did she *look* as if she needed a good rest? Very well, she would *have* one, a long one, never once thinking about him. She took walks through dazzling yellow-and-orange woods, went to sleep early and slept late, read *Flight of The Falcon* by Daphne du Maurier, and made glutton's meals on the bottled-gas stove. Never once thinking about him.

On the third day she thought about him. He was vain, self-centred, shallow, and deceitful. He had married her to have an audience, not a mate. (Little Miss Just-out-of-Omaha, what a *goop* she had been! 'Oh, I'm *used* to actors; I've been here almost a year now.' And she had all but followed him around the studio carrying his newspaper in her mouth.) She would give him a year to shape up and become a good husband; if he didn't make it she would pull out, and with no religious qualms whatever. And meanwhile she would go back to work and get again that sense of independence and self-sufficiency she had been so eager to get rid of. She would be strong and proud and ready to go if he failed to meet her standards.

Those glutton's meals – man-size cans of beef stew and chili con carne – began to disagree with her, and on that third day she was mildly nauseated and could eat only soup and crackers.

On the fourth day she awoke missing him and cried. What was she doing there, alone in that cold crummy cabin? What had he done that was so terrible? He had gotten drunk and had grabbed her without saying may I. Well that was really an earth-shaking offence, now wasn't it? There he was, facing the biggest challenge of his career, and *she* – instead of being there to help him, to cue and encourage him – was off in the middle of nowhere, eating herself sick and feeling sorry for herself. Sure he was vain and self-centred; he was an actor, wasn't he? Laurence *Olivier* was probably vain and self-centred. And yes he might lie now and then; wasn't that exactly what had attracted her and still did? – that freedom and nonchalance so different from her own boxed-in propriety?

She drove into Brewster and called him. Service answered, the Friendly One: 'Oh hi, dear, are you back from the country? Oh. Guy is out, dear; can he call you? *You'll* call *him* at five. Right. You've certainly got lovely weather. Are you enjoying yourself? Good.'

At five he was still out, her message waiting for him. She ate in a diner and went to the one movie theatre. At nine he was still out and Service was someone new and automatic with a message for her: she should call him before eight the next morning or after six in the evening.

That next day she reached what seemed like a sensible and realistic view of things. They were both at fault; he for being thoughtless and self-absorbed, she for failing to express and explain her discontent. He could hardly be expected to change until she showed him that change was called for. She had only to talk – no, *they* had only to talk, for he might be harbouring a similar discontent of which she was similarly unaware – and matters couldn't help but improve. Like so many unhappinesses, this one had begun with silence in the place of honest open talk.

She went into Brewster at six and called and he was there. 'Hi, darling,' he said. 'How are you?'

'Fine. How are you?'

'All right. I miss you.'

She smiled at the phone. 'I miss *you*,' she said. 'I'm coming home tomorrow.'

'Good, that's great,' he said. 'All kinds of things have

been going on here. Rehearsals have been postponed until January.'

'Oh?'

'They haven't been able to cast the little girl. It's a break for me though; I'm going to do a pilot next month. A half-hour comedy series.'

'You are?'

'It fell into my lap, Ro. And it really looks good. ABC loves the idea. It's called *Greenwich Village*; it's going to be filmed there, and I'm a way-out writer. It's practically the lead.'

'That's marvellous, Guy!'

'Allan says I'm suddenly very hot.'

'That's wonderful!'

'Listen, I've got to shower and shave; he's taking me to a screening that Stanley Kubrick is going to be at. When are you going to get in?'

'Around noon, maybe earlier.'

'I'll be waiting. Love you.'

'Love you!'

She called Hutch, who was out, and left word with his service that she would return the car the following afternoon.

The next morning she cleaned the cabin, closed it up and locked it, and drove back to the city. Traffic on the Saw Mill River Parkway was bottlenecked by a three-car collision, and it was close to one o'clock when she parked the car half-in half-out-of the bus stop in front of the Bramford. With her small suitcase she hurried into the house.

The elevator man hadn't taken Guy down, but he had been off duty from eleven-fifteen to twelve.

He was there, though. The *No Strings* album was playing. She opened her mouth to call and he came out of the bedroom in a fresh shirt and tie, headed for the kitchen with a used coffee cup in his hand.

They kissed, lovingly and fully, he hugging her one-armed because of the cup.

'Have a good time?' he asked.

'Terrible. Awful. I missed you so.'

88

'How are you?'

'Fine. How was Stanley Kubrick?'

'Didn't show, the fink.'

They kissed again.

She brought her suitcase into the bedroom and opened it on the bed. He came in with two cups of coffee, gave her one, and sat on the vanity bench while she unpacked. She told him about the yellow-and-orange woods and the still nights; he told her about *Greenwich Village*, who else was in it and who the producers, writers, and director were.

'Are you *really* fine?' he asked when she was zipping closed the empty case.

She didn't understand.

'Your period,' he said. 'It was due on Tuesday.'

'It was?'

He nodded.

'Well, it's just two days,' she said – matter-of-factly, as if her heart weren't racing, leaping. 'It's probably the change of water, or the food I ate up there.'

'You've never been late before,' he said.

'It'll probably come tonight. Or tomorrow.'

'You want to bet?'

'Yes.'

'A quarter?'

'Okay.'

'You're going to lose, Ro.'

'Shut up. You're getting me all jumpy. It's only two days. It'll probably come tonight.'

CHAPTER TEN

IT DIDN'T COME that night or the next day. Or the day after that or the day after that. Rosemary moved gently, walked lightly, so as not to dislodge what might possibly have taken hold inside her.

Talk with Guy? No, that could wait.

Everything could wait.

She cleaned, shopped, and cooked, breathing carefully. Laura-Louise came down one morning and asked her to vote for Buckley. She said she would, to get rid of her.

'Give me my quarter,' Guy said.

'Shut up,' she said, giving his arm a backhand punch.

She made an appointment with an obstetrician and, on Thursday, October 28th, went to see him. His name was Dr Hill. He had been recommended to her by a friend, Elise Dunstan, who had used him through two pregnancies and swore by him. His office was on West Seventy-second Street.

He was younger than Rosemary had expected – Guy's age or even less – and he looked a little bit like Dr Kildare on television. She liked him. He asked her questions slowly and with interest, examined her, and sent her to a lab on Sixtieth Street where a nurse drew blood from her right arm.

He called the next afternoon at three-thirty.

'Mrs Woodhouse?'

'Dr Hill?'

'Yes. Congratulations.'

'Really?'

'Really.'

She sat down on the side of the bed, smiling past the phone. *Really, really, really, really, really.*

'Are you there?'

'What happens now?' she asked.

'Very little. You come in and see me again next month. And you get those Natalin pills and start taking them. One

90

a day. And you fill out some forms that I'm going to mail you – for the hospital; it's best to get the reservation in as soon as possible.'

'When will it be?' she asked.

'If your last period was September twenty-first,' he said, 'it works out to June twenty-eighth.'

'That sounds so far away.'

'It is. Oh, one more thing, Mrs Woodhouse. The lab would like another blood sample. Could you drop by there tomorrow or Monday and let them have it?'

'Yes, of course,' Rosemary said. 'What for?'

'The nurse didn't take as much as she should have.'

'But – I'm pregnant, aren't I?'

'Yes, they did *that* test,' Dr Hill said, 'but I generally have them run a few others besides – blood sugar and so forth – and the nurse didn't know and only took enough for the one. It's nothing to be concerned about. You're pregnant. I give you my word.'

'All right,' she said. 'I'll go back tomorrow morning.'

'Do you remember the address?'

'Yes, I still have the card.'

'I'll put those forms in the mail, and let's see you again – the last week in November.'

They made an appointment for November 29th at one o'clock and Rosemary hung up feeling that something was wrong. The nurse at the lab had seemed to know exactly what she was doing, and Dr Hill's offhandedness in speaking about her hadn't quite rung true. Were they afraid a mistake had been made? – vials of blood mixed up and wrongly labelled? – and was there still a possibility that she wasn't pregnant? But wouldn't Dr Hill have told her so frankly and not have been as definite as he had?

She tried to shake it away. Of course she was pregnant; she had to be, with her period so long overdue. She went into the kitchen, where a wall calendar hung, and in the next day's square wrote *Lab*; and in the square for November 29th, *Dr Hill – 1:00*.

When Guy came in she went to him without saying a word

and put a quarter in his hand. 'What's this for?' he asked, and then caught on. 'Oh, that's great, honey!' he said. 'Just great!' – and taking her by the shoulders he kissed her twice and then a third time.

'Isn't it?' she said.

'Just great. I'm so happy.'

'Father.'

'Mother.'

'Guy, listen,' she said, and looked up at him, suddenly serious. 'Let's make this a new beginning, okay? A new openness and talking-to-each-other. Because we haven't been open. You've been so wrapped up in the show and the pilot and the way things have been breaking for you – I'm not saying you shouldn't be; it wouldn't be normal if you weren't. But that's why I went to the cabin, Guy. To settle in my mind what was going wrong between us. And that's what it was, and is: a lack of openness. On my part too. On my part as much as yours.'

'It's true,' he said, his hands holding her shoulders, his eyes meeting hers earnestly. 'It's true. I felt it too. Not as much as you did, I guess. I'm so God-damned self-centred, Ro. That's what the whole trouble is. I guess it's why I'm in this idiot nutty profession to begin with. You know I love you though, don't you? I *do*, Ro. I'll try to make it plainer from now on, I swear to God I will. I'll be as open as —'

'It's my fault as much as —'

'Bull. It's mine. Me and my self-centredness. Bear with me, will you, Ro? I'll try to do better.'

'Oh, Guy,' she said in a tide of remorse and love and forgiveness, and met his kisses with fervent kisses of her own.

'Fine way for parents to be carrying on,' he said.

She laughed, wet-eyed.

'Gee, honey,' he said, 'do you know what I'd love to do?'

'What?'

'Tell Minnie and Roman.' He raised a hand. 'I know, I know; we're supposed to keep it a deep dark secret. But I told them we were trying and they were so pleased, and, well, with people that old,' – he spread his hands ruefully –

'if we wait too long they might never get to know at all.'

'Tell them,' she said, loving him.

He kissed her nose. 'Back in two minutes,' he said, and turned and hurried to the door. Watching him go, she saw that Minnie and Roman had become deeply important to him. It wasn't surprising; his mother was a busy self-involved chatterer and none of his fathers had been truly fatherly. The Castevets were filling a need in him, a need of which he himself was probably unaware. She was grateful to them and would think more kindly of them in the future.

She went into the bathroom and splashed cold water on her eyes and fixed her hair and lips. 'You're pregnant,' she told herself in the mirror. (*But the lab wants another blood sample. What for?*)

As she came back out they came in at the front door: Minnie in a housedress, Roman holding in both hands a bottle of wine, and Guy behind them flushed and smiling. 'Now *that's* what I call good news!' Minnie said. 'Con*grat-u-la*-tions!' She bore down on Rosemary, took her by the shoulders, and kissed her cheek hard and loud.

'Our best wishes to you, Rosemary,' Roman said, putting his lips to her other cheek. 'We're more pleased than we can say. We have no champagne on hand, but this 1961 Saint Julien, I think, will do just as nicely for a toast.'

Rosemary thanked them.

'When are you due, dear?' Minnie asked.

'June twenty-eighth.'

'It's going to be so exciting,' Minnie said, 'between now and then.'

'We'll do all your shopping for you,' Roman said.

'Oh, no,' Rosemary said. 'Really.'

Guy brought glasses and a corkscrew, and Roman turned with him to the opening of the wine. Minnie took Rosemary's elbow and they walked together into the living-room. 'Listen, dear,' Minnie said, 'do you have a good doctor?'

'Yes, a very good one,' Rosemary said.

'One of the top obstetricians in New York,' Minnie said,

'is a dear friend of ours. Abe Sapirstein. A Jewish man. He delivers all the Society babies and he would deliver yours too if we asked him. And he'd do it *cheap*, so you'd be saving Guy some of his hard-earned money.'

'Abe Sapirstein?' Roman asked from across the room. 'He's one of the finest obstetricians in the country, Rosemary. You've heard of him, haven't you?'

'I think so,' Rosemary said, recalling the name from an article in a newspaper or magazine.

'*I* have,' Guy said. 'Wasn't he on *Open End* a couple of years ago?'

'That's right,' Roman said. 'He's one of the finest obstetricians in the country.'

'Ro?' Guy said.

'But what about Dr Hill?' she asked.

'Don't worry, I'll tell him something,' Guy said. 'You know me.'

Rosemary thought about Dr Hill, so young, so Kildare, with his lab that wanted more blood because the nurse had goofed or the technician had goofed or *someone* had goofed, causing her needless bother and concern.

Minnie said, 'I'm not going to *let* you go to no Dr Hill that nobody heard of! The *best* is what *you're* going to have, young lady, and the best is Abe Sapirstein!'

Gratefully Rosemary smiled her decision at them. 'If you're sure he can take me,' she said. 'He might be too busy.'

'He'll take you,' Minnie said. 'I'm going to call him right now. Where's the phone?'

'In the bedroom,' Guy said.

Minnie went into the bedroom. Roman poured glasses of wine. 'He's a brilliant man,' he said, 'with all the sensitivity of his much-tormented race.' He gave glasses to Rosemary and Guy. 'Let's wait for Minnie,' he said.

They stood motionless, each holding a full wineglass, Roman holding two. Guy said, 'Sit down, honey,' but Rosemary shook her head and stayed standing.

Minnie in the bedroom said, 'Abe? Minnie. Fine. Listen, a dear friend of ours just found out today that she's pregnant. Yes, isn't it? I'm in her apartment now. We told her you'd be glad to take care of her and that you wouldn't charge none of your fancy Society prices neither.' She was silent, then said 'Wait a minute,' and raised her voice. 'Rosemary? Can you go see him tomorrow morning at eleven?'

'Yes, that would be fine,' Rosemary called back.

Roman said, 'You see?'

'Eleven's fine, Abe,' Minnie said. 'Yes. You too. No, not at all. Let's hope so. Goodbye.'

She came back. 'There you are,' she said. 'I'll write down his address for you before we go. He's on Seventy-ninth Street and Park Avenue.'

'Thanks a million, Minnie,' Guy said, and Rosemary said, 'I don't know how to thank you. Both of you.'

Minnie took the glass of wine Roman held out to her. 'It's easy,' she said. 'Just do everything Abe tells you and have a fine healthy baby; that's all the thanks we'll ever ask for.'

Roman raised his glass. 'To a fine healthy baby,' he said.

'Hear, hear,' Guy said, and they all drank; Guy, Minnie, Rosemary, Roman.

'Mmm,' Guy said. 'Delicious.'

'Isn't it?' Roman said. 'And not at all expensive.'

'Oh my,' Minnie said, 'I can't wait to tell the news to Laura-Louise.'

Rosemary said, 'Oh, please. Don't tell anyone else. Not yet. It's so early.'

'She's right,' Roman said. 'There'll be plenty of time later on for spreading the good tidings.'

'Would anyone like some cheese and crackers?' Rosemary asked.

'Sit down, honey,' Guy said. 'I'll get it.'

That night Rosemary was too fired with joy and wonder to fall asleep quickly. Within her, under the hands that lay alertly on her stomach, a tiny egg had been fertilized by a tiny seed. Oh miracle, it would grow to be Andrew or Susan! ('Andrew' she was definite about; 'Susan' was open to discussion with Guy.) What was Andrew-or-Susan now, a

95

pin-point speck? No, surely it was more than that; after all, wasn't she in her second month already? Indeed she was. It had probably reached the early tadpole stage. She would have to find a chart or book that told month by month exactly what was happening. Dr Sapirstein would know of one.

A fire engine screamed by. Guy shifted and mumbled, and behind the wall Minnie and Roman's bed creaked.

There were so many dangers to worry about in the months ahead; fires, falling objects, cars out of control; dangers that had never been dangers before but were dangers now, now that Andrew-or-Susan was begun and living. (Yes, living!) She would give up her occasional cigarette, of course. And check with Dr Sapirstein about cocktails.

If only prayer were still possible! How nice it would be to hold a crucifix again and have God's ear: ask Him for safe passage through the eight more months ahead; no German measles, please, no great new drugs with Thalidomide side effects. Eight good months, please, free of accident and illness, full of iron and milk and sunshine.

Suddenly she remembered the good luck charm, the ball of tannis root; and foolish or not, wanted it – no, needed it – around her neck. She slipped out of bed, tiptoed to the vanity, and got it from the Louis Sherry box, freed it from its aluminium-foil wrapping. The smell of the tannis root had changed; it was still strong but no longer repellent. She put the chain over her head.

With the ball tickling between her breasts, she tiptoed back to bed and climbed in. She drew up the blanket and, closing her eyes, settled her head down into the pillow. She lay breathing deeply and was soon asleep, her hands on her stomach shielding the embryo inside her.

Part Two

CHAPTER ONE

NOW SHE WAS alive; was doing, was being, was at last herself and complete. She did what she had done before – cooked, cleaned, ironed, made the bed, shopped, took laundry to the basement, went to her sculpture class – but did everything against a new and serene background of knowing that Andrew-or-Susan (or Melinda) was every day a little bit bigger inside her than the day before, a little bit more clearly defined and closer to readiness.

Dr Sapirstein was wonderful; a tall sunburned man with white hair and a shaggy white moustache (she had seen him somewhere before but couldn't think where; maybe on *Open End*) who despite the Miës van der Rohe chairs and cool marble tables of his waiting-room was reassuringly old-fashioned and direct. 'Please don't read books,' he said. 'Every pregnancy is different, and a book that tells you what you're going to feel in the third week of the third month is only going to make you worry. No pregnancy was ever exactly like the ones described in the books. And don't listen to your friends either. They'll have had experiences very different from yours and they'll be absolutely certain that their pregnancies were the normal ones and that yours is abnormal.'

She asked him about the vitamin pills Dr Hill had prescribed.

'No, no pills,' he said. 'Minnie Castevet has a herbarium and a blender; I'm going to have her make a daily drink for you that will be fresher, safer, and more vitamin-rich than any pill on the market. And another thing: don't be afraid to satisfy your cravings. The theory today is that pregnant women invent cravings because they feel it's expected of them. I don't hold with that. I say if you want pickles in the middle of the night, make your poor husband go out and get some, just like in the old jokes. *Whatever* you want, be sure you get it. You'll be surprised at some of the strange things your body will ask for in these next few months. And any questions you have, call me night or day. Call *me*, not your mother or your Aunt Fanny. That's what I'm here for.'

She was to come in once a week, which was certainly closer attention than Dr Hill gave his patients, and he would make a reservation at Doctors Hospital without any bother of filling out forms.

Everything was right and bright and lovely. She got a Vidal Sassoon haircut, finished with the dentist, voted on Election Day (for Lindsay for mayor), and went down to Greenwich Village to watch some of the outdoor shooting of Guy's pilot. Between takes – Guy, running with a stolen hotdog wagon down Sullivan Street – she crouched on her heels to talk to small children and smiled *Me too* at pregnant women.

Salt, she found, even a few grains of it, made food inedible. 'That's perfectly normal,' Dr Sapirstein said on her second visit. 'When your system needs it, the aversion will disappear. Meanwhile, obviously, no salt. Trust your aversions the same as you do your cravings.'

She didn't have any cravings though. Her appetite, in fact, seemed smaller than usual. Coffee and toast was enough for breakfast, a vegetable and a small piece of rare meat for dinner. Each morning at eleven Minnie brought over what looked like a watery pistachio milkshake. It was cold and sour.

'What's in it?' Rosemary asked.

'Snips and snails and puppy-dogs' tails,' Minnie said, smiling.

Rosemary laughed. 'That's fine,' she said, 'but what if we want a girl?'

'Do you?'

'Well of course we'll take what we get, but it *would* be nice if the first one were a *boy*.'

'Well there you are,' Minnie said.

Finished drinking, Rosemary said, 'No, really, what's in it?'

100

'A raw egg, gelatin, herbs . . .'

'Tannis root?'

'Some of that, some of some other things.'

Minnie brought the drink every day in the same glass, a large one with blue and green stripes, and stood waiting while Rosemary drained it.

One day Rosemary got into a conversation by the elevator with Phyllis Kapp, young Lisa's mother. The end of it was a brunch invitation for Guy and her on the following Sunday, but Guy vetoed the idea when Rosemary told him of it. In all likelihood he would be in Sunday's shooting, he explained, and if he weren't he would need the day for rest and study. They were having little social life just then. Guy had broken a dinner-and-theatre date they had made a few weeks earlier with Jimmy and Tiger Haenigsen, and he had asked Rosemary if she would mind putting off Hutch for dinner. It was because of the pilot, which was taking longer to shoot than had been intended.

It turned out to be just as well though, for Rosemary began to develop abdominal pains of an alarming sharpness. She called Dr Sapirstein and he asked her to come in. Examining her, he said that there was nothing to worry about; the pains came from an entirely normal expansion of her pelvis. They would disappear in a day or two, and meanwhile she could fight them with ordinary doses of aspirin.

Rosemary, relieved, said, 'I was afraid it might be an ectopic pregnancy.'

'Ectopic?' Dr Sapirstein asked, and looked sceptically at her. She coloured. He said, 'I thought you weren't going to read books, Rosemary.'

'It was staring me right in the face at the drug store,' she said.

'And all it did was worry you. Will you go home and throw it away, please?'

'I will. I promise.'

'The pains will be gone in two days,' he said. ' "Ectopic pregnancy." ' He shook his head.

But the pains weren't gone in two days; they were worse, and grew worse still, as if something inside her were encircled by a wire being drawn tighter and tighter to cut it in two. There would be pain for hour after hour, and then a few minutes of relative painlessness that was only the pain gathering itself for a new assault. Aspirin did little good, and she was afraid of taking too many. Sleep, when it finally came, brought harried dreams in which she fought against huge spiders that had cornered her in the bathroom, or tugged desperately at a small black bush that had taken root on the middle of the living-room rug. She woke tired, to even sharper pain.

'This happens sometimes,' Dr Sapirstein said. 'It'll stop any day now. Are you sure you haven't been lying about your age? Usually it's the older women with less flexible joints who have this sort of difficulty.'

Minnie, bringing in the drink, said, 'You poor thing. Don't fret, dear; a niece of mine in Toledo had exactly the same kind of pains and so did two other women I know of. And their deliveries were real easy and they had beautiful healthy babies.'

'Thanks,' Rosemary said.

Minnie drew back righteously. 'What do you mean? That's the gospel truth! I swear to God it is, Rosemary!'

Her face grew pinched and wan and shadowed; she looked awful. But Guy insisted otherwise. 'What are you talking about?' he said. 'You look great. It's that *haircut* that looks awful, if you want the truth, honey. That's the biggest mistake you ever made in your whole life.'

The pain settled down to a constant presence, with no respite whatever. She endured it and lived with it, sleeping a few hours a night and taking one aspirin where Dr Sapirstein allowed two. There was no going out with Joan or Elise, no sculpture class or shopping. She ordered groceries by phone and stayed in the apartment, making nursery curtains and starting, finally, on *The Decline and Fall of The Roman Empire*. Sometimes Minnie or Roman came in of an afternoon, to talk a while and see if there was anything she wanted. Once Laura-Louise brought down a tray of gingerbread. She hadn't been told yet that Rosemary was pregnant. 'Oh my, I *do* like that haircut, Rosemary,' she said. 'You look so pretty and up-to-date.' She was surprised to hear she wasn't feeling well.

When the pilot was finally finished Guy stayed home most of the time. He had stopped studying with Dominick, his vocal coach, and no longer spent afternoons auditioning and being seen. He had two good commercials on deck – for Pall Mall and Texaco – and rehearsals of *Don't I know You From Somewhere?* were definitely scheduled to begin in mid-January. He gave Rosemary a hand with the cleaning, and they played time-limit Scrabble for a dollar a game. He answered the phone and, when it was for Rosemary, made plausible excuses.

She had planned to give a Thanksgiving dinner for some of their friends who, like themselves, had no family nearby; with the constant pain, though, and the constant worry over Andrew-or-Melinda's well-being, she decided not to, and they ended up going to Minnie and Roman's instead.

CHAPTER TWO

ONE AFTERNOON in December, while Guy was doing the Pall Mall commercial, Hutch called. 'I'm around the corner at City Centre picking up tickets for Marcel Marceau,' he said. 'Would you and Guy like to come on Friday night?'

'I don't think so, Hutch,' Rosemary said. 'I haven't been feeling too well lately. And Guy's got two commercials this week.'

'What's the matter with you?'

'Nothing, really. I've just been a bit under the weather.'

'May I come up for a few minutes?'

'Oh do; I'd love to see you.'

She hurried into slacks and a jersey top, put on lipstick and brushed her hair. The pain sharpened – locking her for a moment with shut eyes and clenched teeth – and then it sank back to its usual level and she breathed out gratefully and went on brushing.

Hutch, when he saw her, stared and said, 'My God.'

'It's Vidal Sassoon and it's very in,' she said.

'What's *wrong* with you?' he said. 'I don't mean your hair.'

'Do I look that bad?' She took his coat and hat and hung them away, smiling a fixed bright smile.

'You look terrible,' Hutch said. 'You've lost God-knows-how-many pounds and you have circles around your eyes that a panda would envy. You aren't on one of those "Zen diets", are you?'

'No.'

'Then what is it? Have you seen a doctor?'

'I suppose I might as well tell you,' Rosemary said. 'I'm pregnant. I'm in my third month.'

Hutch looked at her, nonplussed. 'That's ridiculous,' he said. 'Pregnant women *gain* weight, they don't lose it. And they look *healthy*, not —'

'There's a slight complication,' Rosemary said, leading

the way into the living-room. 'I have stiff joints or something, so I have pains that keep me awake most of the night. Well, *one* pain, really; it just sort of continues. It's not serious, though. It'll probably stop any day now.'

'I never heard of "stiff joints" being a problem,' Hutch said.

'Stiff pelvic joints. It's fairly common.'

Hutch sat in Guy's easy chair. 'Well, congratulations,' he said doubtfully. 'You must be very happy.'

'I am,' Rosemary said. 'We both are.'

'Who's your obstetrician?'

'His name is Abraham Sapirstein. He's —'

'I know him,' Hutch said. 'Or *of* him. He delivered two of Doris's babies.' Doris was Hutch's elder daughter.

'He's one of the best in the city,' Rosemary said.

'When did you see him last?'

'The day before yesterday. And he said just what I told you; it's fairly common and it'll probably stop any day now. Of course he's been saying *that* since it started . . .'

'How much weight have you lost?'

'Only three pounds. It looks —'

'Nonsense! You've lost *far* more than that!'

Rosemary smiled. 'You sound like our bathroom scale,' she said. 'Guy finally threw it out, it was scaring me so. No, I've lost only three pounds and one little space more. And it's perfectly normal to lose a little during the first few months. Later on I'll be gaining.'

'I certainly hope so,' Hutch said. 'You look as if you're being drained by a vampire. Are you sure there aren't any puncture marks?' Rosemary smiled. 'Well,' Hutch said, leaning back and smiling too, 'we'll assume that Dr Sapirstein knows whereof he speaks. God knows he should; he charges enough. Guy must be doing sensationally.'

'He is,' Rosemary said. 'But we're getting bargain rates. Our neighbours the Castevets are close friends of his; they sent me to him and he's charging us his special non-Society prices.'

'Does that mean Doris and Axel are Society?' Hutch said. 'They'll be delighted to hear about it.'

The doorbell rang. Hutch offered to answer it but Rosemary wouldn't let him. 'Hurts less when I move around,' she said, going out of the room; and went to the front door trying to recall if there was anything she had ordered that hadn't been delivered yet.

It was Roman, looking slightly winded. Rosemary smiled and said, 'I mentioned your name two seconds ago.'

'In a favourable context, I hope,' he said. 'Do you need anything from outside? Minnie is going down in a while and our house phone doesn't seem to be functioning.'

'No, nothing,' Rosemary said. 'Thanks so much for asking. I phoned out for things this morning.'

Roman glanced beyond her for an instant, and then, smiling, asked if Guy was home already.

'No, he won't be back until six at the earliest,' Rosemary said; and, because Roman's pallid face stayed waiting with its questioning smile, added, 'A friend of ours is here.' The questioning smile stayed. She said, 'Would you like to meet him?'

'Yes, I would,' Roman said. 'If I won't be intruding.'

'Of course you won't.' Rosemary showed him in. He was wearing a black-and-white checked jacket over a blue shirt and a wide paisley tie. He passed close to her and she noticed for the first time that his ears were pierced – that the left one was, at any rate.

She followed him to the living-room archway. 'This is Edward Hutchins,' she said, and to Hutch, who was rising and smiling, 'This is Roman Castevet, the neighbour I just mentioned.' She explained to Roman: 'I was telling Hutch that it was you and Minnie who sent me to Dr Sapirstein.'

The two men shook hands and greeted each other. Hutch said, 'One of my daughters used Dr Sapirstein too. On two occasions.'

'He's a brilliant man,' Roman said. 'We met him only last spring but he's become one of our closest friends.'

'Sit down, won't you?' Rosemary said. The men seated themselves and Rosemary sat by Hutch.

Roman said, 'So Rosemary has told you the good news, has she?'

'Yes, she has,' Hutch said.

'We must see that she gets plenty of rest,' Roman said, 'and complete freedom from worry and anxiety.'

Rosemary said, 'That would be heaven.'

'I was a bit alarmed by her appearance,' Hutch said, looking at Rosemary as he took out a pipe and a striped rep tobacco pouch.

'Were you?' Roman said.

'But now that I know she's in Dr Sapirstein's care I feel considerably relieved.'

'She's only lost two or three pounds,' Roman said. 'Isn't that so, Rosemary?'

'That's right,' Rosemary said.

'And that's quite normal in the early months of pregnancy,' Roman said. 'Later on she'll gain – probably far too much.'

'So I gather,' Hutch said, filling his pipe.

Rosemary said, 'Mrs Castevet makes a vitamin drink for me every day, with a raw egg and milk and fresh herbs that she grows.'

'All according to Dr Sapirstein's directions, of course,' Roman said. 'He's inclined to be suspicious of commercially prepared vitamin pills.'

'Is he really?' Hutch asked, pocketing his porch. 'I can't think of anything I'd be less suspicious of; they're surely manufactured under every imaginable safeguard.' He struck two matches as one and sucked flame into his pipe, blowing out puffs of aromatic white smoke. Rosemary put an ashtray near him.

'That's true,' Roman said, 'but commercial pills can sit for months in a warehouse or on a druggist's shelf and lose a great deal of their original potency.'

'Yes, I hadn't thought of that,' Hutch said; 'I suppose they can.'

Rosemary said, 'I like the *idea* of having everything fresh and natural. I'll bet expectant mothers chewed bits of tannis root hundreds and hundreds of years ago when nobody'd even heard of vitamins.'

'Tannis root?' Hutch said.

'It's one of the herbs in the drink,' Rosemary said. 'Or *is* it a herb?' She looked to Roman. 'Can a root be a herb?' But Roman was watching Hutch and didn't hear.

' "Tannis"?' Hutch said. 'I've never heard of it. Are you sure you don't mean "anise" or "orris root"?'

Roman said, 'Tannis.'

'Here,' Rosemary said, drawing out her charm. 'It's good luck too, theoretically. Brace yourself; the smell takes a little getting-used-to.' She held the charm out, leaning forward to bring it closer to Hutch.

He sniffed at it and drew away, grimacing. 'I should say it does,' he said. He took the chained ball between two finger-tips and squinted at it from a distance. 'It doesn't look like root matter at all,' he said; 'it looks like mould or fungus of some kind.' He looked at Roman. 'Is it ever called by another name?' he asked.

'Not to my knowledge,' Roman said.

'I shall look it up in the encyclopedia and find out all about it,' Hutch said. 'Tannis. What a pretty holder or charm or whatever-it-is. Where did you get it?'

With a quick smile at Roman, Rosemary said, 'The Castevets gave it to me.' She tucked the charm back inside her top.

Hutch said to Roman, 'You and your wife seem to be taking better care of Rosemary than her own parents would.'

Roman said, 'We're very fond of her, and of Guy too.' He pushed against the arms of his chair and raised himself to his feet. 'If you'll excuse me, I have to go now,' he said. 'My wife is waiting for me.'

'Of course,' Hutch said, rising. 'It's a pleasure to have met you.'

'We'll meet again, I'm sure,' Roman said. 'Don't bother, Rosemary.'

'It's no bother.' She walked along with him to the front door. His right ear was pierced too, she saw, and there were many small scars on his neck like a flight of distant birds. 'Thanks again for stopping by,' she said.

'Don't mention it,' Roman said. 'I like your friend Mr

Hutchins; he seems extremely intelligent.'

Rosemary, opening the door, said, 'He is.'

'I'm glad I met him,' Roman said. With a smile and a handwave he started down the hall.

' 'Bye,' Rosemary said, waving back.

Hutch was standing by the bookshelves. 'This room is glorious,' he said. 'You're doing a beautiful job.'

'Thanks,' Rosemary said. 'I was until my pelvis intervened. Roman has pierced ears. I just noticed it for the first time.'

'Pierced ears and piercing eyes,' Hutch said. 'What was he before he became a Golden Ager?'

'Just about everything. And he's been everywhere in the world. Really everywhere.'

'Nonsense; nobody has. Why did he ring your bell? – if I'm not being too inquisitive.'

'To see if I needed anything from outside. The house phone isn't working. They're fantastic neighbours. They'd come in and do the cleaning if I let them.'

'What's *she* like?'

Rosemary told him. 'Guy's gotten very close to them,' she said. 'I think they've become sort of parent-figures for him.'

'And you?'

'I'm not sure. Sometimes I'm so grateful I could kiss them, and sometimes I get a sort of smothery feeling, as if they're being *too* friendly and helpful. Yet how can I complain? You remember the power failure?'

'Shall I ever forget it? I was in an elevator.'

'No.'

'Yes indeed. Five hours in total darkness with three women and a John Bircher who were all sure that the Bomb had fallen.'

'How awful.'

'You were saying?'

'We were here, Guy and I, and two minutes after the lights went out Minnie was at the door with a handful of candles.' She gestured towards the mantel. 'Now how can you find fault with neighbours like that?'

'You can't, obviously,' Hutch said, and stood looking at the mantel. 'Are those the ones?' he asked. Two pewter candlesticks stood between a bowl of polished stones and a brass microscope; in them were three-inch lengths of black candle ribbed with drippings.

'The last survivors,' Rosemary said. 'She brought a whole month's worth. What is it?'

'Were they all black?' he asked.

'Yes,' she said. 'Why?'

'Just curious.' He turned from the mantel, smiling at her. 'Offer me coffee, will you? And tell me more about Mrs Castevet. Where does she grow those herbs of hers? In window boxes?'

They were sitting over cups at the kitchen table some ten minutes later when the front door unlocked and Guy hurried in. 'Hey, what a surprise,' he said, coming over and grabbing Hutch's hand before he could rise. 'How are you, Hutch? Good to see you!' He clasped Rosemary's head in his other hand and bent and kissed her cheek and lips. 'How you doing, honey?' He still had his make-up on; his face was orange, his eyes black-lashed and large.

'You're the surprise,' Rosemary said. 'What happened?'

'Ah, they stopped in the middle for a rewrite, the dumb bastards. We start again in the morning. Stay where you are, nobody move; I'll just get rid of my coat.' He went out to the closet.

'Would you like some coffee?' Rosemary called.

'Love some!'

She got up and poured a cup, and refilled Hutch's cup and her own. Hutch sucked at his pipe, looking thoughtfully before him.

Guy came back in with his hands full of packs of Pall Mall. 'Loot,' he said, dumping them on the table. 'Hutch?'

'No, thanks.'

Guy tore a pack open, jammed cigarettes up, and pulled one out. He winked at Rosemary as she sat down again.

Hutch said, 'It seems congratulations are in order.'

Guy, lighting up, said, 'Rosemary told you? It's wonderful, isn't it? We're delighted. Of course I'm scared stiff that I'll be a lousy father, but Rosemary'll be such a great mother that it won't make much difference.'

'When is the baby due?' Hutch asked.

Rosemary told him, and told Guy that Dr Sapirstein had delivered two of Hutch's grandchildren.

Hutch said, 'I met your neighbour, Roman Castevet.'

'Oh, did you?' Guy said. 'Funny old duck, isn't he? He's got some interesting stories, though, about Otis Skinner and Modjeska. He's quite a theatre buff.'

Rosemary said, 'Did you ever notice that his ears are pierced?'

'You're kidding,' Guy said.

'No I'm not; I saw.'

They drank their coffee, talking of Guy's quickening career and of a trip Hutch planned to make in the spring to Greece and Turkey.

'It's a shame we haven't seen more of you lately,' Guy said, when Hutch had excused himself and risen. 'With me so busy and Ro being the way she is, we really haven't seen anyone.'

'Perhaps we can have dinner together soon,' Hutch said; and Guy, agreeing, went to get his coat.

Rosemary said, 'Don't forget to look up tannis root.'

'I won't,' Hutch said. 'And you tell Dr Sapirstein to check his scale; I still think you've lost more than three pounds.'

'Don't be silly,' Rosemary said. 'Doctors' scales aren't wrong.'

Guy, holding open a coat, said, 'It's not mine, it must be yours.'

'Right you are,' Hutch said. Turning, he put his arms back into it. 'Have you thought about names yet?' he asked Rosemary, 'or is it too soon?'

'Andrew or Douglas if it's a boy,' she said. 'Melinda or Sarah if it's a girl.'

' "Sarah"?' Guy said. 'What happened to "Susan"?' He gave Hutch his hat.

Rosemary offered her cheek for Hutch's kiss.

'I do hope the pain stops soon,' he said.

'It will,' she said, smiling. 'Don't worry.'

Guy said, 'It's a pretty common condition.'

Hutch felt his pockets. 'Is there another one of these around?' he asked, and showed them a brown fur-lined glove and felt his pockets again.

Rosemary looked around at the floor and Guy went to the closet and looked down on the floor and up on to the shelf. 'I don't see it, Hutch,' he said.

'Nuisance,' Hutch said. 'I probably left it at City Centre. I'll stop back there. Let's really have that dinner, shall we?'

'Definitely,' Guy said, and Rosemary said, 'Next week.'

They watched him around the first turn of the hallway and then stepped back inside and closed the door.

'That was a nice surprise,' Guy said. 'Was he here long?'

'Not very,' Rosemary said. 'Guess what he said.'

'What?'

'I look terrible.'

'Good old Hutch,' Guy said, 'spreading cheer wherever he goes.' Rosemary looked at him questioningly. 'Well he *is* a professional crepe-hanger, honey,' he said. 'Remember how he tried to sour us on moving in here?'

'He isn't a professional crepe-hanger,' Rosemary said, going into the kitchen to clear the table.

Guy leaned against the door jamb. 'Then he sure is one of the top-ranking amateurs,' he said.

A few minutes later he put his coat on and went out for a newspaper.

The telephone rang at ten-thirty that evening, when Rosemary was in bed reading and Guy was in the den watching television. He answered the call and a minute later brought the phone into the bedroom. 'Hutch wants to speak to you,' he said, putting the phone on the bed and crouching to plug it in. 'I told him you were resting but he said it couldn't wait.'

Rosemary picked up the receiver. 'Hutch?' she said.

'Hello, Rosemary,' Hutch said. 'Tell me, dear, do you go out at all or do you stay in your apartment all day?'

'Well I haven't *been* going out,' she said, looking at Guy;

but I could. Why?' Guy looked back at her, frowning, listening.

'There's something I want to speak to you about,' Hutch said. 'Can you meet me tomorrow morning at eleven in front of the Seagram Building?'

'Yes, if you want me to,' she said. 'What is it? Can't you tell me now?'

'I'd rather not,' he said. 'It's nothing terribly important so don't brood about it. We can have a late brunch or early lunch if you'd like.'

'That would be nice.'

'Good. Eleven o'clock then, in front of the Seagram Building.'

'Right. Did you get your glove?'

'No, they didn't have it,' he said, 'but it's time I got some new ones anyway. Goodnight, Rosemary. Sleep well.'

'You too. Goodnight.'

She hung up.

'What was that?' Guy asked.

'He wants me to meet him tomorrow morning. He has something he wants to talk to me about.'

'And he didn't say what?'

'Not a word.'

Guy shook his head, smiling. 'I think those boys' adventure stories are going to his head,' he said. 'Where are you meeting him?'

'In front of the Seagram Building at eleven o'clock.'

Guy unplugged the phone and went out with it to the den; almost immediately, though, he was back. 'You're the pregnant one and I'm the one with yens,' he said, plugging the phone back in and putting it on the night table. 'I'm going to go out and get an ice cream cone. Do you want one?'

'Okay,' Rosemary said.

'Vanilla?'

'Fine.'

'I'll be as quick as I can.'

He went out, and Rosemary leaned back against her pillows, looking ahead at nothing with her book forgotten in her lap. What was it Hutch wanted to talk about? Nothing terribly important, he had said. But it must be something not *un*-important too, or else he wouldn't have summoned her as he had. Was it something about Joan? – or one of the other girls who had shared the apartment?

Far away she heard the Castevets' doorbell give one short ring. Probably it was Guy, asking them if they wanted ice cream or a morning paper. Nice of him.

The pain sharpened inside her.

CHAPTER THREE

THE FOLLOWING morning Rosemary called Minnie on the house phone and asked her not to bring the drink over at eleven o'clock; she was on her way out and wouldn't be back until one or two.

'Why, that's fine, dear,' Minnie said. 'Don't you worry about a thing. You don't have to take it at no fixed time; just so you take it *sometime*, that's all. You go on out. It's a nice day and it'll do you good to get some fresh air. Buzz me when you get back and I'll bring the drink in then.'

It was indeed a nice day; sunny, cold, clear, and invigorating. Rosemary walked through it slowly, ready to smile, as if she weren't carrying her pain inside her. Salvation Army Santa Clauses were on every corner, shaking their bells in their fool-nobody costumes. Stores all had their Christmas windows; Park Avenue had its centre line of trees.

She reached the Seagram Building at a quarter of eleven and, because she was early and there was no sign yet of Hutch, sat for a while on the low wall at the side of the building's forecourt, taking the sun on her face and listening with pleasure to busy footsteps and snatches of conversation, to cars and trucks and a helicopter's racketing. The dress beneath her coat was – for the first satisfying time – snug over her stomach; maybe after lunch she would go to Bloomingdale's and look at maternity dresses. She was glad Hutch had called her out this way (but what did he want to talk about?); pain, even constant pain, was no excuse for staying indoors as much as she had. She would fight it from now on, fight it with air and sunlight and activity, not succumb to it in Bramford gloom under the well-meant pamperings of Minnie and Guy and Roman. *Pain, begone!* she thought; *I will have no more of thee!* The pain stayed, immune to Positive Thinking.

At five of eleven she went and stood by the building's glass doors, at the edge of their heavy flow of traffic. Hutch would probably be coming from inside, she thought, from an earlier appointment; or else why had he chosen here rather than someplace else for their meeting? She scouted the out-coming faces as best she could, saw him but was mistaken, then saw a man she had dated before she met Guy and was mistaken again. She kept looking, stretching now and then on tiptoes; not anxiously, for she knew that even if she failed to see him, Hutch would see her.

He hadn't come by five after eleven, nor by ten after. At a quarter after she went inside to look at the building's directory, thinking she might see a name there that he had mentioned at one time or another and to which she might make a call of inquiry. The directory proved to be far too large and many-named for careful reading, though; she skimmed over its crowded columns and, seeing nothing familiar, went outside again.

She went back to the low wall and sat where she had sat before, this time watching the front of the building and glancing over occasionally at the shallow steps leading up from the sidewalk. Men and women met other men and women, but there was no sign of Hutch, who was rarely if ever late for appointments.

At eleven-forty Rosemary went back into the building and was sent by a maintenance man down to the basement where at the end of a white institutional corridor there was a pleasant lounge area with black modern chairs, an abstract mural, and a single stainless-steel phone booth. A Negro girl was in the booth, but she finished soon and came out with a friendly smile. Rosemary slipped in and dialled the number at the apartment. After five rings Service answered; there were no messages for Rosemary, and the one message for Guy was from a Rudy Horn, not a Mr. Hutchins. She had another dime and used it to call Hutch's number, thinking that his service might know where he was or have a message from him. On the first ring a woman answered with a worried non-service 'Yes?'

'Is this Edward Hutchins' apartment?' Rosemary asked.

'Yes. Who is this, please?' She sounded like a woman neither young nor old – in her forties, perhaps.

Rosemary said, 'My name is Rosemary Woodhouse. I had an eleven o'clock appointment with Mr Hutchins and he hasn't shown up yet. Do you have any idea whether he's coming or not?'

There was silence, and more of it. 'Hello?' Rosemary said.

'Hutch has told me about you, Rosemary,' the woman said. 'My name is Grace Cardiff. I'm a friend of his. He was taken ill last night. Or early this morning, to be exact.'

Rosemary's heart dropped. 'Taken ill?' she said.

'Yes. He's in a deep coma. The doctors haven't been able to find out yet what's causing it. He's at St Vincent's Hospital.'

'Oh, that's *awful*,' Rosemary said. 'I spoke to him last night around ten-thirty and he sounded *fine*.'

'I spoke to him not much later than that,' Grace Cardiff said, 'and he sounded fine to me too. But his cleaning woman came in this morning and found him unconscious on the bedroom floor.'

'And they don't know what from?'

'Not yet. It's early though, and I'm sure they'll find out soon. And when they do, they'll be able to treat him. At the moment he's totally unresponsive.'

'How awful,' Rosemary said. 'And he's never had anything like this before?'

'Never,' Grace Cardiff said. 'I'm going back to the hospital now, and if you'll give me a number where I can reach you, I'll let you know when there's any change.'

'Oh, thank you,' Rosemary said. She gave the apartment number and then asked if there was anything she could do to help.

'Not really,' Grace Cardiff said. 'I just finished calling his daughters, and that seems to be the sum total of what has to be done, at least until he comes to. If there should be anything else I'll let you know.'

Rosemary came out of the Seagram Building and walked across the forecourt and down the steps and north to the corner of Fifty-third Street. She crossed Park Avenue and walked slowly towards Madison, wondering whether Hutch would live or die, and if he died, whether she (selfishness!) would ever again have anyone on whom she could so effortlessly and completely depend. She wondered too about Grace Cardiff, who sounded silver-grey and attractive; had she and Hutch been having a quiet middle-aged affair? She hoped so. Maybe this brush with death – that's what it would be, a *brush* with death, not death itself; it couldn't be – maybe this brush with death would nudge them both towards marriage, and turn out in the end to have been a disguised blessing. Maybe. Maybe.

She crossed Madison, and somewhere between Madison and Fifth found herself looking into a window in which a small crèche was spotlighted, with exquisite porcelain figures of Mary and the Infant and Joseph, the Magi and the shepherds and the animals of the stable. She smiled at the tender scene, laden with meaning and emotion that survived her agnosticism; and then saw in the window glass, like a veil hung before the Nativity, her own reflection smiling, with the skeletal cheeks and black-circled eyes that yesterday had alarmed Hutch and now alarmed her.

'Well *this* is what I call the long arm of coincidence!' Minnie exclaimed, and came smiling to her when Rosemary turned, in a white mock-leather coat and a red hat and her neckchained eyeglasses. 'I said to myself, "As long as *Rosemary's* out, *I* might as well go out, and do the last little bit of my Christmas shopping." And here *you* are and here *I* am! It looks like we're just two of a kind that go the same places and do the same things! Why, what's the matter, dear? You look so sad and downcast.'

'I just heard some bad news,' Rosemary said. 'A friend of mine is very sick. In the hospital.'

'Oh, no,' Minnie said. 'Who?'

'His name is Edward Hutchins,' Rosemary said.

'The one Roman met yesterday afternoon? Why, he was going on for an *hour* about what a nice intelligent man he was! Isn't that a pity! What's troubling him?'

Rosemary told her.

'My land,' Minnie said, 'I hope it doesn't turn out the way it did for poor Lily Gardenia! And the doctors don't even know? Well at least they admit it; usually they cover up what they don't know with a lot of high-flown Latin. If the money spent putting those astronauts up where they are was spent on medical research down here, we'd *all* be a lot better off, if you want *my* opinion. Do you feel all right, Rosemary?'

'The pain is a little worse,' Rosemary said.

'You poor thing. You know what I think? I think we ought to be going home now. What do you say?'

'No, no, you have to finish your Christmas shopping.'

'Oh, shoot,' Minnie said, 'there's two whole weeks yet. Hold on to your ears.' She put her wrist to her mouth and blew stabbing shrillness from a whistle on a gold-chain bracelet. A taxi veered towards them. 'How's *that* for service?' she said. 'A nice big Checker one too.'

Soon after, Rosemary was in the apartment again. She drank the cold sour drink from the blue-and-green-striped glass while Minnie looked on approvingly.

CHAPTER FOUR

SHE HAD BEEN eating her meat rare; now she ate it nearly raw – broiled only long enough to take away the refrigerator's chill and seal in the juices.

The weeks before the holidays and the holiday season itself were dismal. The pain grew worse, grew so grinding that something shut down in Rosemary – some centre of resistance and remembered well-being – and she stopped reacting, stopped mentioning pain to Dr Sapirstein, stopped referring to pain even in her thoughts. Until now it had been inside her; now *she* was inside *it*; pain was the weather around her, was time, was the entire world. Numbed and exhausted, she began to sleep more, and to eat more too – more nearly raw meat.

She did what had to be done: cooked and cleaned, sent Christmas cards to the family – she hadn't the heart for phone calls – and put new money into envelopes for the elevator men, doormen, porters, and Mr Micklas. She looked at newspapers and tried to be interested in students burning draft cards and the threat of a city-wide transit strike, but she couldn't: this was news from a world of fantasy; nothing was real but her world of pain. Guy bought Christmas presents for Minnie and Roman; for each other they agreed to buy nothing at all. Minnie and Roman gave them coasters.

They went to nearby movies a few times, but most evenings they stayed in or went around the hall to Minnie and Roman's where they met couples named Fountain and Gilmore and Wees, a woman named Mrs Sabatini who always brought her cat, and Dr Shand, the retired dentist who had made the chain for Rosemary's tannis-charm. These were all elderly people who treated Rosemary with kindness and concern, seeing, apparently, that she was less than well. Laura-Louise was there too, and sometimes Dr

Sapirstein joined the group. Roman was an energetic host, filling glasses and launching new topics of conversation. On New Year's Eve he proposed a toast – 'To 1966, The Year One,' – that puzzled Rosemary, although everyone else seemed to understand and approve of it. She felt as if she had missed a literary or political reference – not that she really cared. She and Guy usually left early, and Guy would see her into bed and go back. He was the favourite of the women, who gathered around him and laughed at his jokes.

Hutch stayed as he was, in his deep and baffling coma. Grace Cardiff called every week or so. 'No change, no change at all,' she would say. 'They still don't know. He could wake up tomorrow morning or he could sink deeper and never wake up at all.'

Twice Rosemary went to St Vincent's Hospital to stand beside Hutch's bed and look down powerlessly at the closed eyes, the scarcely discernible breathing. The second time, early in January, his daughter Doris was there, sitting by the window working a piece of needlepoint. Rosemary had met her a year earlier at Hutch's apartment; she was a short pleasant woman in her thirties, married to a Swedish-born psychoanalyst. She looked, unfortunately, like a younger wigged Hutch.

Doris didn't recognize Rosemary, and when Rosemary had re-introduced herself she made a distressed apology.

'Please don't,' Rosemary said, smiling. 'I know. I look awful.'

'No, you haven't changed at all,' Doris said. 'I'm terrible with faces. I forget my *children*, really I do.'

She put aside her needlepoint and Rosemary drew up another chair and sat with her. They talked about Hutch's condition and watched a nurse come in and replace the hanging bottle that fed into his taped arm.

'We have an obstetrician in common,' Rosemary said when the nurse had gone; and then they talked about Rosemary's pregnancy and Dr Sapirstein's skill and eminence. Doris was surprised to hear that he was seeing Rosemary every week. 'He only saw me once a month,' she said. 'Till near the end, of course. Then it was every two weeks, and *then* every week, but only in the last month. I thought that was fairly standard.'

Rosemary could find nothing to say, and Doris suddenly looked distressed again. 'But I suppose every pregnancy is a law unto itself,' she said, with a smile meant to rectify tactlessness.

'That's what *he* told me,' Rosemary said.

That evening she told Guy that Dr Sapirstein had only seen Doris once a month. 'Something is wrong with me,' she said. 'And he knew it right from the beginning.'

'Don't be silly,' Guy said. 'He would tell you. And even if he wouldn't, he would certainly tell *me*.'

'Has he? Has he said *anything* to you?'

'Absolutely not, Ro. I swear to God.'

'Then why do I have to go every week?'

'Maybe that's the way he does it now. Or maybe he's giving you better treatment, because you're Minnie and Roman's friend.'

'No.'

'Well *I* don't know; ask *him*,' Guy said. 'Maybe you're more fun to examine than she was.'

She asked Dr Sapirstein two days later. 'Rosemary, Rosemary,' he said to her; 'what did I tell you about talking to your friends? Didn't I say that every pregnancy is different?'

'Yes, but —'

'And the treatment has to be different too. Doris Allert had had two deliveries before she ever came to me, and there had been no complications whatever. She didn't require the close attention a first-timer does.'

'Do you always see first-timers every week?'

'I try to,' he said. 'Sometimes I can't. There's nothing wrong with you, Rosemary. The pain will stop very soon.'

'I've been eating raw meat,' she said. 'Just warmed a little.'

'Anything else out of the ordinary?'

'No,' she said, taken aback; wasn't that enough?

'Whatever you want, eat it,' he said. 'I told you you'd get

some strange cravings. I've had women eat paper. And stop worrying. I don't keep things from my patients; it makes life too confusing. I'm telling you the truth. Okay?'

She nodded.

'Say hello to Minnie and Roman for me,' he said. 'And Guy too.'

She began the second volume of *The Decline and Fall*, and began knitting a red-and-orange striped muffler for Guy to wear to rehearsals. The threatened transit strike had come about but it affected them little since they were both at home most of the time. Late in the afternoon they watched from their bay windows the slow-moving crowds far below. 'Walk, you peasants!' Guy said. 'Walk! Home, home, and be quick about it!'

Not long after telling Dr Sapirstein about the nearly raw meat, Rosemary found herself chewing on a raw and dripping chicken heart – in the kitchen one morning at four-fifteen. She looked at herself in the side of the toaster, where her moving reflection had caught her eye, and then looked at her hand, at the part of the heart she hadn't yet eaten held in red-dripping fingers. After a moment she went over and put the heart in the garbage, and turned on the water and rinsed her hand. Then, with the water still running, she bent over the sink and began to vomit.

When she was finished she drank some water, washed her face and hands, and cleaned the inside of the sink with the spray attachment. She turned off the water and dried herself and stood for a while, thinking; and then she got a memo pad and a pencil from one of the drawers and went to the table and sat down and began to write.

Guy came in just before seven in his pyjamas. She had the *Life* Cookbook open on the table and was copying a recipe out of it. 'What the hell are you doing?' he asked.

She looked at him. 'Planning the menu,' she said. 'For a party. We're giving a party on January twenty-second. A week from next Saturday.' She looked among several slips of paper on the table and picked one up. 'We're inviting

Elise Dunstan and her husband,' she said, 'Joan and a date, Jimmy and Tiger, Allan and a date, Lou and Claudia, the Chens, the Wendells, Dee Bertillon and a date unless you don't want him, Mike and Pedro, Bob and Thea Goodman, the Kapps' – she pointed in the Kapps' direction – 'and Doris and Axel Allert, if they'll come. That's Hutch's daughter.'

'I know,' Guy said.

She put down the paper. 'Minnie and Roman are not invited,' she said. 'Neither is Laura-Louise. Neither are the Fountains and the Gilmores and the Weeses. Neither is Dr Sapirstein. This is a very special party. You have to be under sixty to get in.'

'Whew,' Guy said. 'For a minute there I didn't think I was going to make it.'

'Oh, you make it,' Rosemary said. 'You're the bartender.'

'Swell,' Guy said. 'Do you really think this is such a great idea?'

'I think it's the best idea I've had in months.'

'Don't you think you ought to check with Sapirstein first?'

'Why? I'm just going to give a party; I'm not going to swim the English Channel or climb Annapurna.'

Guy went to the sink and turned on the water. He held a glass under it. 'I'll be in rehearsal then, you know,' he said. 'We start on the seventeenth.'

'You won't have to do a thing,' Rosemary said. 'Just come home and be charming.'

'And tend bar.' He turned off the water and raised his glass and drank.

'We'll *hire* a bartender,' Rosemary said. 'The one Joan and Dick used to have. And when you're ready to go to sleep I'll chase everyone out.'

Guy turned around and looked at her.

'I want to see them,' she said. 'Not Minnie and Roman. I'm tired of Minnie and Roman.'

He looked away from her, and then at the floor, and then at her eyes again. 'What about the pain?' he asked.

She smiled drily. 'Haven't you heard?' she said. 'It's going to be gone in a day or two. Dr Sapirstein told me so.'

Everyone could come except the Allerts, because of Hutch's condition, and the Chens, who were going to be in London taking pictures of Charlie Chaplin. The bartender wasn't available but knew another one who was. Rosemary took a loose brown velvet hostess gown to the cleaner, made an appointment to have her hair done, and ordered wine and liquor and ice cubes and the ingredients of a Chilean seafood casserole called *chupe*.

On the Thursday morning before the party, Minnie came with the drink while Rosemary was picking apart crabmeat and lobster tails. 'That looks interesting,' Minnie said, glancing into the kitchen. 'What is it?'

Rosemary told her, standing at the front door with the striped glass cold in her hand. 'I'm going to freeze it and then bake it Saturday evening,' she said. 'We're having some people over.'

'Oh, you feel up to entertaining?' Minnie asked.

'Yes, I do,' Rosemary said. 'These are old friends whom we haven't seen in a long time. They don't even know yet that I'm pregnant.'

'I'd be glad to give you a hand if you'd like,' Minnie said. 'I could help you dish things out.'

'Thank you, that's sweet of you,' Rosemary said, 'but I really can manage by myself. It's going to be buffet, and there'll be very little to do.'

'I could help you take the coats.'

'No, really, Minnie, you do enough for me as it is. Really.'

Minnie said, 'Well, let me know if you change your mind. Drink your drink now.'

Rosemary looked at the glass in her hand. 'I'd rather not,' she said, and looked up at Minnie. 'Not this minute. I'll drink it in a little while and bring the glass back to you.'

Minnie said, 'It doesn't do to let it stand.'

'I won't wait long,' Rosemary said. 'Go on. You go back and I'll bring the glass to you later on.'

'I'll wait and save you the walk.'

'You'll do no such thing,' Rosemary said. 'I get very nervous if anyone watches me while I'm cooking. I'm going out later so I'll be passing right by your door.'

'Going out?'

'Shopping. Scoot now, go on. You're too nice to me, really you are.'

Minnie backed away. 'Don't wait too long,' she said. 'It's going to lose its vitamins.'

Rosemary closed the door. She went into the kitchen and stood for a moment with the glass in her hand, and then went to the sink and tipped out the drink in a pale green spire drilling straight down into the drain.

She finished the *chupe*, humming and feeling pleased with herself. When it was covered and stowed away in the freezer compartment she made her own drink out of milk, cream, an egg, sugar, and sherry. Shaken in a covered jar, it poured out tawny and delicious-looking. 'Hang on, David-or-Amanda,' she said, and tasted it and found it great.

CHAPTER FIVE

FOR A LITTLE while around half past nine it looked as if no one was going to come. Guy put another chunk of cannel coal on the fire, then racked the tongs and brushed his hands with his handkerchief; Rosemary came from the kitchen and stood motionless in her pain and her just-right hair and her brown velvet; and the bartender, by the bedroom door, found things to do with lemon peel and napkins and glasses and bottles. He was a prosperous-looking Italian named Renato who gave the impression that he tended bar only as a pastime and would leave if he got more bored than he already was.

Then the Wendells came – Ted and Carole – and a minute later Elise Dunstan and her husband Hugh, who limped. And then Allan Stone, Guy's agent, with a beautiful Negro model named Rain Morgan, and Jimmy and Tiger, and Lou and Claudia Comfort and Claudia's brother Scott.

Guy put the coats on the bed; Renato mixed drinks quickly, looking less bored. Rosemary pointed and gave names: 'Jimmy, Tiger, Rain, Allan, Elise, Hugh, Carole, Ted – Claudia and Lou and Scott.'

Bob and Thea Goodman brought another couple, Peggy and Stan Keeler. 'Of *course* it's all right,' Rosemary said; 'don't be silly, the more the merrier!' The Kapps came without coats. 'What a trip!' Mr Kapp ('It's Bernard') said. 'A bus, three trains, and a ferry! We left five hours ago!'

'Can I look around?' Claudia asked. 'If the rest of it's as nice as this I'm going to cut my throat.'

Mike and Pedro brought bouquets of bright red roses. Pedro, with his cheek against Rosemary's, murmured, 'Make him feed you baby; you look like a bottle of iodine.'

Rosemary said, 'Phyllis, Bernard, Peggy, Stan, Thea, Bob, Lou, Scott, Carole . . .'

She took the roses into the kitchen. Elise came in with a drink and a fake cigarette for breaking the habit. 'You're so lucky,' she said; 'it's the greatest apartment I've ever seen. Will you look at this kitchen? Are you all right, Rosie? You look a little tired.'

'Thanks for the understatement,' Rosemary said. 'I'm not all right but I will be. I'm pregnant.'

'You aren't! How *great*! When?'

'June twenty-eighth. I go into my fifth month on Friday.'

'That's *great*!' Elise said. 'How do you like C. C. Hill? Isn't he the dreamboy of the western world?'

'Yes, but I'm not using him,' Rosemary said.

'No!'

'I've got a doctor named Sapirstein, an older man.'

'What *for*? He can't be better than Hill!'

'He's fairly well known and he's a friend of some friends of ours,' Rosemary said.

Guy looked in.

Elise said, 'Well congratulations, Dad.'

'Thanks,' Guy said. 'Weren't nothin' to it. Do you want me to bring in the dip, Ro?'

'Oh, yes, would you? Look at these roses! Mike and Pedro brought them.'

Guy took a tray of crackers and a bowl of pale pink dip from the table. 'Would you get the other one?' he asked Elise.

'Sure,' she said, and took a second bowl and followed after him.

'I'll be out in a minute,' Rosemary called.

Dee Bertillon brought Portia Haynes, an actress, and Joan called to say that she and her date had got stuck at another party and would be there in half an hour.

Tiger said, 'You dirty stinking secret-keeper!' She grabbed Rosemary and kissed her.

'Who's pregnant?' someone asked, and someone else said, 'Rosemary is.'

She put one vase of roses on the mantel – 'Congratulations,' Rain Morgan said, 'I understand you're pregnant' – and the other in the bedroom on the dressing table. When she came out Renato made a Scotch and water for her. 'I make the first ones strong,' he said, 'to get them happy. Then I go light and conserve.'

Mike wig-wagged over heads and mouthed *Congratulations*. She smiled and mouthed *Thanks*.

'The Trench sisters lived here,' someone said; and Bernard Kapp said, 'Adrian Marcato too, and Keith Kennedy.'

'And Pearl Ames,' Phyllis Kapp said.

'The Trent sisters?' Jimmy asked.

'Trench,' Phyllis said. 'They ate little children.'

'And she doesn't mean just ate them,' Pedro said; 'she means *ate them*!'

Rosemary shut her eyes and held her breath as the pain wound tighter. Maybe because of the drink; she put it aside.

'Are you all right?' Claudia asked her.

'Yes, fine,' she said, and smiled. 'I had a cramp for a moment.'

Guy was talking with Tiger and Portia Haynes and Dee. 'It's too soon to say,' he said; 'we've only been in rehearsal six days. It plays much better than it reads, though.'

'It couldn't play much worse,' Tiger said. 'Hey, what ever happened to the other guy? Is he still blind?'

'I don't know,' Guy said.

Portia said, 'Donald Baumgart? You know who *he* is, Tiger; he's the boy Zöe Piper lives with.'

'Oh, is *he* the one?' Tiger said. 'Gee, I didn't know he was someone I knew.'

'He's writing a great play,' Portia said. 'At least the first two scenes are great. Really burning anger, like Osborne before he made it.'

Rosemary said, 'Is he still blind?'

'Oh, yes,' Portia said. 'They've pretty much given up hope. He's going through hell trying to make the adjustment. But this great play is coming out of it. He dictates and Zöe writes.'

Joan came. Her date was over fifty. She took Rosemary's arm and pulled her aside, looking frightened. 'What's the *matter* with you?' she asked. 'What's *wrong*?'

'Nothing's wrong,' Rosemary said. 'I'm pregnant, that's all.'

She was in the kitchen with Tiger, tossing the salad, when Joan and Elise came in and closed the door behind them.

Elise said, 'What did you say your doctor's name was?'

'Sapirstein,' Rosemary said.

Joan said, 'And he's satisfied with your condition?'

Rosemary nodded.

'Claudia said you had a cramp a while ago.'

'I have a pain,' she said. 'But it's going to stop soon; it's not abnormal.'

Tiger said, 'What kind of a pain?'

'A – a *pain*. A sharp pain, that's all. It's because my pelvis is expanding and my joints are a little stiff.'

Elise said, 'Rosie, I've had that – two times – and all it ever meant was a few days of like a Charley horse, an ache through the whole area.'

'Well, everyone is different,' Rosemary said, lifting salad between two wooden spoons and letting it drop back into the bowl again. 'Every pregnancy is different.'

'Not *that* different,' Joan said. 'You look like Miss Concentration Camp of 1966. Are you sure this doctor knows what he's doing?'

Rosemary began to sob, quietly and defeatedly, holding the spoons in the salad. Tears ran from her cheeks.

'Oh, God,' Joan said, and looked for help to Tiger, who touched Rosemary's shoulder and said, 'Shh, ah, shh, don't cry, Rosemary. Shh.'

'It's good,' Elise said. 'It's the best thing. Let her. She's been wound up all night like – like I-don't-*know*-what.'

Rosemary wept, black streaks smearing down her cheeks. Elise put her into a chair; Tiger took the spoons from her hands and moved the salad bowls to the far side of the table.

The door started to open and Joan ran to it and stopped and blocked it. It was Guy. 'Hey, let me in,' he said.

'Sorry,' Joan said. 'Girls only.'

'Let me speak to Rosemary.'

'Can't; she's busy.'

'Look,' he said, 'I've got to wash glasses.'

'Use the bathroom.' She shouldered the door click-closed and leaned against it.

'Damn it, open the door,' he said outside.

Rosemary went on crying, her head bowed, her shoulders heaving, her hands limp in her lap. Elise, crouching, wiped at her cheeks every few moments with the end of a towel; Tiger smoothed her hair and tried to still her shoulders.

The tears slowed.

'It hurts so much,' she said. She raised her face to them. 'And I'm so afraid the baby is going to die.'

'Is he doing anything for you?' Elise asked. 'Giving you any medicine, any treatment?'

'Nothing, nothing.'

Tiger said, 'When did it start?'

She sobbed.

Elise asked, 'When did the pain start, Rosie?'

'Before Thanksgiving,' she said. 'November.'

Elise said, '*In November?*' and Joan at the door said, '*What?*' Tiger said, '*You've been in pain since November and he isn't doing anything for you?*'

'He says it'll stop.'

Joan said, 'Has he brought in another doctor to look at you?'

Rosemary shook her head. 'He's a very good doctor,' she said with Elise wiping at her cheeks. 'He's well known. He was on *Open End*.'

Tiger said, 'He sounds like a sadistic *nut*, Rosemary.'

Elise said, 'Pain like that is a warning that something's not right. I'm sorry to scare you, Rosie, but you go see Dr Hill. See *somebody* besides that —'

'That nut,' Tiger said.

Elise said, 'He *can't* be right, letting you just go on suffering.'

'I won't have an abortion,' Rosemary said.

Joan leaned forward from the door and whispered, 'Nobody's *telling* you to have an abortion! Just go see another doctor, that's all.'

Rosemary took the towel from Elise and pressed it to each eye in turn. 'He said this would happen,' she said, looking at mascara on the towel. 'That my friends would think their pregnancies were normal and mine wasn't.'

'What do you mean?' Tiger asked.

Rosemary looked at her. 'He told me not to listen to what my friends might say,' she said.

Tiger said, 'Well you *do* listen! What kind of sneaky advice is *that* for a doctor to give?'

Elise said, 'All we're telling you to do is check with another doctor. I don't think any reputable doctor would object to that, if it would help his patient's peace of mind.'

'You do it,' Joan said. 'First thing Monday morning.'

'I will,' Rosemary said.

'You promise?' Elise asked.

Rosemary nodded. 'I promise.' She smiled at Elise, and at Tiger and Joan. 'I feel a lot better,' she said. 'Thank you.'

'Well you look a lot worse,' Tiger said, opening her purse. 'Fix your eyes. Fix everything.' She put large and small compacts on the table before Rosemary, and two long tubes and a short one.

'Look at my dress,' Rosemary said.

'A damp cloth,' Elise said, taking the towel and going to the sink with it.

'The garlic bread!' Rosemary cried.

'In or out?' Joan asked.

'In.' Rosemary pointed with a mascara brush at two foil-wrapped loaves on top of the refrigerator.

Tiger began tossing the salad and Elise wiped at the lap of Rosemary's gown. 'Next time you're planning to cry,' she said, 'don't wear velvet.'

Guy came in and looked at them.

Tiger said, 'We're trading beauty secrets. You want some?'

'Are you all right?' he asked Rosemary.

'Yes, fine,' she said with a smile.

'A little spilled salad dressing,' Elise said.

Joan said, 'Could the kitchen staff get a round of drinks, do you think?'

The *chupe* was a success and so was the salad. (Tiger said under her breath to Rosemary, 'It's the tears that give it the extra zing.')

Renato approved of the wine, opened it with a flourish, and served it solemnly.

Claudia's brother Scott, in the den with a plate on his knee, said, 'His name is Altizer and he's down in – Atlanta, I think; and what he says is that the death of God is a specific historic event that happened right now, in our time. That God literally died.' The Kapps and Rain Morgan and Bob Goodman sat listening and eating.

Jimmy, at one of the living-room windows, said, 'Hey, it's beginning to snow!'

Stan Keeler told a string of wicked Polish-jokes and Rosemary laughed out loud at them. 'Careful of the booze,' Guy murmured at her shoulder. She turned and showed him her glass, and said, still laughing, 'It's only ginger ale!'

Joan's over-fifty date sat on the floor by her chair, talking up to her earnestly and fondling her feet and ankles. Elise talked to Pedro; he nodded, watching Mike and Allan across the room. Claudia began reading palms.

They were low on Scotch but everything else was holding up fine.

She served coffee, emptied ashtrays, and rinsed out glasses. Tiger and Carole Wendell helped her.

Later she sat in a bay with Hugh Dunstan, sipping coffee and watching fat wet snowflakes shear down, an endless army of them, with now and then an outrider striking one of the diamond panes and sliding and melting.

'Year after year I swear I'm going to leave the city,' Hugh Dunstan said; 'get away from the crime and the noise and all the rest of it. And every year it snows or the New Yorker has a Bogart Festival and I'm still here.'

Rosemary smiled and watched the snow. 'This is why I wanted this apartment,' she said; 'to sit here and watch the snow, with the fire going.'

Hugh looked at her and said, 'I'll bet you still read Dickens.'

'Of course I do,' she said. 'Nobody stops reading Dickens.'

Guy came looking for her. 'Bob and Thea are leaving,' he said.

By two o'clock everyone had gone and they were alone in the living-room, with dirty glasses and used napkins and spilling-over ashtrays all around. ('Don't forget,' Elise had whispered, leaving. Not very likely.)

'The thing to do now,' Guy said, 'is move.'

'Guy.'

'Yes?'

'I'm going to Dr Hill. Monday morning.'

He said nothing, looking at her.

'I want him to examine me,' she said. 'Dr Sapirstein is either lying or else he's – I don't know, out of his mind. Pain like this is a warning that something is wrong.'

'Rosemary,' Guy said.

'And I'm not drinking Minnie's drink any more,' she said. 'I want vitamins in pills, like everybody else. I haven't drunk it for three days now. I've made her leave it here and I've thrown it away.'

'You've —'

'I've made my own drink instead,' she said.

He drew together all his surprise and anger and, pointing back over his shoulder towards the kitchen, cried it at her. 'Is *that* what those bitches were giving you in there? Is *that* their hint for today? Change doctors?'

'They're my friends,' she said; 'don't call them bitches.'

'They're a bunch of not-very-bright *bitches* who ought to mind their own God-damned business.'

'All they said was get a second opinion.'

'You've got the best doctor in New York, Rosemary. Do you know what Dr Hill is? *Charley Nobody*, that's what he is.'

'I'm tired of hearing how great Dr Sapirstein is,' she said, starting to cry, 'when I've got this *pain* inside me since before Thanksgiving and all he does is tell me it's going to stop!'

'You're not changing doctors,' Guy said. 'We'll have to pay Sapirstein and pay Hill too. It's out of the question.'

'I'm not going to *change*,' Rosemary said; 'I'm just going to let Hill examine me and give his opinion.'

'I won't let you,' Guy said. 'It's – it's not fair to Sapirstein.'

'Not fair to— *What are you talking about?* What about what's fair to *me*?'

'You want another opinion? All right. *Tell* Sapirstein; let *him* be the one who decides who gives it. At least have *that* much courtesy to the top man in his field.'

'I want Dr *Hill*,' she said. 'If you won't pay I'll pay my—' She stopped short and stood motionless, paralysed, no part of her moving. A tear slid on a curved path towards the corner of her mouth.

'Ro?' Guy said.

The pain had stopped. It was gone. Like a stuck auto horn finally put right. Like anything that stops and is gone and is gone for good and won't ever be back again, thank merciful heaven. Gone and finished and oh, how good she might possibly feel as soon as she caught her breath!

'Ro?' Guy said, and took a step forward, worried.

'It stopped,' she said. 'The pain.'

'Stopped?' he said.

'Just now.' She managed to smile at him. 'It stopped. Just like that.' She closed her eyes and took a deep breath, and deeper still, deeper than she had been allowed to breathe for ages and ages. Since before Thanksgiving.

When she opened her eyes Guy was still looking at her, still looking worried.

'What was in the drink you made?' he asked.

Her heart dropped out of her. She had killed the baby. With the sherry. Or a bad egg. Or the combination. The baby had died, the pain had stopped. The pain was the baby and she had killed it with her arrogance.

'An egg,' she said. 'Milk. Cream. Sugar.' She blinked, wiped at her cheek, looked at him. 'Sherry,' she said, trying to make it sound non-toxic.

'How *much* sherry?' he asked.

Something moved in her.

'A lot?'

Again, where nothing had ever moved before. A rippling little pressure. She giggled.

'*Rosemary, for Christ's sake, how much?*'

'It's alive,' she said, and giggled again. 'It's moving. It's all right; it isn't dead. It's moving.' She looked down at her brown-velvet stomach and put her hands on it and pressed in lightly. Now two things were moving, two hands or feet; one here, one there.

She reached for Guy, not looking at him; snapped her fingers quickly for his hand. He came closer and gave it. She put it to the side of her stomach and held it there. Obligingly the movement came. 'You feel it?' she asked, looking at him. 'There, again; you feel it?'

Her jerked his hand away, pale. 'Yes,' he said. 'Yes. I felt it.'

'It's nothing to be afraid of,' she said, laughing. 'It won't bite you.'

'It's wonderful,' he said.

'Isn't it?' She held her stomach again, looking down at it. 'It's alive. It's kicking. It's in there.'

'I'll clean up some of this mess,' Guy said, and picked up an ashtray and a glass and another glass.

'All right now, David-or-Amanda,' Rosemary said, 'you've made your presence known, so kindly settle down and let Mommy attend to the cleaning up.' She laughed. 'My God,' she said, 'it's so active! That means a boy, doesn't it?'

She said, 'All right, you, just take it easy. You've got five more months yet, so save your energy.'

And laughing, 'Talk to it, Guy; you're its father. Tell it not to be so impatient.'

And she laughed and laughed and was crying too, holding her stomach with both hands.

CHAPTER SIX

As bad as it had been before, that was how good it was now. With the stopping of the pain came sleep, great dreamless ten-hour spans of it; and with the sleep came hunger, for meat that was cooked, not raw, for eggs and vegetables and cheese and fruit and milk. Within days Rosemary's skull-face had lost its edges and sunk back behind filling-in flesh; within weeks she looked the way pregnant women are supposed to look: lustrous, healthy, proud, prettier than ever.

She drank Minnie's drink as soon as it was given to her, and drank it to the last chill drop, driving away as by a ritual the remembered guilt of *I-killed-the-baby*. With the drink now came a cake of white gritty sweet stuff like marzipan; this too she ate at once, as much from enjoyment of its candy-like taste as from a resolve to be the most conscientious expectant mother in all the world.

Dr Sapirstein might have been smug about the pain's stopping, but he wasn't, bless him. He simply said 'It's about time' and put his stethoscope to Rosemary's really-showing-now belly. Listening to the stirring baby, he betrayed an excitement that was unexpected in a man who had guided hundreds upon hundreds of pregnancies. It was his undimmed first-time excitement, Rosemary thought, that probably marked the difference between a great obstetrician and a merely good one.

She bought maternity clothes; a two-piece black dress, a beige suit, a red dress with white polka dots. Two weeks after their own party, she and Guy went to one given by Lou and Claudia Comfort. 'I can't get over the *change* in you!' Claudia said, holding on to both Rosemary's hands. 'You look a hundred per cent better, Rosemary! A *thousand* per cent!'

And Mrs Gould across the hall said, 'You know, we were

137

quite concerned about you a few weeks ago; you looked so drawn and uncomfortable. But now you look like an entirely different person, really you do. Arthur remarked on the change just last evening.'

'I feel much better now,' Rosemary said. 'Some pregnancies start out bad and turn good, and some go the other way around. I'm glad I've had the bad first and have gotten it out of the way.'

She was aware now of minor pains that had been overshadowed by the major one – aches in her spinal muscles and her swollen breasts – but these discomforts had been mentioned as typical in the paperback book Dr Sapirstein had made her throw away; they *felt* typical too, and they increased rather than lessened her sense of well-being. Salt was still nauseating, but what, after all, was salt?

Guy's show, with its director changed twice and its title changed three times, opened in Philadelphia in mid February. Dr Sapirstein didn't allow Rosemary to go along on the try-out tour, and so on the afternoon of the opening she and Minnie and Roman drove to Philadelphia with Jimmy and Tiger, in Jimmy's antique Packard. The drive was a less than joyous one. Rosemary and Jimmy and Tiger had seen a bare-stage run-through of the play before the company left New York and they were doubtful of its chances. The best they hoped for was that Guy would be singled out for praise by one or more of the critics, a hope Roman encouraged by citing instances of great actors who had come to notice in plays of little or no distinction.

With sets and costumes and lighting the play was still tedious and verbose; the party afterwards was broken up into small separate enclaves of silent gloom. Guy's mother having flown down from Montreal, insisted to their group that Guy was superb and the play was superb. Small, blonde, and vivacious, she chirped her confidence to Rosemary and Allan Stone and Jimmy and Tiger and Guy himself and Minnie and Roman. Minnie and Roman smiled serenely; the others sat and worried. Rosemary thought that Guy had been even better than superb, but she had thought so too on seeing him in *Luther* and *Nobody Loves*

n Albatross, in neither of which he had attracted critical
tention.

Two reviews came in after midnight; both panned the
lay and lavished Guy with enthusiastic praise, in one case
vo solid paragraphs of it. A third review, which appeared
ae next morning, was headed *Dazzling Performance
barks New Comedy-Drama* and spoke of Guy as 'a virtu-
ly unknown young actor of slashing authority' who was
ure to go on to bigger and better productions'.

The ride back to New York was far happier than the ride
ut.

Rosemary found much to keep her busy while Guy was
way. There was the white-and-yellow nursery wallpaper
nally to be ordered, and the crib and the bureau and the
athinette. There were long-postponed letters to be written,
:lling the family all the news; there were baby clothes and
ore maternity clothes to be shopped for; there were
ssorted decisions to be made, about birth announcements
nd breast-or-bottle and the name, the name, the name.
ndrew or Douglas or David; Amanda or Jenny or Hope.

And there were exercises to be done, morning and even-
ig, for she was having the baby by Natural Childbirth.
he had strong feelings on the subject and Dr Sapirstein
oncurred with them wholeheartedly. He would give her an
naesthetic only if at the very last moment she asked for
ne. Lying on the floor, she raised her legs straight up in
he air and held them there for a count of ten; she prac-
sed shallow breathing and panting, imagining the sweaty
riumphant moment when she would see whatever-its-
ame-was coming inch by inch out of her effectively help-
ig body.

She spent evenings at Minnie and Roman's, one at the
Kapps', and another at Hugh and Elise Dunstan's. ('You
on't have a nurse yet?' Elise asked. 'You should have
rranged for one long ago; they'll all be booked by now.'
But Dr Sapirstein, when she called him about it the next
lay, told her that he had lined up a fine nurse who would
tay with her for as long as she wanted after the delivery.

Hadn't he mentioned it before? Miss Fitzpatrick; one o
the best.)

Guy called every second or third night after the show. H
told Rosemary of the changes that were being made and o
the rave he had got in *Variety*; she told him about Mis
Fitzpatrick and the wallpaper and the shaped-all-wrong
bootees that Laura-Louise was knitting.

The show folded after fifteen performances and Guy wa
home again, only to leave two days later for California an
a Warner Brothers screen test. And then he was home fo
good, with two great next-season parts to choose from an
thirteen half-hour *Greenwich Village*'s to do. Warne
Brothers made an offer and Allan turned it down.

The baby kicked like a demon. Rosemary told it to sto
or she would start kicking back.

Her sister Margaret's husband called to tell of the birtl
of an eight-pound boy, Kevin Michael, and later a too-cut
announcement came – an impossibly rosy baby megaphon
ing his name, birth date, weight, and length. (Guy saic
'What, no blood type?') Rosemary decided on simple en
graved announcements, with nothing but the baby's name
their name, and the date. And it would be Andrew John o
Jennifer Susan. Definitely. Breast-fed, not bottle-fed.

They moved the television set into the living-room an
gave the rest of the den furniture to friends who could us
it. The wallpaper came, was perfect, and was hung; the cril
and bureau and bathinette came and were placed first on
way and then another. Into the bureau Rosemary put re
ceiving blankets, waterproof pants, and shirts so tiny tha
holding one up, she couldn't keep from laughing.

'Andrew John Woodhouse,' she said, '*stop* it! You've go
two whole months yet!'

They celebrated their second anniversary and Guy'
thirty-third birthday; they gave another party – a sit-dow
dinner for the Dunstans, the Chens, and Jimmy and Tige
they saw *Morgan!* and a preview of *Mame*.

Bigger and bigger Rosemary grew, her breasts liftin
higher atop her ballooning belly that was drum-solid wit
its navel flattened away, that rippled and jutted with th

movements of the baby inside it. She did her exercises morning and evening, lifting her legs, sitting on her heels, shallow-breathing, panting.

At the end of May, when she went into her ninth month, she packed a small suitcase with the things she would need at the hospital – nightgowns, nursing brassieres, a new quilted housecoat and so on – and set it ready by the bedroom door.

On Friday, June 3rd, Hutch died in his bed at St Vincent's Hospital. Axel Allert, his son-in-law, called Rosemary on Saturday morning and told her the news. There would be a memorial service on Tuesday morning at eleven, he said, at the Ethical Culture Centre on West Sixty-fourth Street.

Rosemary wept, partly because Hutch was dead and partly because she had all but forgotten him in the past few months and felt now as if she had hastened his dying. Once or twice Grace Cardiff had called and once Rosemary had called Doris Allert; but she hadn't gone to see Hutch; there had seemed no point in it when he was still frozen in coma, and having been restored to health herself, she had been averse to being near someone sick, as if she and the baby might somehow have been endangered by the nearness.

Guy, when he heard the news, turned bloodless grey and was silent and self-enclosed for several hours. Rosemary was surprised by the depth of his reaction.

She went alone to the memorial service; Guy was filming and couldn't get free and Joan begged off with a virus. Some fifty people were there, in a handsome panelled auditorium. The service began soon after eleven and was quite short. Axel Allert spoke, and then another man who apparently had known Hutch for many years. Afterwards Rosemary followed the general movement towards the front of the auditorium and said a word of sympathy to the Allerts and to Hutch's other daughter, Edna, and her husband. A woman touched her arm and said, 'Excuse me, you're Rosemary, aren't you?' – a stylishly dressed woman in her early fifties, with grey hair and an exceptionally fine complexion. 'I'm Grace Cardiff.'

Rosemary took her hand and greeted her and thanked her for the phone calls she had made.

'I was going to mail this last evening,' Grace Cardiff said, holding a book-size brown-paper package, 'and then I realized that I'd probably be seeing you this morning.' She gave Rosemary the package; Rosemary saw her own name and address printed on it, and Grace Cardiff's return address.

'What is it?' she asked.

'It's a book Hutch wanted you to have; he was very emphatic about it.'

Rosemary didn't understand.

'He was conscious at the end for a few minutes,' Grace Cardiff said. 'I wasn't there, but he told a nurse to tell me to give you the book on his desk. Apparently he was reading it the night he was stricken. He was very insistent, told the nurse two or three times and made her promise not to forget. And I'm to tell you that "the name is an anagram".'

'The name of the book?'

'Apparently. He was delirious, so it's hard to be sure. He seemed to fight his way out of the coma and then die of the effort. First he thought it was the next morning, the morning after the coma began, and he spoke about having to meet you at eleven o'clock —'

'Yes, we had an appointment,' Rosemary said.

'And then he seemed to realize what had happened and he began telling the nurse that I was to give you the book. He repeated himself a few times and that was the end.' Grace Cardiff smiled as if she were making pleasant conversation. 'It's an English book about witchcraft,' she said.

Rosemary, looking doubtfully at the package, said, 'I can't imagine why he wanted me to have it.'

'He did though, so there you are. And the name is an anagram. Sweet Hutch. He made everything sound like a boy's adventure, didn't he?'

They walked together out of the auditorium and out of the building on to the sidewalk.

'I'm going uptown; can I drop you anywhere?' Grace Cardiff asked.

'No, thank you,' Rosemary said. 'I'm going down and across.'

They went to the corner. Other people who had been at the service were hailing taxis; one pulled up, and the two men who had got it offered it to Rosemary. She tried to decline and, when the men insisted, offered it to Grace Cardiff, who wouldn't have it either. 'Certainly not,' she said. 'Take full advantage of your lovely condition. When is the baby due?'

'June twenty-eighth,' Rosemary said. Thanking the men, she got into the cab. It was a small one and getting into it wasn't easy.

'Good luck,' Grace Cardiff said, closing the door.

'Thank you,' Rosemary said, 'and thank you for the book.' To the driver she said, 'The Bramford, please.' She smiled through the open window at Grace Cardiff as the cab pulled away.

CHAPTER SEVEN

SHE THOUGHT OF unwrapping the book there in the cab, but it was a cab that had been fitted out by its driver with extra ashtrays and mirrors and hand-lettered pleas for cleanliness and consideration, and the string and the paper would have been too much of a nuisance. So she went home first and got out of her shoes, dress, and girdle, and into slippers and a new gigantic peppermint-striped smock.

The doorbell rang and she went to answer it holding the still-unopened package; it was Minnie with the drink and the little white cake. 'I heard you come in,' she said. 'It certainly wasn't very long.'

'It was nice,' Rosemary said, taking the glass. 'His son-in-law and another man talked a little about what he was like and why he'll be missed, and that was it.' She drank some of the thin pale-green.

'That sounds like a sensible way of doing it,' Minnie said. 'You got mail already?'

'No, someone gave it to me,' Rosemary said, and drank again, deciding not to go into *who* and *why* and the whole story of Hutch's return to consciousness.

'Here, I'll hold it,' Minnie said, and took the package – 'Oh, thanks,' Rosemary said – so that Rosemary could take the white cake.

Rosemary ate and drank.

'A book?' Minnie asked, weighing the package.

'Mm-hmm. She was going to mail it and then she realized she'd be seeing me.'

Minnie read the return address. 'Oh, I know that house,' she said. 'The Gilmores used to live there before they moved over to where they are now.'

'Oh?'

'I've been there lots of times. "Grace." That's one of my favourite names. One of your girl friends?'

'Yes,' Rosemary said; it was easier than explaining and it made no difference really.

She finished the cake and the drink, and took the package from Minnie and gave her the glass. 'Thanks,' she said, smiling.

'Say listen,' Minnie said, 'Roman's going down to the cleaner in a while; do you have anything to go or pick up?'

'No, nothing, thanks. Will we see you later?'

'Sure. Take a nap, why don't you?'

'I'm going to. 'Bye.'

She closed the door and went into the kitchen. With a paring knife she cut the string of the package and undid its brown paper. The book within was *All Of Them Witches* by J. R. Hanslet. It was a black book, not new, its gold lettering all but worn away. On the flyleaf was Hutch's signature, with the inscription *Torquay, 1934* beneath it. At the bottom of the inside cover was a small blue sticker imprinted *J. Waghorn & Son, Booksellers.*

Rosemary took the book into the living-room, riffling its pages as she went. There were occasional photographs of respectable-looking Victorians, and, in the text, several of Hutch's underlinings and marginal checkmarks that she recognized from books he had lent her in the Higgins–Eliza period of their friendship. One underlined phrase was 'the fungus they call "Devil's Pepper".'

She sat in one of the window bays and looked at the table of contents. The name Adrian Marcato jumped to her eye; it was the title of the fourth chapter. Other chapters dealt with other people – all of them, it was to be presumed from the book's title, witches: Gilles de Rais, Jane Wenham, Aleister Crowley, Thomas Weir. The final chapters were *Witch Practices* and *Witchcraft and Satanism.*

Turning to the fourth chapter, Rosemary glanced over its twenty-odd pages; Marcato was born in Glasgow in 1846, he was brought soon after to New York (underlined), and he died on the island of Corfu in 1922. There were accounts of the 1896 tumult when he claimed to have called forth Satan and was attacked by a mob outside the Bramford (not in the lobby as Hutch had said), and of similar happenings in Stockholm in 1898 and Paris in 1899. He was a hypnotic-eyed black-bearded man who, in a standing portrait, looked fleetingly familiar to Rosemary. Overleaf there was a less formal photograph of him sitting at a Paris café table with his wife Hessia and his son Steven (underlined).

Was this why Hutch had wanted her to have the book; so that she could read in detail about Adrian Marcato? But why? Hadn't he issued his warnings long ago, and acknowledged later on that they were unjustified? She flipped through the rest of the book, pausing near the end to read other underlinings. 'The stubborn fact remains,' one read, 'that whether or not *we* believe, *they* most assuredly do.' And a few pages later: 'the universally held belief in the power of fresh blood'. And 'surrounded by candles, which needless to say are also black'.

The black candles Minnie had brought over on the night of the power failure. Hutch had been struck by them and had begun asking questions about Minnie and Roman. Was this the book's meaning; that they were *witches*? Minnie with her herbs and tannis-charms, Roman with his piercing eyes? But there *were* no witches, were there? Not *really*.

She remembered then the other part of Hutch's message, that the name of the book was an anagram. *All Of Them Witches*. She tried to juggle the letters in her head, to transpose them into something meaningful, revealing. She couldn't; there were too many of them to keep track of. She needed a pencil and paper. Or better yet, the Scrabble set.

She got it from the bedroom and, sitting in the bay again, put the unopened board on her knees and picked out from the box beside her the letters to spell *All Of Them Witches*. The baby, which had been still all morning, began moving inside her. *You're going to be a born Scrabble-player*, she thought, smiling. It kicked. 'Hey, easy,' she said.

With *All Of Them Witches* laid out on the board, she jumped the letters and mixed them around, then looked to see what else could be made of them. She found *comes with the fall* and, after a few minutes of rearranging the flat wood tiles, *how is hell fact met*. Neither of which seemed to mean anything. Nor was there revelation in *who shall meet it, we that chose ill,* and *if she shall come,* all of which weren't real anagrams anyway, since they used less than the full complement of letters. It was foolishness. How could the title of a book have a hidden anagram message for her and her alone? Hutch had been delirious; hadn't Grace Cardiff said so? Time-wasting. *Elf shot lame witch. Tell me which fatso.*

But maybe it was the name of the author, not the book, that was the anagram. Maybe J. R. Hanslet was a pen name; it didn't sound like a real one, when you stopped to think about it.

She took new letters.

The baby kicked.

J. R. Hanslet was *Jan Shrelt.* Or *J. H. Snartle.*

Now that *really* made sense.

Poor Hutch.

She took up the board and tilted it, spilling the letters back into the box.

The book, which lay open on the window seat beyond the box, had turned its pages to the picture of Adrian Marcato and his wife and son. Perhaps Hutch had pressed hard there, holding it open while he underlined 'Steven'.

The baby lay quiet in her, not moving.

She put the board on her knees again and took from the box the letters of *Steven Marcato.* When the name lay spelled before her, she looked at it for a moment and then began transposing the letters. With no false moves and no wasted motion she made them into *Roman Castevet.*

And then again into *Steven Marcato.*

And then again into *Roman Castevet.*

The baby stirred ever so slightly.

She read the chapter on Adrian Marcato and the one called *Witch Practices,* and then she went into the kitchen and ate some tuna salad and lettuce and tomatoes, thinking about what she had read.

She was just beginning the chapter called *Witchcraft and Satanism* when the front door unlocked and was pushed against the chain. The doorbell rang as she went to see who it was. It was Guy.

'What's with the chain?' he asked when she had let him in.

She said nothing, closing the door and rechaining it.

'What's the matter?' He had a bunch of daisies and a box from Bronzini.

'I'll tell you inside,' she said as he gave her the daisies and a kiss.

'Are you all right?' he asked.

'Yes,' she said. She went into the kitchen.

'How was the memorial?'

'Very nice. Very short.'

'I got the shirt that was in *The New Yorker*,' he said, going to the bedroom. 'Hey,' he called, '*On A Clear Day* and *Skyscraper* are both closing.'

She put the daisies in a blue pitcher and brought them into the living-room. Guy came in and showed her the shirt. She admired it.

Then she said, 'Do you know who Roman really is?'

Guy looked at her, blinked, and frowned. 'What do you mean, honey?' he said. 'He's Roman.'

'He's Adrian Marcato's son,' she said. 'The man who said he conjured up Satan and was attacked downstairs by a mob. Roman is his son Steven. "Roman Castevet" is "Steven Marcato" rearranged – an anagram.'

Guy said, 'Who told you?'

'Hutch,' Rosemary said. She told Guy about *All Of Them Witches* and Hutch's message. She showed him the book, and he put aside his shirt and took it and looked at it, looked at the title page and the table of contents and then sprung the pages out slowly from under his thumb, looking at all of them.

'There he is when he was thirteen,' Rosemary said. 'See the eyes?'

'It might just *possibly* be a coincidence,' Guy said.

'And another coincidence that he's living here? In the same house Steven Marcato was brought up in?' Rosemary shook her head. 'The ages match too,' she said. 'Steven

Marcato was born in August, 1886, which would make him seventy-nine now. Which is what Roman is. It's no coincidence.'

'No, I guess it's not,' Guy said, springing out more pages. 'I guess he's Steven Marcato, all right. The poor old geezer. No wonder he switched his name around, with a crazy father like that.'

Rosemary looked at Guy uncertainly and said, 'You don't think he's – the same as his father?'

'What do you mean?' Guy said, and smiled at her. 'A witch? A devil worshipper?'

She nodded.

'Ro,' he said. 'Are you *kidding*? Do you *really* —' He laughed and gave the book back to her. 'Ah, Ro, *honey*,' he said.

'It's a religion,' she said. 'It's an early religion that got – pushed into the corner.'

'All right,' he said, 'but *today*?'

'His father was a *martyr* to it,' she said. 'That's how it must look to him. Do you know where Adrian Marcato died? In a stable. On Corfu. Wherever *that* is. Because they wouldn't let him into the hotel. Really. "No room at the inn." So he died in the stable. And *he* was with him. Roman. Do you think he's given it up after *that*?'

'Honey, it's 1966,' Guy said.

'This book was published in 1933,' Rosemary said; 'there were covens in Europe – that's what they're called, the groups, the congregations; covens – in Europe, in North and South America, in Australia; do you think they've all died out in just thirty-three years? They've got a coven *here*, Minnie and Roman, with Laura-Louise and the Fountains and the Gilmores and the Weeses; those parties with the flute and the chanting, those are *sabbaths* or *esbats* or whatever-they-are!'

'Honey,' Guy said, 'don't get excited. Let's—'

'Read what they do, Guy,' she said, holding the book open at him and jabbing a page with her forefinger. 'They use *blood* in their rituals, because blood has *power*, and the blood that has the *most* power is a *baby's* blood, a baby that

149

hasn't been baptized; and they use *more* than the blood, they use the *flesh* too!'

'For God's sake, Rosemary!'

'Why have they been so friendly to us?' she demanded.

'Because they're friendly people! What do you think they are, maniacs?'

'Yes! Yes. Maniacs who think they have magic power, who think they're real storybook witches, *who perform all sorts of crazy rituals and practices* because they're – sick and crazy maniacs!'

'Honey —'

'Those black candles Minnie brought us were from the black mass! That's how Hutch caught on. And their living-room is clear in the middle so that they have *room*.'

'Honey,' Guy said, 'they're old people and they have a bunch of old friends, and Dr Shand happens to play the recorder. You can get black candles right down in the hardware store, and red ones and green ones and blue ones. And their living-room is clear because Minnie is a lousy decorator. Roman's father was a nut, okay; but that's no reason to think that Roman is too.'

'They're not setting foot in this apartment ever again,' Rosemary said. 'Either one of them. Or Laura-Louise or any of the others. And they're not coming within fifty feet of the baby.'

'The fact that Roman changed his name *proves* that he's not like his father,' Guy said. 'If he were he'd be proud of the name and would have kept it.'

'He did keep it,' Rosemary said. 'He switched it around, but he didn't really change it for something else. And this way he can get into hotels.' She went away from Guy, to the window where the Scrabble set lay. 'I won't let them in again,' she said. 'And as soon as the baby is old enough I want to sublet and move. I don't want them near us. Hutch was right; we never should have moved in here.' She looked out the window, holding the book clamped in both hands, trembling.

Guy watched her for a moment. 'What about Dr Sapirstein?' he said. 'Is he in the coven too?'

She turned and looked at him.

'After all,' he said, 'there've been maniac doctors, haven't there? His big ambition is probably to make house calls on a broomstick.'

She turned to the window again, her face sober. 'No, I don't think he's one of them,' she said. 'He's – too intelligent.'

'And besides, he's Jewish,' Guy said and laughed. 'Well, I'm glad you've exempted *somebody* from your McCarthy-type smear campaign. Talk about witch-hunting, wow! And guilt by association.'

'I'm not saying they're really witches,' Rosemary said. 'I know they haven't got *real* power. But there are people who *do* believe, even if we don't; just the way my family believes that God hears their prayers and that the wafer is the actual body of Jesus. Minnie and Roman believe *their* religion, believe it and practise it, I know they do; and I'm not going to take any chances with the baby's safety.'

'We're not going to sub-let and move,' Guy said.

'Yes we are,' Rosemary said, turning to him.

He picked up his new shirt. 'We'll talk about it later,' he said.

'He lied to you,' she said. 'His father wasn't a producer. He didn't have anything to do with the theatre at all.'

'All right, so he's a bullthrower,' Guy said; 'who the hell isn't?' He went into the bedroom.

Rosemary sat down next to the Scrabble set. She closed it and, after a moment, opened the book and began again to read the final chapter, *Witchcraft and Satanism*.

Guy came back in without the shirt. 'I don't think you ought to read any more of that,' he said.

Rosemary said, 'I just want to read this last chapter.'

'Not today, honey,' Guy said, coming to her; 'you've got yourself worked up enough as it is. It's not good for you *or* the baby.' He put his hand out and waited for her to give him the book.

'I'm not worked up,' she said.

'You're shaking,' he said. 'You've *been* shaking for five

minutes now. Come on, give it to me. You'll read it to-morrow.'

'Guy—'

'No,' he said. 'I mean it. Come on, give it to me.'

She said 'Ohh' and gave it to him. He went over to the bookshelves, stretched up, and put it as high as he could reach, across the tops of the two Kinsey Reports.

'You'll read it tomorrow,' he said. 'You've had too much stirring-up today already, with the memorial and all.'

CHAPTER EIGHT

DR SAPIRSTEIN was amazed. 'Fantastic,' he said. 'Absolutely fantastic. What did you say the name was, "Machado"?'

'Marcato,' Rosemary said.

'Fantastic,' Dr Sapirstein said. 'I had no idea whatsoever. I think he told me once that his father was a coffee importer. Yes, I remember him going on about different grades and different ways of grinding the beans.'

'He told Guy that he was a producer.'

Dr Sapirstein shook his head. 'It's no wonder he's ashamed of the truth,' he said. 'And it's no wonder that *you*'re upset at having discovered it. I'm as sure as I am of anything on earth that Roman doesn't hold any of his father's weird beliefs, but I can understand completely how disturbed you must be to have him for a close neighbour.'

'I don't want anything more to do with him or Minnie,' Rosemary said. 'Maybe I'm being unfair, but I don't want to take even the slightest chance where the baby's safety is concerned.'

'Absolutely,' Dr Sapirstein said. 'Any mother would feel the same way.'

Rosemary leaned forward. 'Is there any chance at all,' she said, 'that Minnie put something harmful in the drink or in those little cakes?'

Dr Sapirstein laughed. 'I'm sorry, dear,' he said; 'I don't mean to laugh, but really, she's such a kind old woman and so concerned for the baby's well-being ... No, there's no chance at all that she gave you anything harmful. I would have seen evidence of it long ago, in you or in the baby.'

'I called her on the house phone and told her I wasn't feeling well. I won't take anything else from her.'

'You won't have to,' Dr Sapirstein said. 'I can give you some pills that will be more than adequate in these last few weeks. In a way this may be the answer to Minnie and Roman's problem too.'

'What do you mean?' Rosemary said.

'They want to go away,' Dr Sapirstein said, 'and rather soon. Roman isn't well, you know. In fact, and in the strictest of confidence, he hasn't got more than a month or two left in him. He wants to pay a last visit to a few of his favourite cities and they were afraid you might take offence at their leaving on the eve of the baby's birth, so to speak. They broached the subject to me the night before last, wanted to know how I thought you would take it. They don't want to upset you by telling you the real reason for the trip.'

'I'm sorry to hear that Roman isn't well,' Rosemary said.

'But glad at the prospect of his leaving?' Dr Sapirstein smiled. 'A perfectly reasonable reaction,' he said, 'all things considered. Suppose we do this, Rosemary: I'll tell them that I've sounded you out and you aren't at all offended by the idea of their going; and until they do go – they mentioned Sunday as a possibility – you continue as before, not letting Roman know that you've learned his true identity. I'm sure he would be embarrassed and unhappy if he knew, and it seems a shame to upset him when it's only a matter of three or four more days.'

Rosemary was silent for a moment, and then she said, 'Are you sure they'll be leaving on Sunday?'

'I know they'd like to,' Dr Sapirstein said.

Rosemary considered. 'All right,' she said; 'I'll go on as before, but only until Sunday.'

'If you'd like,' Dr Sapirstein said, 'I can have those pills sent over to you tomorrow morning; you can get Minnie to leave the drink and the cake with you and throw them away and take a pill instead.'

'That would be wonderful,' Rosemary said. 'I'd be much happier that way.'

'That's the main thing at this stage,' Dr Sapirstein said, 'keeping you happy.'

Rosemary smiled. 'If it's a boy,' she said, 'I may just name him Abraham Sapirstein Woodhouse.'

'God forbid,' Dr Sapirstein said.

Guy, when he heard the news, was as pleased as Rosemary. 'I'm sorry Roman is on his last lap,' he said, 'but I'm glad for your sake that they're going away. I'm sure you'll feel more relaxed now.'

'Oh, I will,' Rosemary said. 'I feel better already, just knowing about it.'

Apparently Dr Sapirstein didn't waste any time in telling Roman about Rosemary's supposed feelings, for that same evening Minnie and Roman stopped by and broke the news that they were going to Europe. 'Sunday morning at ten,' Roman said. 'We fly directly to Paris, where we'll stay for a week or so, and then we'll go on to Zürich, Venice, and the loveliest city in all the world, Dubrovnik, in Yugoslavia.'

'I'm green with envy,' Guy said.

Roman said to Rosemary, 'I gather this doesn't come as a complete bolt from the blue, does it, my dear?' A conspirator's gleam winked from his deep-socketed eyes.

'Dr Sapirstein mentioned you were thinking of going,' Rosemary said.

Minnie said, 'We'd have loved to stay till the baby came—'

'You'd be foolish to,' Rosemary said, 'now that the hot weather is here.'

'We'll send you all kinds of pictures,' Guy said.

'But when Roman gets the wanderlust,' Minnie said, 'there's just no holding him.'

'It's true, it's true,' Roman said. 'After a lifetime of traveling I find it all but impossible to stay in one city for more than a year; and it's been fourteen months now since we came back from Japan and the Philippines.'

He told them about Dubrovnik's special charms, and Madrid's, and the Isle of Skye's. Rosemary watched him, wondering which he really was, an amiable old talker or the mad son of a mad father.

The next day Minnie made no fuss at all about leaving the drink and the cake; she was on her way out with a long list of going-away jobs to do. Rosemary offered to pick up a dress at the cleaner's for her and buy toothpaste and dramamine. When she threw away the drink and the cake and took one of the large white capsules Dr Sapirstein had sent, she felt just the slightest bit ridiculous.

On Saturday morning Minnie said, 'You know, don't you, about who Roman's father was.'

Rosemary nodded, surprised.

'I could tell by the way you turned sort of cool to us,' Minnie said. 'Oh, don't apologize, dear; you're not the first and you won't be the last. I can't say that I really blame you. Oh, I could *kill* that crazy old man if he wasn't dead already! He's been the bane in poor Roman's existence. That's why he likes to travel so much; he always wants to leave a place before people can find out who he is. Don't let on to him that you know, will you? He's so fond of you and Guy, it would near about break his heart. I want him to have a real happy trip with no sorrows, because there aren't likely to be many more. Trips, I mean. Would you like the perishables in my icebox? Send Guy over later on and I'll load him up.'

Laura-Louise gave a bon voyage party Saturday night in her small dark tannis-smelling apartment on the twelfth floor. The Weeses and the Gilmores came, and Mrs Sabatini with her cat Flash, and Dr Shand. (How had Guy known that it was Dr Shand who played the recorder, Rosemary wondered. And that it was a recorder, not a flute or a clarinet? She would have to ask him.) Roman told of his and Minnie's planned itinerary, surprising Mrs Sabatini who couldn't believe they were bypassing Rome and Florence. Laura-Louise served home-made cookies and a mildly alcoholic fruit punch. Conversation turned to tornadoes and civil rights. Rosemary, watching and listening to these people who were much like her aunts and uncles in Omaha, found it hard to maintain her belief that they were in fact a coven of witches. Little Mr Wees, listening to Guy talking about Martin Luther King; could such a feeble old man, even in his dreams, imagine himself a caster of spells, a maker of charms? And dowdy old women like Laura-

Louise and Minnie and Helen Wees; could they really bring themselves to cavort naked in mock-religious orgies? (Yet hadn't she seen them that way, seen all of them naked? No, no, that was a dream, a wild dream that she'd had a long, long time ago.)

The Fountains phoned a goodbye to Minnie and Roman, and so did Dr Sapirstein and two or three other people whose names Rosemary didn't know. Laura-Louise brought out a gift that everyone had chipped in for, a transistor radio in a pigskin carrying case, and Roman accepted it with an eloquent thank-you speech, his voice breaking. *He knows he's going to die*, Rosemary thought, and was genuinely sorry for him.

Guy insisted on lending a hand the next morning despite Roman's protests; he set the alarm clock for eight-thirty and, when it went off, hopped into chinos and a T shirt and went around to Minnie and Roman's door. Rosemary went with him in her peppermint-striped smock. There was little to carry; two suitcases and a hatbox. Minnie wore a camera and Roman his new radio. 'Anyone who needs more than one suitcase,' he said as he double-locked their door, 'is a tourist, not a traveller.'

On the sidewalk, while the doorman blew his whistle at oncoming cars, Roman checked through tickets, passport, traveller's cheques, and French currency. Minnie took Rosemary by the shoulders. 'No matter where we are,' she said, 'our thoughts are going to be with you every minute, darling, till you're all happy and thin again with your sweet little boy or girl lying safe in your arms.'

'Thank you,' Rosemary said, and kissed Minnie's cheek. 'Thank you for everything.'

'You make Guy send us lots of pictures, you hear?' Minnie said, kissing Rosemary back.

'I will. I will,' Rosemary said.

Minnie turned to Guy. Roman took Rosemary's hand. 'I won't wish you luck,' he said, 'because you won't need it. You're going to have a happy, happy life.'

She kissed him. 'Have a wonderful trip,' she said, 'and come back safely.'

'Perhaps,' he said, smiling. 'But I may stay on in Dubrovnik, or Pescara or maybe Mallorca. We shall see, we shall see . . .'

'Come back,' Rosemary said, and found herself meaning it. She kissed him again.

A taxi came. Guy and the doorman stowed the suitcases beside the driver. Minnie shouldered and grunted her way in, sweating under the arms of her white dress. Roman folded himself in beside her. 'Kennedy Airport,' he said; 'the TWA Building.'

There were more goodbyes and kisses through open windows, and then Rosemary and Guy stood waving at the taxi that sped away with hands ungloved and white-gloved waving from either side of it.

Rosemary felt less happy than she had expected.

That afternoon she looked for *All Of Them Witches,* to reread parts of it and perhaps find it foolish and laughable. The book was gone. It wasn't atop the Kinsey Reports or anywhere else that she could see. She asked Guy and he told her he had put it in the garbage Thursday morning.

'I'm sorry, honey,' he said, 'but I just didn't want you reading any more of that stuff and upsetting yourself.'

She was surprised and annoyed. 'Guy,' she said, 'Hutch *gave* me that book. He *left* it to me.'

'I didn't think about that part of it,' Guy said. 'I just didn't want you upsetting yourself. I'm sorry.'

'That's a *terrible* thing to do.'

'I'm sorry. I wasn't thinking about Hutch.'

'Even if he *hadn't* given it to me, you don't throw away another person's books. If I want to read something, I want to read it.'

'I'm sorry,' he said.

It bothered her all day long. And she had forgotten something that she meant to ask him; that bothered her too.

She remembered it in the evening, while they were walking back from La Scala, a restaurant not far from the ouse. 'How did you know Dr Shand plays the recorder?' he said.

He didn't understand.

'The other day,' she said, 'when I read the book and we argued about it; you said that Dr Shand just happened to play the recorder. How did you know?'

'Oh,' Guy said. 'He told me. A long time ago. And I said we'd heard a flute or something through the wall once or twice, and he said that was him. How did you *think* I knew?'

'I didn't think,' Rosemary said. 'I just wondered, that's all.'

She couldn't sleep. She lay awake on her back and frowned at the ceiling. The baby inside her was sleeping fine, but she couldn't; she felt unsettled and worried, without knowing what she was worried about.

Well the *baby* of course, and whether everything would go the way it should. She had cheated on her exercises lately. No more of *that*; solemn promise.

It was really Monday already, the thirteenth. Fifteen more days. Two weeks. Probably all women felt edgy and unsettled two weeks before. And couldn't sleep from being sick and tired of sleeping on their backs! The first thing she was going to do after it was all over was sleep twenty-four solid hours on her stomach, hugging a pillow with her face snuggled deep down into it.

She heard a sound in Minnie and Roman's apartment, but it must have been from the floor above or the floor below. Sounds were masked and confused with the air conditioner going.

They were in Paris already. Lucky them. Some day she and Guy would go, with their three lovely children.

The baby woke up and began moving.

CHAPTER NINE

SHE BOUGHT COTTON balls and cotton swabs and
talcum powder and baby lotion; engaged a diaper service
and rearranged the baby's clothing in the bureau drawers.
She ordered the announcements – Guy would phone in the
name and date later – and addressed and stamped a boxful
of small ivory envelopes. She read a book called *Summerhill*
that presented a seemingly irrefutable case for permissive
child-rearing, and discussed it at Sardi's East with Elise and
Joan, their treat.

She began to feel contractions; one one day, one the next,
then none, then two.

A postcard came from Paris, with a picture of the Arc de
Triomphe and a neatly written message: *Thinking of you
both. Lovely weather, excellent food. The flight over was
perfect. Love, Minnie.*

The baby dropped low inside her, ready to be born.

Early in the afternoon of Friday, June 24th, at the station-
ery counter at Tiffany's where she had gone for twenty-five
more envelopes, Rosemary met Dominick Pozzo, who in the
past had been Guy's vocal coach. A short, swarthy, hump-
backed man with a voice that was rasping and unpleasant,
he seized Rosemary's hand and congratulated her on her
appearance and on Guy's recent good fortune, for which he
disavowed all credit. Rosemary told him of the play Guy
was signing for and of the latest offer Warner Brothers had
made. Dominick was delighted; now, he said, was when
Guy could truly benefit from intensive coaching. He explained why, made Rosemary promise to have Guy call
him, and, with final good wishes, turned towards the elevators. Rosemary caught his arm. 'I never thanked you for
the tickets to *The Fantasticks*,' she said. 'I just loved it. It's
going to go on and on forever, like that Agatha Christie
play in London.'

'*The Fantasticks*?' Dominick said.

'You gave Guy a pair of tickets. Oh, long ago. In the fall. I went with a friend. Guy had seen it already.'

'I never gave Guy tickets for *The Fantasticks*,' Dominick said.

'You did. Last fall.'

'No, my dear. I never gave *anybody* tickets to *The Fantasticks*; I never had any to give. You're mistaken.'

'I'm sure he said he got them from you,' Rosemary said.

'Then *he* was mistaken,' Dominick said. 'You'll tell him to call me, yes?'

'Yes. Yes, I will.'

It was strange, Rosemary thought when she was waiting to cross Fifth Avenue. Guy *had* said that Dominick had given him the tickets, she was certain of it. She remembered wondering whether or not to send Dominick a thank-you note and deciding finally that it wasn't necessary. She *couldn't* be mistaken.

Walk, the light said, and she crossed the avenue.

But *Guy* couldn't have been mistaken either. He didn't get free tickets every day of the week; he *must* have remembered who gave them to him. Had he deliberately lied to her? Perhaps he hadn't been given the tickets at all, but had found and kept them. No, there might have been a scene at the theatre; he wouldn't have exposed her to that.

She walked west on Fifty-seventh Street, walked very slowly with the bigness of the baby hanging before her and her back aching from withstanding its forward-pulling weight. The day was hot and humid; ninety-two already and still rising. She walked very slowly.

Had he wanted to get her out of the apartment that night for some reason? Had he gone down and bought the tickets himself? To be free to study the scene he was working on? But there wouldn't have been any need for trickery if that had been the case; more than once in the old one-room apartment he had asked her to go out for a couple of hours and she had gone gladly. Most of the time, though, he wanted her to stay, to be his line-feeder, his audience.

Was it a girl? One of his old flames for whom a couple of hours hadn't been enough, and whose perfume he had been washing off in the shower when she got home? No, it was tannis root not perfume that the apartment had smelled of that night; she had had to wrap the charm in foil because of it. And Guy had been far too energetic and amorous to have spent the earlier part of the night with someone else. He had made unusually violent love to her, she remembered; later, while he slept, she had heard the flute and the chanting at Minnie and Roman's.

No, not the flute. Dr Shand's recorder.

Was that how Guy knew about it? Had he been there that evening? At a sabbath ...

She stopped and looked in Henri Bendel's windows, because she didn't want to think any more about witches and covens and baby's blood and Guy being over there. Why had she met that stupid Dominick? She should never have gone out today at all. It was too hot and sticky.

There was a great raspberry crepe dress that looked like a Rudi Gernreich. After Tuesday, after she was her own real shape again, maybe she would go in and price it. And a pair of lemon-yellow hip-huggers and a raspberry blouse ...

Eventually, though, she had to go on. Go on walking, go on thinking, with the baby squirming inside her.

The book (*which Guy had thrown away*) had told of initiation ceremonies, of covens inducting novice members with vows and baptism, with anointing and the infliction of a 'witch mark'. Was it possible (the shower to wash away the smell of a tannis anointing) that Guy had joined the coven? That he (no, he couldn't be!) was one of them, with a secret mark of membership somewhere on his body?

There had been a flesh-coloured band-aid on his shoulder. It had been there in his dressing-room in Philadelphia ('That damn pimple,' he had said when she had asked him) and it had been there a few months before ('Not the same one!' she had said). Was it still there now?

She didn't know. He didn't sleep naked any more. He had

in the past, especially in hot weather. But not any more, not for months and months. Now he wore pyjamas every night. When had she last seen him naked?

A car honked at her; she was crossing Sixth Avenue. 'For God's sake, lady,' a man behind her said.

But why, *why*? He was *Guy*, he wasn't a crazy old man with nothing better to do, with no other way to find purpose and self-esteem! He had a *career*, a busy, exciting, every-day-getting-better career! What did he need with wands and witch knives and censers and – and *junk*; with the Weeses and the Gilmores and Minnie and Roman? What could they give him that he couldn't get elsewhere?

She had known the answer before she asked herself the question. Formulating the question had been a way to put off facing the answer.

The blindness of Donald Baumgart.

If you believed.

But she didn't. She didn't.

Yet there Donald Baumgart was, blind, only a day or two after that Saturday. With Guy staying home to grab the phone every time it rang. Expecting the news.

The blindness of Donald Baumgart.

Out of which had come everything; the play, the reviews, the new play, the movie offer ... Maybe Guy's part in *Greenwich Village*, too, would have been Donald Baumgart's if he hadn't gone inexplicably blind a day or two after Guy had joined (maybe) a coven (maybe) of witches (maybe).

There were spells to take an enemy's sight or hearing, the book had said. *All Of Them Witches.* (Not Guy!) The united mental force of the whole coven, a concentrated battery of malevolent wills, could blind, deafen, paralyse, and ultimately kill the chosen victim.

Paralyse and ultimately kill.

'Hutch?' she asked aloud, standing motionless in front of Carnegie Hall. A girl looked up at her, clinging to her mother's hand.

He had been reading the book that night and had asked her to meet him the next morning. To tell her that Roman

163

was Steven Marcato. And Guy knew of the appointment, and knowing, went out for – what, ice cream? – and rang Minnie and Roman's bell. Was a hasty meeting called? The united mental force ... But how had they known what Hutch would be telling her? She hadn't known herself; only he had known.

Suppose, though, that 'tannis root' wasn't 'tannis root' at all. Hutch hadn't heard of it, had he? Suppose it was – that other stuff he underlined in the book, Devil's Fungus or whatever it was. He had told Roman he was going to look into it; wouldn't that have been enough to make Roman wary of him? *And right then and there Roman had taken one of Hutch's gloves,* because the spells can't be cast without one of the victim's belongings! And then, when Guy told them about the appointment for the next morning, they took no chances and went to work.

But no, Roman couldn't have taken Hutch's glove; she had shown him in and shown him out, walking along with him both times.

Guy had taken the glove. He had rushed home with his make-up still on – which he *never* did – and had gone by himself to the closet. Roman must have called him, must have said, 'This man Hutch is getting suspicious about "tannis root"; go home and get one of his belongings, just in case!' And Guy had obeyed. To keep Donald Baumgart blind.

Waiting for the light at Fifty-fifth Street, she tucked her handbag and the envelopes under her arm, unhooked the chain at the back of her neck, drew the chain and the tannis-charm out of her dress and dropped them together down through the sewer grating.

So much for 'tannis root'. Devil's Fungus.

She was so frightened she wanted to cry.

Because she knew what Guy was giving them in exchange for his success.

The baby. To use in their rituals.

He had never *wanted* a baby until after Donald Baumgart was blind. He didn't like to feel it moving; he didn't like to talk about it; he kept himself as distant and busy as if it weren't his baby at all.

Because he knew what they were planning to do to it as soon as he gave it to them.

In the apartment, in the blessedly-cool shaded apartment, she tried to tell herself that she was mad. *You're going to have your baby in four days, Idiot Girl. Maybe even less. So you're all tense and nutty and you've built up a whole lunatic persecution thing out of a bunch of completely un-related coincidences. There are no real witches. There are no real spells. Hutch died a natural death, even if the doctors couldn't give a name to it. Ditto for Donald Baum-gart's blindness. And how, pray tell, did Guy get one of Donald Baumgart's belongings for the big spell-casting? See, Idiot Girl? It all falls apart when you pick at it.*

But why had he lied about the tickets?

She undressed and took a long cool shower, turned clumsily around and around and then pushed her face up into the spray, trying to think sensibly, rationally.

There *must* be another reason why he had lied. Maybe he'd spent the day hanging around Downey's, yes, and had gotten the tickets from one of the gang there; wouldn't he then have said Dominick had given them to him, so as not to let her know he'd been goofing off?

Of course he would have.

There, you see, Idiot Girl?

But why hadn't he shown himself naked in so many months and months?

She was glad, anyway, that she had thrown away that damned charm. She should have done it long ago. She never should have taken it from Minnie in the first place. What a pleasure it was to be rid of its revolting smell! She dried herself and splashed on cologne, lots and lots of it.

He hadn't shown himself naked because he had a little rash of some kind and was embarrassed about it. Actors are vain, aren't they? Elementary.

But why had he thrown out the book? And spent so much time at Minnie and Roman's? And waited for the news of Donald Baumgart's blindness? And rushed home wearing his make-up just before Hutch missed his glove?

She brushed her hair and tied it, and put on a brassiere and panties. She went into the kitchen and drank two glasses of cold milk.

She didn't know.

She went into the nursery, moved the bathinette away from the wall, and thumbtacked a sheet of plastic over the wallpaper to protect it when the baby splashed in its bath.

She didn't know.

She didn't know if she was going mad or going sane, if witches had only the longing for power or power that was real and strong, if Guy was her loving husband or the treacherous enemy of the baby and herself.

It was almost four. He would be home in an hour or so.

She called Actors Equity and got Donald Baumgart's telephone number.

The phone was answered on the first ring with a quick impatient 'Yeh?'

'Is this Donald Baumgart?'

'That's right.'

'This is Rosemary Woodhouse,' she said. 'Guy Woodhouse's wife.'

'Oh?'

'I wanted —'

'My God,' he said, 'you must be a happy little lady these days! I hear you're living in baronial splendour in the "Bram", sipping vintage wine from crystal goblets, with scores of uniformed lackeys in attendance.'

She said, 'I wanted to know how you are; if there's been any improvement.'

He laughed. 'Why bless your heart, Guy Woodhouse's wife,' he said, 'I'm fine! I'm splendid! There's been enormous improvement! I only broke six glasses today, only fell down three flights of stairs, and only went tap-a-tap-tapping in front of two speeding fire engines! Every day in every way I'm getting better and better and better and better.'

Rosemary said, 'Guy and I are both very unhappy that he

got his break because of your misfortune.'

Donald Baumgart was silent for a moment, and then said, 'Oh, what the hell. That's the way it goes. Somebody's up, somebody's down. He would've made out all right anyway. To tell you the truth, after that second audition we did for *Two Hours of Solid Crap*, I was dead certain he was going to get the part. He was terrific.'

'He thought *you* were going to get it,' Rosemary said. 'And he was right.'

'Briefly.'

'I'm sorry I didn't come along that day he came to visit you,' Rosemary said. 'He asked me to, but I couldn't.'

'Visit me? You mean the day we met for drinks?'

'Yes,' she said. 'That's what I meant.'

'It's good you *didn't* come,' he said; 'they don't allow women, do they? No, after four they *do*, that's right; and it was after four. That was awfully good-natured of Guy. Most people wouldn't have had the – well, *class*, I guess. *I* wouldn't have had it, I can tell you that.'

'The loser buying the winner a drink,' Rosemary said.

'And little did we know that a week later – less than a week, in fact —'

'That's right,' Rosemary said. 'It was only a few days before you —'

'Went blind. Yes. It was a Wednesday or Thursday, because I'd been to a matinee – Wednesday, I think – and the following Sunday was when it happened. Hey,' – he laughed – 'Guy didn't put anything *in* that drink, did he?'

'No, he didn't,' Rosemary said. Her voice was shaking. 'By the way,' she said, 'he has something of yours, you know.'

'What do you mean?'

'Don't you know?'

'No,' he said.

'Didn't you miss anything that day?'

'No. Not that I remember.'

'You're sure?'

'You don't mean my tie, do you?'

'Yes,' she said.

'Well he's got mine and I've got his. Does he want his back? He can have it; it doesn't matter to *me* what tie I'm wearing, or if I'm wearing one at all.'

'No, he doesn't want it back,' Rosemary said. 'I didn't understand. I thought he had only borrowed it.'

'No, it was a trade. It sounded as if you thought he had *stolen* it.'

'I have to hang up now,' Rosemary said. 'I just wanted to know if there was any improvement.'

'No, there isn't. It was nice of you to call.'

She hung up.

It was nine minutes after four.

She put on her girdle and a dress and sandals. She took the emergency money Guy kept under his underwear – a not very thick fold of bills – and put it into her handbag, put in her address book too and the bottle of vitamin capsules. A contraction came and went, the second of the day. She took the suitcase that stood by the bedroom door and went down the hallway and out of the apartment.

Halfway to the elevator, she turned and doubled back.

She rode down in the service elevator with two delivery boys.

On Fifty-fifth Street she got a taxi.

Miss Lark, Dr Sapirstein's receptionist, glanced at the suitcase and said, smiling, 'You aren't in labour, are you?'

'No,' Rosemary said, 'but I have to see the doctor. It's very important.'

Miss Lark glanced at her watch. 'He has to leave at five,' she said, 'and there's Mrs Byron' – she looked over at a woman who sat reading and then smiled at Rosemary – 'but I'm sure he'll see you. Sit down. I'll let him know you're here as soon as he's free.'

'Thank you,' Rosemary said.

She put the suitcase by the nearest chair and sat down. The handbag's white patent was damp in her hands. She opened it, took out a tissue, and wiped her palms and then her upper lip and temples. Her heart was racing.

'How is it out there?' Miss Lark asked.

'Terrible,' Rosemary said. 'Ninety-four.'

Miss Lark made a pained sound.

A woman came out of Dr Sapirstein's office, a woman in her fifth or sixth month whom Rosemary had seen before. They nodded at each other. Miss Lark went in.

'You're due any day now, aren't you?' the woman said, waiting by the desk.

'Tuesday,' Rosemary said.

'Good luck,' the woman said. 'You're smart to get it over with before July and August.'

Miss Lark came out again. 'Mrs Byron,' she said, and to Rosemary, 'He'll see you right after.'

'Thank you,' Rosemary said.

Mrs Byron went into Dr Sapirstein's office and closed the door. The woman by the desk conferred with Miss Lark about another appointment and then went out, saying goodbye to Rosemary and wishing her luck again.

Miss Lark wrote. Rosemary took up a copy of *Time* that lay at her elbow. *Is God Dead?* it asked in red letters on a black background. She found the index and turned to Show Business. There was a piece on Barbra Streisand. She tried to read it.

'That smells nice,' Miss Lark said, sniffing in Rosemary's direction. 'What is it?'

'It's called "Detchema",' Rosemary said.

'It's a big improvement over your regular, if you don't mind my saying.'

'That wasn't a cologne,' Rosemary said. 'It was a good luck charm. I threw it away.'

'Good,' Miss Lark said. 'Maybe the doctor will follow your example.'

Rosemary, after a moment, said, 'Dr Sapirstein?'

Miss Lark said, 'Mm-hmm. He has the after-shave. But it isn't, is it? Then he has a good luck charm. Only he isn't superstitious. I don't *think* he is. *Anyway*, he has the same *smell* once in a while, *whatever* it is, and when he does, I can't come within five feet of him. Much stronger than yours was. Haven't you ever noticed?'

'No,' Rosemary said.

'I guess you haven't been here on the right days,' Miss Lark said. 'Or maybe you thought it was your own you were smelling. What is it, a chemical thing?'

Rosemary stood up and put down *Time* and picked up her suitcase. 'My husband is outside; I have to tell him something,' she said. 'I'll be back in a minute.'

'You can leave your suitcase,' Miss Lark said.

Rosemary took it with her though.

CHAPTER TEN

$\mathcal{S}$HE WALKED UP Park to Eighty-first Street, where she found a glass-walled phone booth. She called Dr Hill. It was very hot in the booth.

A service answered. Rosemary gave her name and the phone number. 'Please ask him to call me back right away,' she said. 'It's an emergency and I'm in a phone booth.'

'All right,' the woman said and clicked to silence.

Rosemary hung up and then lifted the receiver again, but kept a hidden finger on the hook. She held the receiver to her ear as if listening, so that no one should come along and ask her to give up the phone. The baby kicked and twisted in her. She was sweating. *Quickly, please, Dr Hill. Call me. Rescue me.*

All of them. All of them. They were all in it together. Guy, Dr Sapirstein, Minnie, and Roman. All of them witches. *All of Them Witches.* Using her to produce a baby for them, so that they could take it and — *Don't you worry, Andy-or-Jenny, I'll kill them before I let them touch you!*

The phone rang. She jumped her finger from the hook. 'Yes?'

'Is this Mrs Woodhouse?' It was the service again.

'Where's Dr *Hill*?' she said.

'Did I get the name right?' the woman asked. 'Is it "Rosemary Woodhouse"?'

'Yes!'

'And you're Dr Hill's patient?'

She explained about the one visit back in the fall. 'Please, please,' she said, 'he *has* to speak to me! It's important! It's - please. Please tell him to call me.'

'All right,' the woman said.

Holding the hook again, Rosemary wiped her forehead with the back of her hand. *Please, Dr Hill.* She cracked open the door for air and then pushed it closed again as a woman came near and waited. 'Oh, I didn't know that,' Rosemary said to the mouthpiece, her finger on the hook. 'Really? What else did he say?' Sweat trickled down her back and from under her arms. The baby turned and rolled.

It had been a mistake to use a phone so near Dr Sapirstein's office. She should have gone to Madison or Lexington. 'That's wonderful,' she said. 'Did he say anything else?' At this very moment he might be out of the door and looking for her, and wouldn't the nearest phone booth be the first place he'd look? She should have gotten right into a taxi, gotten far away. She put her back as much as she could in the direction he would come from if he came. The woman outside was walking away, thank God.

And now, too, Guy would be coming home. He would see the suitcase gone and call Dr Sapirstein, thinking she was in the hospital. Soon the two of them would be looking for her. And all the others too; the Weeses, the—

'Yes?' – stopping the ring in its middle.

'Mrs Woodhouse?'

It was Dr Hill, Dr Saviour-Rescuer-Kildare-Wonderful Hill. 'Thank you,' she said. 'Thank you for calling me.'

'I thought you were in California,' he said.

'No,' she said. 'I went to another doctor, one some friends sent me to, and he isn't good, Dr Hill; he's been lying to me and giving me unusual kinds of – drinks and capsules. The baby is due on Tuesday – remember, you told me, June twenty-eighth? – and I want *you* to deliver it. I'll pay you whatever you want, the same as if I'd been coming to you all along.'

'Mrs Woodhouse—'

'Please, let me talk to you,' she said, hearing refusal. 'Let me come and explain what's been going on. I can't stay too long where I am right now. My husband and this doctor and the people who sent me to him, they've all been involved in – well, in a plot; I know that sounds crazy, Doctor, and you're probably thinking, "My God, this poor girl has completely flipped," but I *haven't* flipped, Doctor, I swear by all the saints I haven't. Now and then there *are* plots against people, aren't there?'

172

'Yes, I suppose there are,' he said.

'There's one against me and my baby,' she said, 'and if you'll let me come talk to you I'll tell you about it. And I'm not going to ask you to do anything unusual or wrong or anything; all I want you to do is get me into a hospital and deliver my baby for me.'

He said, 'Come to my office tomorrow after —'

'Now,' she said. 'Now. Right now. They're going to be looking for me.'

'Mrs Woodhouse,' he said, 'I'm not at my office now, I'm home. I've been up since yesterday morning and —'

'I beg you,' she said. 'I beg you.'

He was silent.

She said, 'I'll come there and explain to you. I can't stay here.'

'My office at eight o'clock,' he said. 'Will that be all right?'

'Yes,' she said. 'Yes. Thank you. Dr Hill?'

'Yes?'

'My husband may call you and ask if I called.'

'I'm not going to speak to *anyone*,' he said. 'I'm going to take a nap.'

'Would you tell your service? Not to say that I called? Doctor?'

'All right, I will,' he said.

'Thank you,' she said.

'Eight o'clock.'

'Yes. Thank you.'

A man with his back to the booth turned as she came out; he wasn't Dr Sapirstein though, he was somebody else.

She walked to Lexington Avenue and uptown to Eighty-sixth Street, where she went into the theatre there, used the ladies' room, and then sat numbly in the safe cool darkness facing a loud colour movie. After a while she got up and went with her suitcase to a phone booth, where she placed a person-to-person collect call to her brother Brian. There was no answer. She went back with her suitcase and sat in a different seat. The baby was quiet, sleeping. The movie

173

changed to something with Keenan Wynn.

At twenty of eight she left the theatre and took a taxi to Dr Hill's office on West Seventy-second Street. It would be safe to go in, she thought; they would be watching Joan's place and Hugh and Elise's, but not Dr Hill's office at eight o'clock, not if his service had said she hadn't called. To be sure, though, she asked the driver to wait and watch until she was inside the door.

Nobody stopped her. Dr Hill opened the door himself, more pleasantly than she had expected after his reluctance on the telephone. He had grown a moustache, blond and hardly noticeable, but he still looked like Dr Kildare. He was wearing a blue-and-yellow plaid sport shirt.

They went into his consulting room, which was a quarter the size of Dr Sapirstein's, and there Rosemary told him her story. She sat with her hands on the chair arms and her ankles crossed and spoke quietly and calmly, knowing that any suggestion of hysteria would make him disbelieve her and think her mad. She told him about Adrian Marcato and Minnie and Roman; about the months of pain she had suffered and the herbal drinks and the little white cakes; about Hutch and *All Of Them Witches* and the *Fantasticks* tickets and black candles and Donald Baumgart's necktie. She tried to keep everything coherent and in sequence but she couldn't. She got it all out without getting hysterical though; Dr Shand's recorder and Guy throwing away the book and Miss Lark's final unwitting revelation.

'Maybe the coma and the blindness were only coincidences,' she said, 'or maybe they *do* have some kind of ESP way of hurting people. But that's not important. The important thing is that they want the baby. I'm sure they do.'

'It certainly seems that way,' Dr Hill said, 'especially in light of the interest they've taken in it right from the beginning.'

Rosemary shut her eyes and could have cried. He believed her. He didn't think she was mad. She opened her eyes and looked at him, staying calm and composed. He was writing. Did all his patients love him? Her palms were et; she slid them from the chair arms and pressed them against her dress.

'The doctor's name is Shand, you say,' Dr Hill said.

'No, Dr Shand is just one of the group,' Rosemary said. 'One of the coven. The doctor is Dr Sapirstein.'

'Abraham Sapirstein?'

'Yes,' Rosemary said uneasily. 'Do you know him?'

'I've met him once or twice,' Dr Hill said, writing more.

'Looking at him,' Rosemary said, 'or even talking to him, you would never think he —'

'Never in a million years,' Dr Hill said, putting down his pen, 'which is why we're told not to judge books by their covers. Would you like to go into Mount Sinai right now, this evening?'

Rosemary smiled. 'I would *love* to,' she said. 'Is it possible?'

'It'll take some wire-pulling and arguing,' Dr Hill said. He rose and went to the open door of his examining room. 'I want you to lie down and get some rest,' he said, reaching into the darkened room behind him. It blinked into ice-blue fluorescent light. 'I'll see what I can do and then I'll check you over.'

Rosemary hefted herself up and went with her handbag into the examining room. 'Anything they've got,' she said. 'Even a broom closet.'

'I'm sure we can do better than that,' Dr Hill said. He came in after her and turned on an air conditioner in the room's blue-curtained window. It was a noisy one.

'Shall I undress?' Rosemary asked.

'No, not yet,' Dr Hill said. 'This is going to take a good half-hour of high-powered telephoning. Just lie down and rest.' He went out and closed the door.

Rosemary went to the day bed at the far end of the room and sat down heavily on its blue-covered softness. She put her handbag on a chair.

God bless Dr Hill.

She would make a sampler to that effect some day.

She shook off her sandals and lay back gratefully. The air conditioner sent a small stream of coolness to her; the baby turned over slowly and lazily, as if feeling it.

Everything's okay now, Andy-or-Jenny. We're going
be in a nice clean bed at Mount Sinai Hospital, with
visitors and —

Money. She sat up, opened her handbag, and found Guy
money that she had taken. There was a hundred and eigh
dollars. Plus sixteen-and-change of her own. It would
enough, certainly, for any advance payments that had to
made, and if more were needed Brian would wire it
Hugh and Elise would lend it to her. Or Joan. Or Gra
Cardiff. She had plenty of people she could turn to.

She took the capsules out, put the money back in, ar
closed the handbag; and then she lay back again on the da
bed, with the handbag and the bottle of capsules on th
chair beside her. She would give the capsules to Dr Hill;
would analyse them and make sure there was nothin
harmful in them. There *couldn't* be. They would want th
baby to be healthy, wouldn't they, for their insane ritual:

She shivered.

The – monsters.

And Guy.

Unspeakable, unspeakable.

Her middle hardened in a straining contraction, th
strongest one yet. She breathed shallowly until it ended.

Making three that day.

She would tell Dr Hill.

She was living with Brian and Dodie in a large conten
porary house in Los Angeles, and Andy had just starte
talking (though only four months old) when Dr Hill looke
in and she was in his examining room again, lying on th
day bed in the coolness of the air conditioner. She shielde
her eyes with her hand and smiled at him. 'I've been slee
ing,' she said.

He pushed the door all the way open and withdrew. I
Sapirstein and Guy came in.

Rosemary sat up, lowering her hand from her eyes.

They came and stood close to her. Guy's face was ston
and blank. He looked at the walls, only at the walls, not

her. Dr Sapirstein said, 'Come with us quietly, Rosemary. Don't argue or make a scene, because if you say anything more about witches or witchcraft we're going to be forced to take you to a mental hospital. The facilities there for delivering the baby will be less than the best. You don't want that, do you? So put your shoes on.'

'We're just going to take you home,' Guy said, finally looking at her. 'No one's going to hurt you.'

'Or the baby,' Dr Sapirstein said. 'Put your shoes on.' He picked up the bottle of capsules, looked at it, and put it in his pocket.

She put her sandals on and he gave her her handbag.

They went out, Dr Sapirstein holding her arm, Guy touching her other elbow.

Dr Hill had her suitcase. He gave it to Guy.

'She's fine now,' Dr Sapirstein said. 'We're going to go home and rest.'

Dr Hill smiled at her. 'That's all it takes, nine times out of ten,' he said.

She looked at him and said nothing.

'Thank you for your trouble, Doctor,' Dr Sapirstein said, and Guy said, 'It's a shame you had to come in here and —'

'I'm glad I could be of help, sir,' Dr Hill said to Dr Sapirstein, opening the front door.

They had a car. Mr Gilmore was driving it. Rosemary sat between Guy and Dr Sapirstein in back.

Nobody spoke.

They drove to the Bramford.

The elevator man smiled at her as they crossed the lobby towards him. Diego. Smiled because he liked her, favoured her over some of the other tenants.

The smile, reminding her of her individuality, wakened something in her, revived something.

She snicked open her handbag at her side, worked a finger through her key ring, and, near the elevator door, turned the handbag all the way over, spilling out every-thing except the keys. Rolling lipstick, coins, Guy's tens and twenties fluttering, everything. She looked down stupidly.

They picked things up, Guy and Dr Sapirstein, while she stood mute, pregnant-helpless. Diego came out of the elevator, making tongue-teeth sounds of concern. He bent and helped. She backed in to get out of the way and, watching them, toed the big round floor button. The rolling door rolled. She pulled closed the inner gate.

Diego grabbed for the door but saved his fingers smacked on the outside of it. 'Hey, Mrs Woodhouse!'

Sorry, Diego.

She pushed the handle and the car lurched upward.

She would call Brian. Or Joan or Elise or Grace Cardiff. Someone.

We're not through yet, Andy!

She stopped the car at nine, then at six, then halfway past seven, and then close enough to seven to open the gate and the door and step four inches down.

She walked through the turns of hallway as quickly as she could. A contraction came but she marched right through it, paying no heed.

The service elevator's indicator blinked from four to five and she knew it was Guy and Dr Sapirstein coming up to intercept her.

So of course the key wouldn't go into the lock.

But finally did, and she was inside, slamming the door as the elevator door opened, hooking in the chain as Guy's key went into the lock. She turned the bolt and the key turned it right back again. The door opened and pushed in against the chain.

'Open up, Ro,' Guy said.

'Go to hell,' she said.

'I'm not going to hurt you, honey.'

'You promised them the baby. Get away.'

'I didn't promise them anything,' he said. 'What are you talking about? Promised who?'

'Rosemary,' Dr Sapirstein said.

'You too. Get away.'

'You seem to have imagined some sort of conspiracy against you.'

'Get away,' she said, and pushed the door shut and bolted it.

It stayed bolted.

She backed away, watching it, and then went into the bedroom.

It was nine-thirty.

She wasn't sure of Brian's number and her address book was in the lobby or Guy's pocket, so the operator had to get Omaha Information. When the call was finally put through there was still no answer. 'Do you want me to try again in twenty minutes?' the operator asked.

'Yes, please,' Rosemary said; 'in *five* minutes.'

'I can't try again in five minutes,' the operator said, 'but I'll try in twenty minutes if you want me to.'

'Yes, please,' Rosemary said and hung up.

She called Joan, and Joan was out too.

Elise and Hugh's number was – she didn't know. Information took forever to answer but, having answered, supplied it quickly. She dialled it and got an answering service. They were away for the weekend. 'Are they anywhere where I can reach them? This is an emergency.'

'Is this Mr Dunstan's secretary?'

'No, I'm a close friend. It's very important that I speak to them.'

'They're on Fire Island,' the woman said. 'I can give you a number.'

'Please.'

She memorized it, hung up, and was about to dial it when she heard whispers outside the doorway and footsteps on the vinyl floor. She stood up.

Guy and Mr Fountain came into the room – 'Honey, we're *not* going to hurt you,' Guy said – and behind them Dr Sapirstein with a loaded hypodermic, the needle up and dripping, his thumb at the plunger. And Dr Shand and Mrs Fountain and Mrs Gilmore. 'We're your friends,' Mrs Gilmore said, and Mrs Fountain said, 'There's nothing to be afraid of, Rosemary; honest and truly there isn't.'

'This is nothing but a mild sedative,' Dr Sapirstein said. 'To calm you down so that you can get a good night's sleep.'

She was between the bed and the wall, and too gross to climb over the bed and evade them.

They came towards her – 'You know I wouldn't let anyone hurt you, Ro,' – and she picked up the phone and struck with the receiver at Guy's head. He caught her wrist and Mr Fountain caught her other arm and the phone fell as he pulled her around with startling strength. *'Help me, somebod—'* she screamed, and a handkerchief or something was jammed into her mouth and held there by a small strong hand.

They dragged her away from the bed so Dr Sapirstein could come in front of her with the hypodermic and a dab of cotton, and a contraction far more gruelling than any of the others clamped her middle and clenched shut her eyes. She held her breath, then sucked air in through her nostrils in quick little pulls. A hand felt her belly, deft all-over fingertipping, and Dr Sapirstein said, 'Wait a minute, wait a minute now; we happen to be in labour here.'

Silence; and someone outside the room whispered the news: 'She's in labour!'

She opened her eyes and stared at Dr Sapirstein, dragging air through her nostrils, her middle relaxing. He nodded to her, and suddenly took her arm that Mr Fountain was holding, touched it with cotton, and stabbed it with the needle.

She took the injection without trying to move, too afraid, too stunned.

He withdrew the needle and rubbed the spot with his thumb and then with the cotton.

The women, she saw, were turning down the bed.

Here?

Here?

It was supposed to be Doctors Hospital! Doctors Hospital with equipment and nurses and everything clean and sterile!

They held her while she struggled, Guy saying in her ear, 'You'll be all right, honey, I swear to God you will! I swear to God you're going to be perfectly all right! Don't go on fighting like this, Ro, please don't! I give you my absolute word of honour you're going to be perfectly all right!'

And then there was another contraction.

And then she was on the bed, with Dr Sapirstein giving her another injection.

And Mrs Gilmore wiped her forehead.

And the phone rang.

And Guy said, 'No, just cancel it, operator.'

And there was another contraction, faint and disconnected from her floating eggshell head.

All the exercises had been for nothing. All wasted energy. This wasn't Natural Childbirth at all; she wasn't helping, she wasn't seeing.

Oh, Andy, Andy-or-Jenny! I'm sorry, my little darling! Forgive me!

Part Three

CHAPTER ONE

LIGHT.

The ceiling.

And pain between her legs.

And Guy. Sitting beside the bed, watching her with an anxious, uncertain smile.

'Hi,' he said.

'Hi,' she said back.

The pain was terrible.

And then she remembered. It was over. It was over. The baby was born.

'Is it all right?' she asked.

'Yes, fine,' he said.

'What is it?'

'A boy.'

'Really? A boy?'

He nodded.

'And it's all right?'

'Yes.'

She let her eyes close, then managed to open them again.

'Did you call Tiffany's?' she asked.

'Yes,' he said.

She let her eyes close and slept.

Later she remembered more. Laura-Louise was sitting by the bed reading the *Reader's Digest* with a magnifying glass.

'Where is it?' she asked.

Laura-Louise jumped. 'My goodness, dear,' she said, the magnifying glass at her bosom showing red ropes interwoven, 'what a *start* you gave me, waking up so suddenly! My goodness!' She closed her eyes and breathed deeply.

'The baby; where is it?' she asked.

'You just wait here a minute,' Laura-Louise said, getting

up with the *Digest* closed on a finger. 'I'll get Guy and Doctor Abe. They're right in the kitchen.'

'Where's the baby?' she asked, but Laura-Louise went out the door without answering.

She tried to get up but fell back, her arms boneless. And there was pain between her legs like a bundle of knife points. She lay and waited, remembering, remembering.

It was night. Five after nine, the clock said.

They came in, Guy and Dr Sapirstein, looking grave and resolute.

'Where's the baby?' she asked them.

Guy came around to the side of the bed and crouched down and took her hand. 'Honey,' he said.

'Where is it?'

'Honey . . .' He tried to say more and couldn't. He looked across the bed for help.

Dr Sapirstein stood looking down at her. A shred of coconut was caught in his moustache. 'There were complications, Rosemary,' he said, 'but nothing that will affect future births.'

'It's —'

She stared at him.

'Dead,' he said.

He nodded.

She turned to Guy.

He nodded too.

'It was in the wrong position,' Dr Sapirstein said. 'In the hospital I might have been able to do something, but there simply wasn't time to get you there. Trying anything here would have been – too dangerous for you.'

Guy said, 'We can have others, honey, and we will, just as soon as you're better. I promise you.'

Dr Sapirstein said, 'Absolutely. You can start on another in a very few months and the odds are thousands to one against anything similar happening. It was a tragic-one-in-ten thousand mishap; the baby itself was perfectly healthy and normal.'

Guy squeezed her hand and smiled encouragingly at her. 'As soon as you're better,' he said.

She looked at them, at Guy, at Dr Sapirstein with the shred of coconut in his moustache. 'You're lying,' she said. 'I don't believe you. You're both lying.'

'Honey,' Guy said.

'It didn't die,' she said. 'You took it. You're lying. You're witches. You're lying. You're lying! You're lying! *You're lying! You're lying! You're lying!*'

Guy held her shoulders to the bed and Dr Sapirstein gave her an injection.

She ate soup and triangles of buttered white bread. Guy sat on the side of the bed, nibbling at one of the triangles. 'You were crazy,' he said. 'You were really ka-pow out of your mind. It happens sometimes in the last couple of weeks. That's what Abe says. He has a name for it. Prepartum I-don't-know, some kind of hysteria. You had it, honey, and with a vengeance.'

She said nothing. She took a spoonful of soup.

'Listen,' he said, 'I know where you got the idea that Minnie and *Roman* were witches, but what made you think Abe and I had joined the party?'

She said nothing.

'That's stupid of me, though,' he said. 'I guess prepartum whatever-it-is doesn't *need* reasons.' He took another of the triangles and bit off first one point and then another.

She said, 'Why did you trade ties with Donald Baumgart?'

'Why did I – well what has *that* got to do with anything?'

'You needed one of his personal belongings,' she said, 'so they could cast the spell and make him blind.'

He stared at her. 'Honey,' he said, 'for God's sake what are you *talking* about?'

'You know.'

'Holy mackerel,' he said. 'I traded ties with him because I liked his and didn't like mine, and *he* liked mine and didn't like his. I didn't tell you about it because afterwards it seemed like a slightly faggy thing to have done and I was a little embarrassed about it.'

'Where did you get the tickets for *The Fantasticks*?' she asked him.

'*What?*'

'You said you got them from Dominick,' she said; 'you didn't.'

'Boy oh *boy*,' he said. 'And that makes me a witch? I got them from a girl named Norma-something that I met at an audition and had a couple of drinks with. What did Abe do? Tie his shoelaces the wrong way?'

'He uses tannis root,' she said. 'It's a witch thing. His receptionist told me she smelled it on him.'

'Maybe Minnie gave him a good luck charm, just the way she gave you one. You mean only witches use it? That doesn't sound very likely.'

Rosemary was silent.

'Let's face it, darling,' Guy said, 'you had the prepartum crazies. And now you're going to rest and get over them.' He leaned closer to her and took her hand. 'I know this has been the worst thing that ever happened to you,' he said, 'but from now on everything's going to be roses. Warners is within an inch of where we want them, and suddenly Universal is interested too. I'm going to get some more good reviews and then we're going to blow this town and be in the beautiful hills of Beverly, with the pool and the spice garden and the whole schmeer. And the kids too, Ro. Scout's honour. You heard what Abe said.' He kissed her hand. 'Got to run now and get famous.'

He got up and started for the door.

'Let me see your shoulder,' she said.

He stopped and turned.

'Let me see your shoulder,' she said.

'Are you kidding?'

'No,' she said. 'Let me see you. Your left shoulder.'

He looked at her and said, 'All right, whatever you say, honey.'

He undid the collar of his shirt, a short-sleeved blue knit, and peeled the bottom of it up and over his head. He had a white T shirt on underneath. 'I generally prefer doing this to music,' he said, and took off the T shirt too. He went close to the bed and, leaning, showed Rosemary his left shoulder. It was unmarked. There was only the faint scar of a boil or pimple. He showed her his other shoulder and his chest and his back.

'This is as far as I go without a blue light,' he said.

'All right,' she said.

He grinned. 'The question now,' he said, 'is do I put my shirt back on or do I go out and give Laura-Louise the thrill of a lifetime.'

Her breasts filled with milk and it was necessary to relieve them, so Dr Sapirstein showed her how to use a rubber-bulbed breast pump, like a glass auto horn; and several times a day Laura-Louise or Helen Wees or whoever was there brought it in to her with a Pyrex measuring cup. She drew from each breast an ounce or two of thin faintly-green fluid that smelled ever so slightly of tannis root – in a process that was a final irrefutable demonstration of the baby's absence. When the cup and the pump had been carried from the room she would lie against her pillows broken and lonely beyond tears.

Joan and Elise and Tiger came to see her, and she spoke with Brian for twenty minutes on the phone. Flowers came – roses and carnations and a yellow azalea plant – from Allan, and Mike and Pedro, and Lou and Claudia. Guy bought a new remote-control television set and put it at the foot of the bed. She watched and ate and took pills that were given to her.

A letter of sympathy came from Minnie and Roman, a page from each of them. They were in Dubrovnik.

The stitches gradually stopped hurting.

One morning, when two or three weeks had gone by, she thought she heard a baby crying. She rayed off the television and listened. There was a frail far away wailing. Or was there? She slipped out of bed and turned off the air conditioner.

Florence Gilmore came in with the pump and the cup.

'Do you hear a baby crying?' Rosemary asked her.

Both of them listened.

Yes, there it was. A baby crying.

'No, dear, I don't,' Florence said. 'Get back into bed now; you know you're not supposed to be walking around. Did you turn off the air conditioner? You mustn't do that; it's a *terrible* day. People are actually dying, it's so hot.'

She heard it again that afternoon, and mysteriously her breasts began to leak . . .

'Some new people moved in,' Guy said out of nowhere that evening. 'Up on eight.'

'And they have a baby,' she said.

'Yes. How did you know?'

She looked at him for a moment. 'I heard it crying,' she said.

She heard it the next day. And the next.

She stopped watching television and held a book in front of her, pretending to read but only listening, listening . . .

It wasn't up on eight; it was right there on seven.

And more often than not, the pump and the cup were brought to her a few minutes after the crying began; and the crying stopped a few minutes after her milk was taken away.

'What do you do with it?' she asked Laura-Louise one morning, giving her back the pump and the cup and six ounces of milk.

'Why throw it away, of course,' Laura-Louise said, and went out.

That afternoon, as she gave Laura-Louise the cup, she said, 'Wait a minute,' and started to put a used coffee spoon into it.

Laura-Louise jerked the cup away. 'Don't do that,' she said, and caught the spoon in a finger of the hand holding the pump.

'What difference does it make?' Rosemary asked.

'It's just messy, that's all,' Laura-Louise said.

CHAPTER TWO

IT WAS ALIVE.

It was in Minnie and Roman's apartment.

They were keeping it there, feeding it her milk and please God taking care of it, because, as well as she remembered from Hutch's book, August first was one of their special days, Lammas or Leamas, with special maniacal rituals. Or maybe they were keeping it until Minnie and Roman came back from Europe. For their share.

But it was still alive.

She stopped taking the pills they gave her. She tucked them down into the fold between her thumb and her palm and faked the swallowing, and later pushed the pills as far as she could between the mattress and the box spring beneath it.

She felt stronger and more wide-awake.

Hang on, Andy! I'm coming!

She had learned her lesson with Dr Hill. This time she would turn to no one, would expect no one to believe her and be her saviour. Not the police, not Joan or the Dunstans or Grace Cardiff, not even Brian. Guy was too good an actor, Dr Sapirstein too famous a doctor; between the two of them they'd have even him, even Brian, thinking she had some kind of post-losing-the-baby madness. This time she would do it alone, would go in there and get him herself, with her longest sharpest kitchen knife to fend away those maniacs.

And she was one up on them. Because she knew – and they didn't *know* she knew – that there was a secret way from the one apartment to the other. The door had been chained that night – she knew that as she knew the hand she was looking at was a hand, not a bird or a battleship – and still they had all come pouring in. So there had to be another way.

Which could only be the linen closet, barricaded by dead Mrs Gardenia, who surely had died of the same witchery that had frozen and killed poor Hutch. The closet had been put there to break the one big apartment into two smaller ones, and if Mrs Gardenia had belonged to the coven – she'd given Minnie her herbs; hadn't Terry said so? – then what was more logical than to open the back of the closet in some way and go to and fro with so many steps saved and the Bruhns and Dubin-and-DeVore never knowing of the traffic?

It *was* the linen closet.

In a dream long ago she had been carried through it. That had been no dream; it had been a sign from heaven, a divine message to be stored away and remembered now for assurance in a time of trial.

Oh Father in heaven, forgive me for doubting! Forgive me for turning from you, Merciful Father, and help me, help me in my hour of need! Oh Jesus, dear Jesus, help me save my innocent baby!

The pills, of course, were the answer. She squirmed her arm in under the mattress and caught them out one by one. Eight of them, all alike; small white tablets scored across the middle for breaking in half. Whatever they were, three a day had kept her limp and docile; eight at once, surely, would send Laura-Louise or Helen Wees into sound sleep. She brushed the pills clean, folded them up in a piece of magazine cover, and tucked them away at the bottom of her box of tissues.

She pretended still to be limp and docile; ate her meals and looked at magazines and pumped out her milk.

It was Leah Fountain who was there when everything was right. She came in after Helen Wees had gone out with the milk and said, 'Hi, Rosemary! I've been letting the other girls have the fun of visiting with you, but now *I'm* going to take a turn. You're in a regular movie theatre here! Is there anything good on tonight?'

Nobody else was in the apartment. Guy had gone to meet Allan and have some contracts explained to him.

They watched a Fred Astaire–Ginger Rogers picture, and during a break Leah went into the kitchen and brought back two cups of coffee. 'I'm a little hungry too,' Rosemary said when Leah had put the cups on the night table. 'Would you mind very much fixing me a cheese sandwich?'

'Of course I wouldn't mind, dear,' Leah said. 'How do you like it, with lettuce and mayonnaise?'

She went out again and Rosemary got the fold of magazine cover from her tissue box. There were eleven pills in it now. She slid them all into Leah's cup and stirred the coffee with her own spoon, which she then wiped off with a tissue. She picked up her own coffee, but it shook so much that she had to put it down again.

She was sitting and sipping calmly though when Leah came in with the sandwich. 'Thanks, Leah,' she said, 'that looks great. The coffee's a little bitter; I guess it was sitting too long.'

'Shall I make fresh?' Leah asked.

'No, it's not that bad,' Rosemary said.

Leah sat down beside the bed, took her cup, and stirred it and tasted. 'Mm,' she said and wrinkled her nose; she nodded, agreeing with Rosemary.

'It's drinkable though,' Rosemary said.

They watched the movie, and after two more breaks Leah's head drooped and snapped up sharply. She put down her cup and saucer, the cup two-thirds empty. Rosemary ate the last piece of her sandwich and watched Fred Astaire and two other people dancing on turntables in a glossy unreal fun house.

During the next section of the movie Leah fell asleep.

'Leah?' Rosemary said.

The elderly woman sat snoring, her chin to her chest, her hands palm-upward in her lap. Her lavender-tinted hair, a wig, had slipped forward; sparse white hairs stuck out at the back of her neck.

Rosemary got out of bed, slid her feet into slippers, and put on the blue-and-white quilted housecoat she had bought for the hospital. Going quietly out of the bedroom, she closed the door almost all the way and went to the front door of the apartment and quietly chained and bolted it.

She then went into the kitchen and, from her knife rack, took the longest sharpest knife – a nearly new carving knife with a curved and pointed steel blade and a heavy bone handle with a brass butt. Holding it point-down at her side, she left the kitchen and went down the hallway to the linen-closet door.

As soon as she opened it she knew she was right. The shelves looked neat and orderly enough, but the contents of two of them had been interchanged; the bath towels and hand towels were where the winter blankets ought to have been and vice versa.

She laid the knife on the bathroom threshold and took everything out of the closet except what was on the fixed top shelf. She put towels and linens on the floor, and large and small boxes, and then lifted out the four gingham-covered shelves she had decorated and placed there a thousand thousand years ago.

The back of the closet, below the top shelf, was a single large white-painted panel framed with narrow white moulding. Standing close and leaning aside for better light, Rosemary saw that where the panel and the moulding met, the paint was broken in a continuous line. She pressed at one side of the panel and then at the other; pressed harder, and it swung inward on scraping hinges. Within was darkness; another closet, with a wire hanger glinting on the floor and one bright spot of light, a keyhole. Pushing the panel all the way open, Rosemary stepped into the second closet and ducked down. Through the keyhole she saw, at a distance of about twenty feet, a small curio cabinet that stood at a jog in the hallway of Minnie and Roman's apartment.

She tried the door. It opened.

She closed it and backed out through her own closet and got the knife; then went in and through again, looked out again through the keyhole, and opened the door just the least bit.

Then opened it wide, holding the knife shoulder-high, point forward.

The hallway was empty, but there were distant voices from the living-room. The bathroom was on her right, its door open, dark. Minnie and Roman's bedroom was on the left, with a bedside lamp burning. There was no crib, no baby.

She went cautiously down the hallway. A door on the right was locked; another, on the left, was a linen closet.

Over the curio cabinet hung a small but vivid oil painting of a church in flames. Before, there had been only a clean space and a hook; now there was this shocking painting. St Patrick's, it looked like, with yellow and orange flames bursting from its windows and soaring through its gutted roof.

Where had she seen it? A church burning...

In the dream. The one where they had carried her through the linen closet. Guy and somebody else. 'You've got her too high.' To a ballroom where a church was burning. Where *that* church was burning.

But how could it be?

Had she *really* been carried through the closet, seen the painting as they carried her past it?

Find Andy. Find Andy. Find Andy.

Knife high, she followed the jog to the left and the right. Other doors were locked. There was another painting; nude men and women dancing in a circle. Ahead were the foyer and the front door, the archway on the right to the living-room. The voices were louder. 'Not if he's still waiting for a plane, he isn't!' Mr Fountain said, and there was laughter and then hushing.

In the dream ballroom Jackie Kennedy had spoken kindly to her and gone away, and then all of *them* had been there, the whole coven, naked and singing in a circle round her. Had it been a real thing that had really happened? Roman in a black robe had drawn designs on her. Dr Sapirstein had held a cup of red paint for him. Red paint? Blood?

'Oh hell now, Hayato,' Minnie said, 'you're just making fun of me! "Pulling my leg" is what we say over here.'

Minnie? Back from Europe? And Roman too? But only

yesterday there had been a card from Dubrovnik saying they were staying on!

Had they ever really been away?

She was at the archway now, could see the bookshelves and file cabinets and bridge tables laden with newspapers and stacked envelopes. The coven was at the other end, laughing, talking softly. Ice cubes clinked.

She bettered her grip on the knife and moved a step forward. She stopped, staring.

Across the room, in the one large window bay, stood a black bassinet. Black and only black it was; skirted with black taffeta, hooded and flounced with black organza. A silver ornament turned on a black ribbon pinned to its black hood.

Dead? But no, even as she feared it, the stiff organza trembled, the silver ornament quivered.

He was in there. In that monstrous perverted witches' bassinet.

The silver ornament was a crucifix hanging upside down, with the black ribbon wound and knotted around Jesus' ankles.

The thought of her baby lying helpless amid sacrilege and horror brought tears to Rosemary's eyes, and suddenly a longing dragged at her to do nothing but collapse and weep, to surrender completely before such elaborate and unspeakable evil. She withstood it though; she shut her eyes tight to stop the tears, said a quick Hail Mary, and drew together all her resolve and all her hatred too; hatred of Minnie, Roman, Guy, Dr Sapirstein – of all of them who had conspired to steal Andy away from her and make their loathsome uses of him. She wiped her hands on her housecoat, threw back her hair, found a fresh grip on the knife's thick handle, and stepped out where they could every one of them see her and know she had come.

Insanely, they didn't. They went right on talking, listening, sipping, pleasantly partying, as if she were a ghost, or back in her bed dreaming; Minnie, Roman, Guy (contracts!), Mr Fountain, the Weeses, Laura-Louise, and a studious-looking young Japanese with eyeglasses – al gathered under an over-the-mantel portrait of Adrian Marcato. He alone saw her. He stood glaring at her, motionless, powerful; but powerless, a painting.

Then Roman saw her too; put down his drink and touched Minnie's arm. Silence sprang up, and those who sat with their backs towards her turned around questioningly. Guy started to rise but sat down again. Laura-Louise clapped her hands to her mouth and began squealing. Helen Wees said, 'Get back in bed, Rosemary; you know you aren't supposed to be up and around.' Either mad or trying psychology.

'Is the mother?' the Japanese asked, and when Roman nodded, said 'Ah, sssssss,' and looked at Rosemary with interest.

'She killed Leah,' Mr Fountain said, standing up. 'She killed my Leah. Did you? Where is she? Did you kill my Leah?'

Rosemary stared at them, at Guy. He looked down, red-faced.

She gripped the knife tighter. 'Yes,' she said, 'I killed her. I stabbed her to death. And I cleaned my knife and I'll stab to death whoever comes near me. Tell them how sharp it is, Guy!'

He said nothing. Mr Fountain sat down, a hand to his heart. Laura-Louise squealed.

Watching them, she started across the room towards the bassinet.

'Rosemary,' Roman said.

'Shut up,' she said.

'Before you look at —'

'Shut up,' she said. 'You're in Dubrovnik. I don't hear you.'

'Let her,' Minnie said.

She watched them until she was by the bassinet, which was angled in their direction. With her free hand she caught the black-covered handle at the foot of it and swung the bassinet slowly, gently, around to face her. Taffeta rustled; the back wheels squeaked.

Asleep and sweet, so small and rosy-faced, Andy lay

wrapped in a snug black blanket with little black mitts
ribbon-tied around his wrists. Orange-red hair he had, a surprising amount of it, silky-clean and brushed. *Andy! Oh,
Andy!* She reached out to him, her knife turning away; his
lips pouted and he opened his eyes and looked at her. His
eyes were golden-yellow, all golden-yellow, with neither
whites nor irises; all golden-yellow, with vertical black-slit
pupils.

She looked at him.

He looked at her, golden-yellowly, and then at the swaying upside-down crucifix.

She looked at them watching her and knife-in-hand
screamed at them, '*What have you done to his eyes?*'

They stirred and looked to Roman.

'He has His Father's eyes,' he said.

She looked at him, looked at Guy – whose eyes were
hidden behind a hand – looked at Roman again. 'What are
you *talking* about?' she said. 'Guy's eyes are *brown*, they're
normal! What have you *done* to him, you maniacs?' She
moved from the bassinet, ready to kill them.

'Satan is His Father, not Guy,' Roman said. '*Satan* is His
Father, who came up from Hell and begat a Son of mortal
woman! To avenge the iniquities visited by the God
worshippers upon His never-doubting followers!'

'Hail Satan,' Mr Wees said.

'*Satan* is His Father and His name is Adrian!' Roman
cried, his voice growing louder and prouder, his bearing
more strong and forceful. 'He shall overthrow the mighty
and lay waste their temples! He shall redeem the despised
and wreak vengeance in the name of the burned and the
tortured!'

'Hail Adrian,' they said. 'Hail Adrian.' 'Hail Adrian.'
And 'Hail Satan.' 'Hail Adrian.' 'Hail Satan.'

She shook her head. 'No,' she said.

Minnie said, 'He chose *you* out of all the world, Rosemary. Out of all the women in the whole world, He chose
you. He brought you and Guy to your apartment there, He
made that foolish what's-her-name, Terry, made her get all
scared and silly so we had to change our plans. He arranged

everything that *had* to be arranged, 'cause He wanted *you* to be the mother of His only living Son.'

'His power is stronger than stronger,' Roman said.

'Hail Satan,' Helen Wees said.

'His might will last longer than longer.'

'Hair Satan,' the Japanese said.

Laura-Louise uncovered her mouth. Guy looked out at Rosemary from under his hand.

'No,' she said, 'no,' the knife hanging at her side. 'No. It can't *be*. No.'

'Go look at His hands,' Minnie said. 'And His feet.'

'And His tail,' Laura-Louise said.

'And the buds of His horns,' Minnie said.

'Oh God,' Rosemary said.

'God's dead,' Roman said.

She turned to the bassinet, let fall the knife, turned back to the watching coven. 'Oh God!' she said and covered her face. 'Oh God!' And raised her fists and screamed to the ceiling: *'Oh God! Oh God! Oh God! Oh God! Oh God!'*

'God is DEAD!' Roman thundered. *'God is dead and Satan lives! The year is One, the first year of our Lord! The year is One, God is done! The year is One, Adrian's begun!'*

'Hail Satan!' they cried. 'Hail Adrian!' 'Hail Adrian!' 'Hail Satan!'

She backed away – 'No, no' – backed farther and farther away until she was between two bridge tables. A chair was behind her; she sat down on it and stared at them. 'No.'

Mr Fountain hurried out and down the hallway. Guy and Mr Wees hurried after him.

Minnie went over and, grunting as she stooped, picked up the knife. She took it out to the kitchen.

Laura-Louise went to the bassinet and rocked it posses-ively, making faces into it. The black taffeta rustled; the wheels squeaked.

She sat there and stared. 'No,' she said.

The dream. The dream. It had been true. The yellow eyes he had looked up into. 'Oh God,' she said.

Roman came over to her. 'Clare is just putting on,' he said, 'holding his heart that way over Leah. He's not that sorry. Nobody really liked her; she was stingy, emotionally as well as financially. Why don't you help us out, Rosemary, be a real mother to Adrian; and we'll fix it so you don't get punished for killing her. So that nobody ever even finds out about it. You don't have to *join* if you don't want to; just be a mother to your baby.' He bent over and whispered: 'Minnie and Laura-Louise are too old. It's not right.'

She looked at him.

He stood straight again. 'Think about it, Rosemary,' he said.

'I didn't kill her,' she said.

'Oh?'

'I just gave her pills,' she said. 'She's asleep.'

'Oh,' he said.

The doorbell rang.

'Excuse me,' he said, and went to answer it. 'Think about it anyway,' he said over his shoulder.

'Oh *God*,' she said.

'Shut up with your "Oh God's" or we'll kill you,' Laura-Louise said, rocking the bassinet. 'Milk or no milk.'

'*You* shut up,' Helen Wees said, coming to Rosemary and putting a dampened handkerchief in her hand. 'Rosemary is His mother, no matter how she behaves,' she said. 'You remember that, and show some respect.'

Laura-Louise said something under her breath.

Rosemary wiped her forehead and cheeks with the cool handkerchief. The Japanese, sitting across the room on a hassock, caught her eye and grinned and ducked his head. He held up an opened camera into which he was putting film, and moved it back and forth in the direction of the bassinet, grinning and nodding. She looked down and started to cry. She wiped at her eyes.

Roman came in holding the arm of a robust, handsome dark-skinned man in a snow-white suit and white shoes. He carried a large box wrapped in light blue paper patterned with Teddy bears and candy canes. Musical sounds came from it. Everyone gathered to meet him and shake his

200

and. 'Worried,' they said, and 'pleasure', and 'airport', and 'Stavropoulos', and 'occasion'. Laura-Louise brought the box to the bassinet. She held it up for the baby to see, shook it for him to hear, and put it on the window seat with many other boxes similarly wrapped and a few that were wrapped in black with black ribbon.

'Just after midnight on June twenty-fifth,' Roman said. 'Exactly half the year 'round from you-know. Isn't it perfect?'

'But why are you surprised?' the newcomer asked with both his hands outstretched. 'Didn't Edmond Lautréamont predict June twenty-fifth three hundred years ago?'

'Indeed he did,' Roman said, smiling, 'but it's such a novelty for one of his predictions to prove accurate!' Everyone laughed. 'Come, my friend,' Roman said, drawing the newcomer forward, 'come see Him. Come see the Child.'

They went to the bassinet, where Laura-Louise waited with a shopkeeper's smile, and they closed around it and looked into it silently. After a few moments the newcomer lowered himself to his knees.

Guy and Mr Wees came in.

They waited in the archway until the newcomer had risen, and then Guy came over to Rosemary. 'She'll be all right,' he said; 'Abe is in there with her.' He stood looking down at her, his hands rubbing at his sides. 'They promised me you wouldn't be hurt,' he said. 'And you haven't been, really. I mean, suppose you'd had a baby and lost it; wouldn't it be the same? And we're getting so much in return, Ro.'

She put the handkerchief on the table and looked at him. As hard as she could she spat at him.

He flushed and turned away, wiping at the front of his jacket. Roman caught him and introduced him to the newcomer, Argyron Stavropoulos.

'How proud you must be,' Stravropoulos said, clasping Guy's hand in both his own. 'But surely that isn't the mother there? Why in the name of —' Roman drew him away and spoke in his ear.

'Here,' Minnie said, and offered Rosemary a mug of

steaming tea. 'Drink this and you'll feel a little better.'

Rosemary looked at it, and looked up at Minnie. 'Wha• in it?' she said; 'tannis root?'

'*Nothing* is in it,' Minnie said. 'Except sugar and lemo• It's plain ordinary Lipton tea. You drink it.' She put it dow• by the handkerchief.

The thing to do was kill it. Obviously. Wait till they we• all sitting at the other end, then run over, push away Laur• Louise, and grab it and throw it out the window. And jum• out after it. *Mother Slays Baby and Self at Bramford.*

Save the world from God-knows-what. From Satan-know• what.

A tail! The buds of his horns!

She wanted to scream, to die.

She would do it, throw it out and jump.

They were all milling around now. Pleasant cockta• party. The Japanese was taking pictures; of Guy, of Stavr• poulos, of Laura-Louise holding the baby.

She turned away, not wanting to see.

Those eyes! Like an animal's, a tiger's, not like a huma• being's!

He *wasn't* a human being, of course. He was – som• kind of a half-breed.

And how dear and sweet he had looked before he ha• opened those yellow eyes! The tiny chin, a bit like Brian'• the sweet mouth; all that lovely orange-red hair ... It woul• be nice to look at him again, if only he wouldn't open thos• yellow animal-eyes.

She tasted the tea. It was tea.

No, she *couldn't* throw him out the window. He was he• baby, no matter who the father was. What she had to d• was go to someone who would understand. Like a pries• Yes, that was the answer; a priest. It was a problem for th• Church to handle. For the Pope and all the cardinals t• deal with, not stupid Rosemary Reilly from Omaha.

Killing was wrong, no matter what.

She drank more tea.

He began whimpering because Laura-Louise was rockin•

the bassinet too fast, so of course the idiot began rocking it faster.

She stood it as long as she could and then got up and went over.

'Get away from here,' Laura-Louise said. 'Don't you come near Him. Roman!'

'You're rocking him too fast,' she said.

'Sit down!' Laura-Louise said, and to Roman, 'Get her out of here. Put her back where she belongs.'

Rosemary said, 'She's rocking him too fast; that's why he's whimpering.'

'Mind your own business!' Laura-Louise said.

'Let Rosemary rock Him,' Roman said.

Laura-Louise stared at him.

'Go on,' he said, standing behind the bassinet's hood. 'Sit down with the others. Let Rosemary rock Him.'

'She's liable —'

'*Sit down with the others, Laura-Louise.*'

She huffed, and marched away.

'Rock Him,' Roman said to Rosemary, smiling. He moved the bassinet back and forth towards her, holding it by the hood.

She stood still and looked at him. 'You're trying to – get me to be his mother,' she said.

'*Aren't* you His mother?' Roman said. 'Go on. Just rock Him till He stops complaining.'

She let the black-covered handle come into her hand, and closed her fingers around it. For a few moments they rocked the bassinet between them, then Roman let go and she rocked it alone, nice and slowly. She glanced at the baby, saw his yellow eyes, and looked to the window. 'You should oil the wheels,' she said. 'That could bother him too.'

'I will,' Roman said. 'You see? He's stopped complaining. He knows who you are.'

'Don't be silly,' Rosemary said, and looked at the baby again. He was watching her. His eyes weren't that bad really, now that she was prepared for them. It was the surprise that had upset her. They were pretty in a way. 'What are his hands like?' she asked, rocking him.

'They're very nice,' Roman said. 'He has claws, but they're very tiny and pearly. The mitts are only so He doesn't scratch Himself, not because His hands aren't attractive.'

'He looks worried,' she said.

Dr Sapirstein came over. 'A night of surprises,' he said.

'Go away,' she said, 'or I'm going to spit in your face.'

'Go away, Abe,' Roman said, and Dr Sapirstein nodded and went away.

'Not you,' Rosemary said to the baby. 'It's not *your* fault. I'm angry at *them*, because they tricked me and lied to me. Don't look so worried; I'm not going to hurt you.'

'He knows that,' Roman said.

'Then what does he look so worried for?' Rosemary said. 'The poor little thing. Look at him.'

'In a minute,' Roman said. 'I have to attend to my guests. I'll be right back.' He backed away, leaving her alone.

'Word of honour I'm not going to hurt you,' she said to the baby. She bent over and untied the neck of his gown. 'Laura-Louise made this too tight, didn't she. I'll make it a little looser and then you'll be more comfortable. You have a very cute chin; are you aware of that fact? You have strange yellow eyes, but you have a very cute chin.'

She tied the gown more comfortably for him.

Poor little creature.

He couldn't be *all* bad, he just *couldn't*. Even if he was half Satan, wasn't he half *her* as well, half decent, ordinary, sensible, human being? If she worked *against* them, exerted a good influence to counteract their bad one...

'You have a room of your own, do you know that?' she said, undoing the blanket around him, which was also too tight. 'It has white-and-yellow wallpaper and a white crib with yellow bumpers, and there isn't one drop of witchy old black in the whole place. We'll show it to you when you're ready for your next feeding. In case you're curious, *I* happen to be the lady who's been supplying all that milk you've been drinking. I'll bet you thought it comes in bottles, didn't you. Well it doesn't; it comes in *mothers*, and I'm yours. That's right, Mr Worry-face. You seem to greet e idea with no enthusiasm whatsoever.'

Silence made her look up. They were gathering around to atch her, stopping at a respectful distance.

She felt herself blushing and turned back to tucking the anket around the baby. '*Let* them watch,' she said; 'we n't care, do we? We just want to be all cosy and comrtable, like so. There. Better?'

'Hail Rosemary,' Helen Wees said.

The others took it up. 'Hail Rosemary.' 'Hail Rosemary.' innie and Stavropoulos and Dr Sapirstein. 'Hail Rosemary.' Guy said it too. 'Hail Rosemary.' Laura-Louise oved her lips but made no sound.

'Hail Rosemary, mother of Adrian!' Roman said.

She looked up from the bassinet. 'It's Andrew,' she said. ndrew John Woodhouse.'

'Adrian Steven,' Roman said.

Guy said, 'Roman, look,' and Stavropoulos, at Roman's her side, touched his arm and said, 'Is the name of so eat an importance?'

'It is. Yes. It is,' Roman said. 'His name is Adrian Steven.'

Rosemary said, 'I understand why you'd like to call him at, but I'm sorry; you can't. His name is Andrew John. e's my child, not yours, and this is one point that I'm not en going to argue about. This and the clothes. He can't ear black all the time.'

Roman opened his mouth but Minnie said, 'Hail Andrew' a loud voice, looking right at him.

Everyone else said 'Hail Andrew' and 'Hail Rosemary, other of Andrew' and 'Hail Satan.'

Rosemary tickled the baby's tummy. 'You didn't like Adrian", did you?' she asked him. 'I should think not. Adrian Steven"! Will you *please* stop looking so worried?' he poked the tip of his nose. 'Do you know how to smile et, Andy? Do you? Come on, little funny-eyes Andy, can u smile? Can you smile for Mommy?' She tapped the lver ornament and set it swinging. 'Come on, Andy,' she id. 'One little smile. Come on, Andy-candy.'

The Japanese slipped forward with his camera, crouched, nd took two three four pictures in quick succession.

HOWARD CLEWES

MAN ON A HORSE

A three-fold drama of searing passion and physical violence in the steaming jungles of South America.

'A vivid picture of central Brazil, and the interplay of temperaments among husband, wife and lover — to say nothing of corrupt officials and strong-arm land-stealers — allow an exciting story to be told'
GLASGOW HERALD

'A gripping yarn of love and brutality in the badlands of Brazil'
SUN

THE LONG MEMORY

Betrayed by the woman he loved, Philip Davidson plotted revenge for seventeen long years, his sentence for brutal murder. Now he was free . . . free to slake his lust for vengeance and able to release his long pent-up desires.

'It is a compelling story, the characters being few and strongly drawn, the action continuous, the atmosphere full of suspense'
DAILY TELEGRAPH

Arthur Hailey

The book that remained for over six
months on the American bestseller list,
now filmed with a star-studded cast —

HOTEL 5/-

Against the background of a great
New Orleans hotel move the characters —
tycoons of the hotel industry, guests,
and staff; men and women, young and old,
dedicated and amoral — sealing their
own destinies in five days of
dramatic change.

'Compulsively readable' DAILY EXPRESS

THE FINAL DIAGNOSIS 5/-

The engrossing story of a young
pathologist and his efforts to restore
the standards of a hospital controlled
by an ageing, once brilliant doctor.
'Probably the best and most
potentially popular medical novel
since *Not as a Stranger*'
NEW YORK TIMES BOOK REVIEW

A SELECTION OF POPULAR READING IN PAN